FUTURE SHOCK

The voice of Mr. Kott broke over the boy, harsh and jagged tones that he did not understand. He clasped his hands to his ears. All at once, Mr. Kott shot across the room, then vanished.

Where had he gone?

No matter where he looked the boy could not find him. He began to tremble.

Suddenly he saw that Mr. Kott had reappeared and was chattering to a dark figure.

The dark figure flowed step by step across the room. Awed, Manfred looked directly at him . . . and at that moment, the dark man looked back, meeting his gaze.

"You must die," the dark man said. "Then you will be reborn. Do you see, child?"

"Yes," Manfred said. And then he fled into the blackness of the future . . .

"THIS BOOK HAS THE USUAL PHILIP K. DICK COMPLEX CROSS-CUTTING PLOT. DICK IS SURE TO UNSETTLE AND DISTURB YOU WITH THE INCREASINGLY OUT-OF-KILTER WORLD HE HAS SET UP ON MARS."

—The Magazine of Fantasy and Science Fiction

Martian
Time-Slip

Philip K. Dick

A Del Rey Book

BALLANTINE BOOKS • NEW YORK

A Del Rey Book
Published by Ballantine Books

ISBN 0-345-29560-9

Manufactured in the United States of America

First Edition: April 1964
Fourth Printing: June 1981

Cover art by Darrell Sweet

To Mark and Jodie

one

FROM THE DEPTHS of phenobarbital slumber, Silvia Bohlen heard something that called. Sharp, it broke the layers into which she had sunk, damaging her perfect state of nonself.

"Mom," her son called again, from outdoors.

Sitting up, she took a swallow of water from the glass by the bed; she put her bare feet on the floor and rose with difficulty. Time by the clock: nine-thirty. She found her robe, walked to the window.

I must not take any more of that, she thought. Better to succumb to the schizophrenic process, join the rest of the world. She raised the window shade; the sunlight, with its familiar reddish, dusty tinge, filled her sight and made it impossible to see. She put up her hand, calling, "What is it, David?"

"Mom, the ditch rider's here!"

Then this must be Wednesday. She nodded turned and walked unsteadily from the bedroom to the kitchen, where she managed to put on the good, solid, Earth-made coffeepot.

What must I do? she asked herself. All's ready for him. David will see, anyhow. She turned on the water at the sink and splashed her face. The water, unpleasant and tainted, made her cough. We should drain the tank, she thought. Scour it, adjust the chlorine flow and see how many of the filters are plugged; perhaps all. Couldn't the ditch rider do that? No, not the UN's business.

"Do you need me?" she asked, opening the back door. The air swirled at her, cold and choked with the fine sand; she averted her head and listened for David's answer. He was trained to say no.

"I guess not," the boy grumbled.

Later, as she sat in her robe at the kitchen table drinking coffee, her plate of toast and applesauce before her, she

7

looked out on the sight of the ditch rider arriving in his little flat-bottom boat which put-putted up the canal in its official way, never hurrying and yet always arriving on schedule. This was 1994, the second week in August. They had waited eleven days, and now they would receive their share of water from the great ditch which passed by their line of houses a mile to the Martian north.

The ditch rider had moored his boat at the sluice gate and was hopping up onto dry land, encumbered with his ringed binder—in which he kept his records—and his tools for switching the gate. He wore a gray uniform spattered with mud, high boots almost brown from the dried silt. German? But he was not; when the man turned his head she saw that his face was flat and Slavic and that in the center of the visor of his cap was a red star. It was the Russians' turn, this time; she had lost track.

And she evidently was not the only one who had lost track of the sequence of rotation by the managing UN authorities. For now she saw that the family from the next house, the Steiners, had appeared on their front porch and were preparing to approach the ditch rider: all six of them, father and heavy-set mother and the four blonde, round, noisy Steiner girls.

It was the Steiners' water which the rider was now turning off.

"Bitte, mein Herr," Norbert Steiner began, but then he, too, saw the red star, and became silent.

To herself, Silvia smiled. Too bad, she thought.

Opening the back door, David hurried into the house. "Mom, you know what? The Steiners' tank sprang a leak last night, and around half their water drained out! So they don't have enough water stored up for their garden, and it'll die, Mr. Steiner says."

She nodded as she ate her last bit of toast. She lit a cigarette.

"Isn't that terrible, Mom?" David said.

Silvia said, "And the Steiners want him to leave their water on just a little longer."

"We can't let their garden die. Remember all the trouble we had with our beets? And Mr. Steiner gave us that chemical from Home that killed the beetles, and we were going to give them some of our beets but we never did; we forgot."

That was true. She recalled with a guilty start; we did promise them . . . and they've never said anything, even

8

though they must remember. And David is always over there playing.

"Please go out and talk to the rider," David begged.

She said, "I guess we could give them some of our water later on in the month; we could run a hose over to their garden. But I don't believe them about the leak—they always want more than their share."

"I know," David said, hanging his head.

"They don't deserve more, David. No one does."

"They just don't know how to keep their property going right," David said. "Mr. Steiner, he doesn't know anything about tools."

"Then that's their responsibility." She felt irritable, and it occurred to her that she was not fully awake; she needed a Dexamye, or her eyes would never be open, not until it was nightfall once more and time for another phenobarbital. Going to the medicine cabinet in the bathroom, she got down the bottle of small green heart-shaped pills, opened it, and counted; she had only twenty-three left, and soon she would have to board the big tractor-bus and cross the desert to town, to visit the pharmacy for a refill.

From above her head came a noisy, echoing gurgle. The tank on the roof, their huge tin water storage tank, had begun to fill. The ditch rider had finished switching the sluice gate; the pleas of the Steiners had been in vain.

Feeling more and more guilty, she filled a glass with water in order to take her morning pill. If only Jack were home more, she said to herself; it's so empty around here. It's a form of barbarism, this pettiness we're reduced to. What's the point of all this bickering and tension, this terrible concern over each drop of water, that dominates our lives? There should be something more. . . . We were promised so much, in the beginning.

Loudly, from a nearby house, the racket of a radio blared up suddenly; dance music, and then an announcer giving a commercial for some sort of farm machinery.

". . . Depth and angle of the furrow," the voice declared, echoing in the cold bright morning air, "pre-set and self-adjusting so that even the most unskilled owner can—almost the first time—"

Dance music returned; the people had turned to a different station.

The squabble of children rose up. Is it going to be like this all day? she asked herself, wondering if she could face it.

And Jack, away until the weekend at his job—it was almost like not being married, like not having a man. Did I emigrate from Earth for this? She clapped her hands to her ears, trying to shut out the noise of radios and children.

I ought to be back in bed; that's where I belong, she thought as she at last resumed dressing for the day which lay ahead of her.

In his employer's office in downtown Bunchewood Park, Jack Bohlen talked on the radio-telephone to his father in New York City. The contact, made through a system of satellites over millions of miles of space, was none too good, as always; but Leo Bohlen was paying for the call.

"What do you mean, the Franklin D. Roosevelt Mountains?" Jack said loudly. "You must be mistaken, Dad, there's nothing there—it's a total waste area. Anybody in real estate can tell you that."

His father's faint voice came. "No, Jack, I believe it's sound. I want to come out and have a look and discuss it with you. How's Silvia and the boy?"

"Fine," Jack said. "But listen—don't commit yourself, because it's a known fact that any Mars real estate away from the part of the canal network that works—and remember that only about one-tenth of it works—comes close to being an outright fraud." He could not understand how his father, with his years of business experience, especially in investments in unimproved land, could have gotten on to such a bum steer. It frightened him. Maybe his dad, in the years since he had seen him, had gotten old. Letters told very little; his dad dictated them to one of his company stenographers.

Or perhaps time flowed differently on Earth than on Mars; he had read an article in a psychology journal suggesting that. His father would arrive a tottering, white-haired old relic. Was there any way to get out of the visit? David would be glad to see his grandfather, and Silvia liked him, too. In Jack Bohlen's ear the faint, distant voice related news of New York City, none of any interest. It was unreal to Jack. A decade ago he had made a terrific effort to detach himself from his community on Earth, and he had succeeded; he did not want to hear about it.

And yet the link with his father remained, and it would be shored up in a little while by his father's first trip off Earth; he had always wanted to visit another planet before

10

it was too late—before his death, in other words. Leo was determined. But despite improvements in the big interplan ships, travel was hazardous. That did not bother him. Nothing would deter him; he had already made reservations, in fact.

"Gosh, Dad," Jack said, "it sure is wonderful that you feel able to make such an arduous trip. I hope you're up to it." He felt resigned.

Across from him his employer, Mr. Yee, regarded him and held up a slip of yellow paper on which was written a service call. Skinny, elongated Mr. Yee in his bow tie and single-breasted suit . . . the Chinese style of dress rigorously rooted here on alien soil, as authentic as if Mr. Yee did business in downtown Canton.

Mr. Yee pointed to the slip and then solemnly acted out its meaning: he shivered, poured from left hand to right, then mopped his forehead and tugged at his collar. Then he inspected the wrist watch on his bony wrist. A refrigeration unit on some dairy farm had broken down, Jack Bohlen understood, and it was urgent; the milk would be ruined as the day's heat increased.

"O.K., Dad," he said, "we'll be expecting your wire." He said good-bye and hung up. "Sorry to be on the phone so long," he said to Mr. Yee. He reached for the slip.

"An elderly person should not make the trip here," Mr. Yee said in his placid, implacable voice.

"He's made up his mind to see how we're doing," Jack said.

"And if you are not doing as well as he would wish, can he help you?" Mr. Yee smiled with contempt. "Are you supposed to have struck it rich? Tell him there are no diamonds. The UN got them. As to the call which I gave you: that refrigeration unit, according to the file, was worked on by us two months ago for the same complaint. It is in the power source or conduit. At unpredictable times the motor slows until the safety switch cuts it off to keep it from burning out."

"I'll see what else they have drawing power from their generator," Jack said.

It was hard, working for Mr. Yee, he thought as he went upstairs to the roof where the company's copters were parked. Everything was conducted on a rational basis. Mr. Yee looked and acted like something put together to calculate. Six years ago, at the age of twenty-two, he had calculated that he could operate a more profitable business on Mars than on Earth. There was a crying need on Mars for service maintenance on all sorts of machinery, on anything with moving parts, since the cost of shipping new units from Earth was so great. An old toaster, thoughtlessly scrapped on Earth, would have to be kept working on Mars. Mr. Yee had liked the idea of salvaging. He did not approve of waste, having been reared in the frugal, puritanical atmosphere of People's China. And being an electrical engineer in Honan Province, he possessed training. So in a very calm and methodical way he had come to a decision which for most people meant a catastrophic emotional wrenching; he had made arrangements to emigrate from Earth, exactly as he would have gone about visiting a dentist for a set of stainless steel dentures. He knew to the last UN dollar how far he could cut his overhead, once he had set up shop on Mars. It was a low-margin operation, but extremely professional. In the six years since 1988 he had expanded until now his repairmen held priority in cases of emergency—and what, in a colony which still had difficulty growing its own radishes and cooling its own tiny yield of milk, was not an emergency?

Shutting the 'copter door, Jack Bohlen started up the engine, and soon was rising above the buildings of Bunchewood Park, into the hazy dull sky of midmorning, on his first service call of the day.

Far to his right, an enormous ship, completing its trip from Earth, was settling down onto the circle of basalt which was the receiving field for living cargoes. Other cargoes had to be delivered a hundred miles to the east. This was a first-class carrier, and shortly it would be visited by remote-operated devices which would fleece the passengers of every virus and bactria, insect and weed-seed adhering to them; they would emerge as naked as the day they were born, pass through chemical baths, sputter resentfully through eight hours of tests—and then at last be set free to see about their personal survival, the survival of the colony having been assured. Some might even be sent back to Earth; those whose condition implied genetic defects revealed by the stress of the trip. Jack thought of his dad patiently enduring the immigration processing. Has to be done, my boy, his dad would say. Necessary. The old man, smoking his cigar and meditating . . . a philosopher whose total formal education consisted of seven years in the New York public school system, and during its most feral period. Strange, he thought, how character shows itself. The old man was in touch with some level of knowledge which told him how to behave, not in the social sense, but in a deeper, more permanent way. He'll adjust to this world here, Jack

12

decided. In his short visit he'll come to terms better than Silvia and I. About as David has. . . .

They would get along well, his father and his boy. Both shrewd and practical, and yet both haphazardly romantic, as witness his father's impulse to buy land somewhere in the F.D.R. Mountains. It was a last gasp of hope springing eternal in the old man; here was land selling for next to nothing, with no takers, the authentic frontier which the habitable parts of Mars were patently not. Below him, Jack noted the Senator Taft Canal and aligned his flight with it; the canal would lead him to the McAuliff dairy ranch with its thousands of acres of withered grass, its once prize herd of Jerseys, now bent into something resembling their ancestors by the unjust environment. This was habitable Mars, this almost-fertile spiderweb of lines, radiating and crisscrossing but always barely adequate to support life, no more. The Senator Taft, directly below now, showed a sluggish and repellent green; it was water sluiced and filtered in its final stages, but here it showed the accretions of time, the underlying slime and sand and contaminants which made it anything but potable. God knew what alkalines the population had absorbed and built into its bones by now. However, they were alive. The water had not killed them, yellow-brown and full of sediment as it was. While over to the west—the reaches, which were waiting for human science to rare back and pass its miracle.

The archaeological teams which had landed on Mars early in the '70's had eagerly plotted the stages of retreat of the old civilization which human beings had now begun to replace. It had not at any time settled in the desert proper. Evidently, as with the Tigris and Euphrates civilization on Earth, it had clung to what it could irrigate. At its peak, the old Martian culture had occupied a fifth of the planet's surface, leaving the rest as it had found it. Jack Bohlen's house, for instance, near the junction of the William Butler Yeats Canal with the Herodotus; it stood almost at the edge of the network by which fertility had been attained for the past five thousand years. The Bohlens were latecomers, although no one had known, eleven years ago, that emigration would fall off so startlingly.

The radio in the 'copter made static noises, and then a tinny version of Mr. Yee's voice said, "Jack, I have a service call for you to add. The UN Authority says that the Public School is malfunctioning and their own man is unavailable."

Picking up the microphone, Jack said into it, "I'm sorry, Mr. Yee—as I thought I'd told you, I'm not trained to touch those school units. You'd better have Bob or Pete handle that." As I know I told you, he said to himself.

In his logical way, Mr. Yee said, "This repair is vital, and therefore we can't turn it down, Jack. We have never turned down any repair job. Your attitude is not positive. I will have to insist that you tackle the job. As soon as it is possible I will have another repairman out to the school to join you. Thank you, Jack." Mr. Yee rang off.

Thank you, too, Jack Bohlen said acidly to himself.

Below him now he saw the beginnings of a second settlement; this was Lewistown, the main habitation of the plumbers' union colony which had been one of the first to be organized on the planet, and which had its own union members as its repairmen; it did not patronize Mr. Yee. If his job became too unpleasant, Jack Bohlen could always pack up and migrate to Lewistown, join the union, and go to work at perhaps an even better salary. But recent political events in the plumbers' union colony had not been to his liking. Arnie Kott, president of the Water Workers' Local, had been elected only after much peculiar campaigning and some more-than-average balloting irregularities. His regime did not strike Jack as the sort he wanted to live under; from what he had seen of it, the old man's rule had all the elements of early Renaissance tyranny, with a bit of nepotism thrown in. And yet the colony appeared to be prospering economically. It had an advanced public works program, and its fiscal policies had brought into existence an enormous cash reserve. The colony was not only efficient and prosperous, it was also able to provide decent jobs for all its inhabitants. With the exception of the Israeli settlement to the north, the union colony was the most viable on the planet. And the Israeli settlement had the advantage of possessing die-hard Zionist shock units, encamped on the desert proper, engaged in reclamation projects of all sorts, from growing oranges to refining chemical fertilizers. Alone, New Israel had reclaimed a third of all the desert land now under cultivation. It was, in fact, the only settlement on Mars which exported its produce back to Earth in any quantity.

The water workers' union capital city of Lewistown passed by, and then the monument to Alger Hiss, the first UN martyr; then open desert followed. Jack sat back and lit a cigarette. Under Mr. Yee's prodding scrutiny, he had left without remembering to bring his thermos of coffee, and he now felt its lack. He felt sleepy. They won't get me to work on the Public School, he said to himself, but with more anger than conviction. I'll quit. But he knew he wouldn't quit. He would go to the school, tinker with it for an hour or so, giving the impression of being busy repairing, and then Bob or Pete would show up and do the job; the firm's reputation would be preserved, and they could go back to the office. Everyone would be satisfied, including Mr. Yee.

Several times he had visited the Public School with his son. That was different. David was at the top of his class, attending the most advanced teaching machines along the route. He stayed late, making the most of the tutorial system of which the UN was so proud. Looking at his watch, Jack saw that it was ten o'clock. At this moment, as he recalled from his visits and from his son's accounts, David was with the Aristotle, learning the rudiments of science, philosophy, logic, grammar, poetics, and an archaic physics. Of all the teaching machines, David seemed to derive the most from the Aristotle, which was a relief; many of the children preferred the more dashing teachers at the School: Sir Francis Drake (English history, fundamentals of masculine civility) or Abraham Lincoln (United States history, basics of modern warfare and the contemporary state) or such grim personages as Julius Caesar and Winston Churchill. He himself had been born too soon to take advantage of the tutorial school system, he had gone to classes as a boy where he sat with sixty other children, and later, in high school, he had found himself listening and watching an instructor speaking over closed-circuit TV along with a class of a thousand. If, however, he had been allowed into the new school, he could readily have located his own favorite: on a visit with David, on the first parent-teacher day in fact, he had seen the Thomas Edison Teaching Machine, and that was enough for him. It took David almost an hour to drag his father away.

Below the 'copter, the desert land gave way to sparse, prairie-like grassland. A barbed-wire fence marked the beginning of the McAuliff ranch, and with it the area administered by the State of Texas. McAuliff's father had been a Texas oil millionaire, and had financed his own ships for the emigration to Mars; he had beaten even the plumbers' union people. Jack put out his cigarette and began to lower the 'copter, searching against the glare of the sun for the buildings of the ranch.

A small herd of cows panicked and galloped off at the noise of the 'copter; he watched them scatter, hoping that Mc-

Auliff, who was a short, dour-faced Irishman with an obsessive attitude toward life, hadn't noticed. McAuliff, for good reasons, had a hypochondriacal view of his cows; he suspected that all manner of Martian *things* were out to get them, to make them lean, sick, and fitful in their milk production.

Turning on his radio transmitter, Jack said into the microphone, "This is a Yee Company repairship. Jack Bohlen asking permission to land on the McAuliff strip, in answer to your call."

He waited, and then there came the answer from the huge ranch. "O.K., Bohlen, all clear. No use asking what took you so long." McAuliff's resigned, grumpy voice.

"Be there any minute now," Jack said, with a grimace.

Presently he made out the buildings ahead, white against the sand.

"We've got fifteen thousand gallons of milk here." McAuliff's voice came from the radio speaker. "And it's all going to spoil unless you get this damned refrigeration unit going soon."

"On the double," Jack said. He put his thumbs in his ears and leered a grotesque, repudiating face at the radio speaker.

two

THE EX-PLUMBER, Supreme Goodmember Arnie Kott of the Water Workers' Local, Fourth Planet Branch, rose from his bed at ten in the morning and as was his custom strolled directly to the steam bath.

"Hello, Gus."

"Hi there, Arnie."

Everybody called him by his first name, and that was good. Arnie Kott nodded to Bill and Eddy and Tom, and they all greeted him. The air, full of steam, condensed around his feet and drained off across the tiles, to be voided. That was a touch which pleased him; the baths had been constructed so as not to preserve the run-off. The water drained out onto the hot sand and disappeared forever. Who else could do that? He thought, Let's see if those rich Jews up in New Israel have a steam bath that wastes water.

Placing himself under a shower, Arnie Kott said to the fellows around him, "I heard some rumor I want checked on soon as possible. You know that combine from California, those Portugees that originally held title on the F.D.R. Mountain Range, and they tried to extract iron ore there, but it was too low grade, and the cost was way out of line? I heard they sold their holdings."

"Yeah, I heard that too." All the boys nodded. "I wonder how much they lost. Must have taken a terrible beating."

Arnie said, "No, I heard they found a buyer that was willing to put up more than they paid; they made a profit, after all these years. So it paid them to hold out. I wonder who's nuts enough to want that land. I got some mineral rights there, you know. I want you to check into who bought that land and what kind of operation they represent. I want to know what they're doing over there."

"Good to know those things." Again everyone nodded, and

17

one man—Fred, it looked like—detached himself from his shower and padded off to dress. "I'll check into that, Arnie," Fred said over his shoulder. "I'll get to it right away."

Addressing himself to the remaining men, Arnie soaped himself all over and said, "You know I got to protect my mineral rights; I can't have some smoozer coming in here from Earth and making those mountains into like for instance a national park for picnickers. I tell you what I heard. I know that a bunch of Communist officials from Russia and Hungary, big boys, was over here around a week ago, no doubt looking around. You think because that collective of theirs failed last year they gave up? No. They got the brains of bugs, and like bugs they always come back. Those Reds are aching to establish a successful collective on Mars; it's practically a wet dream of theirs back Home. I wouldn't be surprised if we find out that those Portugees from California sold to Communists, and pretty soon we're seeing the name changed from the F.D.R. Mountains, which is right and proper, to something like the Joe Stalin Mountains."

The men all laughed appreciatively.

"Now, I got a lot of business ahead of me today to conduct," Arnie Kott said, washing the soapsuds from him with furious streams of hot water. "So I can't devote myself to this matter any further; I'm relying on you to dig into it. For example, I have been traveling east where we got that melon experiment in progress, and it seems like we're about to be entirely successful in inducing the New England type of melon into growing here in this environment. I know you all have been wondering about that, because everybody likes a good slice of cantaloupe in the morning for his breakfast, if it's at all possible."

"That's true, Arnie," the boys agreed.

"But," Arnie said, "I got more on my mind than melons. We had one of those UN boys visiting us the other day protesting our regulations concerning the niggers. Or maybe I shouldn't say that; maybe I should talk like the UN boys and say 'indigenous population remnants,' or just Bleekmen. What he had reference to was our licensing the mines owned by our settlement to use Bleekmen at below scale, I mean, below the minimum wage—because even those fairies at the UN don't seriously propose we pay scale to Bleekmen niggers. However, we have this problem that we can't pay any minimum wage to the Bleekmen niggers because their work is so inconsistent that we'd go broke, and we have to use them in mining operations because they're the only ones who can breathe down there, and we can't get oxygen equipment in quantity transported over here at any price less than outrageous. Somebody's making a lot of money back Home on those oxygen tanks and compressors and all that. It's a racket, and we're not going to get gouged, I can tell you."

Everybody nodded somberly.

"Now, we can't allow the UN bureaucrats to dictate to us how we'll run our settlement," Arnie said. "We set up operations here before the UN was anything here but a flag planted in the sand; we had houses built before they had a pot to piss in anywhere on Mars, including all that disputed area in the south between the U.S. and France."

"Right, Arnie," the boys all agreed.

"However," Arnie said, "there's the problem that those UN fruits control the waterways, and we got to have water; we need them for conveyance into and out of the settlement and for source of power and to drink and like now, like we're here bathing. I mean, those buggers can cut off our water any time; they've got us by the short hairs."

He finished his shower and padded across the warm, wet tiles to get a towel from the attendant. Thinking about the UN made his stomach rumble, and his onetime duodenal ulcer began to burn way down in his left side, almost at the groin. Better get some breakfast, he realized.

When he had been dressed by the attendant, in his gray flannel trousers and T-shirt, soft leather boots, and nautical cap, he left the steam bath and crossed the corridor of the Union Hall to his dining room, where Helio, his Bleekman cook, had his breakfast waiting. Shortly, he sat before a stack of hotcakes and bacon, coffee and a glass of orange juice, and the previous week's New York *Times*, the Sunday edition.

"Good morning, Mr. Kott." In answer to his button-pressing, a secretary from the pool had appeared, a girl he had never seen before. Not too good-looking, he decided after a brief glance; he returned to reading the newspaper. And calling him Mr. Kott, too. He sipped his orange juice and read about a ship that had perished in space with all three hundred aboard killed. It was a Japanese merchantman carrying bicycles. That made him laugh. Bicycles in space, and all gone, now; too bad, because on a planet with little mass like Mars, where there was virtually no power source—except the sluggish canal system—and where even kerosene cost a fortune, bicycles were of great economic value. A man could pedal free of cost for hundreds of miles, right over the sand, too. The only people who used kerosene-powered turbine conveyances were vital functionaries, such as the repair and maintenance men, and of course important officials such as himself. There were public transports, of course, such as the tractor-buses which connected one settlement with the next and the outlying residential areas with the world at large . . . but they ran irregularly, being dependent on shipments from Earth for their fuel. And personally speaking the buses gave him a case of claustrophobia, they moved so slow.

Reading the New York *Times* made him feel for a little while as if he were back Home again, in South Pasadena; his family had subscribed to the West Coast edition of the *Times*, and as a boy he remembered bringing it in from the mailbox, in from the street lined with apricot trees, the warm, smoggy little street of neat one-story houses and parked cars and lawns tended from one weekend to the next without fail. It was the lawn, with all its equipment and medicines, that he missed most—the wheelbarrow of fertilizer, the new grass seed, the snippers, the poultry-netting fence in the early spring . . . and always the sprinklers at work throughout the long summer, whenever the law allowed. Water shortage there, too. Once his Uncle Paul had been arrested for washing his car on a water-ration day.

Reading further in the paper he came upon an article about a reception at the White House for a Mrs. Lizner who, as an official of the Birth Control Agency, had performed eight thousand therapeutic abortions and had thereby set an example for American womanhood. Kind of like a nurse, Arnie Kott decided. Noble occupation for females. He turned the page.

There, in big type, was a quarter-page ad which he himself had helped compose, a glowing come-on to get people to emigrate. Arnie sat back in his chair, folded the paper, felt deep pride as he studied the ad; it looked good, he decided. It would surely attract people, if they had any guts at all and a sincere desire for adventure, as the ad said.

The ad listed all the skills in demand on Mars, and it was a long list, excluding only canary raiser and proctologist, if that. It pointed out how hard it was now for a person with only a master's degree to get a job on Earth, and how on Mars there were good-paying jobs for people with only B.A.'s.

That ought to get them, Arnie thought. He himself had emigrated due to his having only a B.A. Every door had been shut to him, and then he had come to Mars as nothing but a union plumber, and within a few short years, look at him. On Earth, a plumber with only a B.A. would be raking up dead locusts in Africa as part of a U.S. foreign aid work gang. In fact, his brother Phil was doing that right now; he had graduated from the University of California and had never had a chance to practice his profession, that of milk tester. In his class, over a hundred milk testers had been graduated, and for what? There were no opportunities on Earth. You have to come to Mars, Arnie said to himself. We can use you here. Look at the pokey cows on those dairy ranches outside of town. They could use some testing.

But the catch in the ad was simply that, once on Mars, the emigrant was guaranteed nothing, not even the certainty of being-able to give up and go home; trips back were much more expensive, due to the inadequate field facilities. Certainly, he was guaranteed nothing in the way of employment. The fault lay with the big powers back Home, China and the U.S. and Russia and West Germany. Instead of properly backing the development of the planets, they had turned their attention to further exploration. Their time and brains and money were all committed to the sidereal projects, such as that frigging flight to Centaurus, which had already wasted billions of dollars and man-hours. Arnie Kott could not see the sidereal projects for beans. Who wanted to take a four-year trip to another solar system which maybe wasn't even there?

And yet at the same time Arnie feared a change in the attitude of the great terrestrial powers. Suppose one morning they woke up and took a new look at the colonies on Mars and Venus? Suppose they eyed the ramshackle developments there and decided something should be done about them? In other words, what became of Arnie Kott when the Great Powers came to their senses? It was a thought to ponder.

However, the Great Powers showed no symptoms of rationality. Their obsessive competitiveness still governed them; right this moment they were locking horns, two light years away, to Arnie's relief.

Reading further in the paper, he came across a brief article having to do with a women's organization in Berne, Switzerland, which had met to declare once more its anxiety about colonization.

COLONIAL SAFETY COMMITTEE ALARMED OVER
CONDITIONS OF MARS LANDING FIELDS

The ladies, in a petition presented to the Colonial Department of the UN, had expressed once more their conviction that the fields on Mars at which ships from Earth landed were too remote from habitation and from the water system. Passengers in some cases had been required to trek over a hundred miles of wasteland, and these included women and children and old people. The Colonial Safety Committee wanted the UN to pass a regulation compelling ships to land at fields within twenty-five miles of a major (named) canal.

Do-gooders, Arnie Kott thought as he read the article. Probably not one of them has ever been off Earth; they just know what somebody wrote home in a letter, some aunt retiring to Mars on a pension, living on free UN land and naturally griping. And of course they also depended on their member in residence on Mars, a certain Mrs. Anne Esterhazy; she circulated a mimeographed newsletter to other public-spirited ladies throughout the settlements. Arnie received and read her newsletter, *The Auditor Speaks Back,* a title at which he gagged. He gagged, too, at the one- and two-line squibs inserted between longer articles:

* * * * * * * *

Pray for potable purification! ! Contact colony charismatic councilors and witness for water filtration we can be proud of!

* * * * * * * *

He could hardly make out the meaning of some of the *Auditor Speaks Back* articles, they were phrased in such special jargon. But evidently the newsletter had attracted an audience of devoted women who grimly took each item to heart and acted out the deeds asked of them. Right now they were undoubtedly complaining, along with the Colonial Safety Committee back on Earth, about the hazardous distances separating most of the landing fields on Mars from water sources and human habitation. They were doing their part in one of the many great fights, and in this particular case, Arnie Kott had managed to gain control of his nausea. For of the twenty or so landing fields on Mars, only one lay within twenty-five miles of a major canal, and that was Samuel Gompers Field, which served his own settlement. If by some chance the pressure of the Colonial Safety Committee was effective, then all incoming passenger ships from Earth would have to land at

Arnie Kott's field, with the revenue received going to his settlement.

It was far from accidental that Mrs. Esterhazy and her newsletter and organization on Earth were advocating a cause which would be of economic value to Arnie. Anne Esterhazy was Arnie's ex-wife. They were still good friends, and still owned jointly a number of economic ventures which they had founded or bought into during their marriage. On a number of levels they still worked together, even though on a strictly personal basis they had no common ground whatsoever. He found her aggressive, domineering, overly masculine, a tall and bony female with a long stride, wearing low-heeled shoes and a tweed coat and dark glasses, a huge leather purse slung from a strap over her shoulder . . . but she was shrewd and intelligent and a natural executive. As long as he did not have to see her outside of the business context, he could get along with her.

The fact that Anne Esterhazy had once been his wife and that they still had financial ties was not well known. When he wanted to get in touch with her he did not dictate a letter to one of the settlement's stenographers; instead he used a little encoding dictation machine which he kept in his desk, sending the reel of tape over to her by special messenger. The messenger dropped off the tape at an art object shop which Anne owned over in the Israeli settlement, and her answer, if any, was deposited the same way at the office of a cement and gravel works on the Bernard Baruch Canal which belonged to Arnie's brother-in-law, Ed Rockingham, his sister's husband.

A year ago, when Ed Rockingham had built a house for himself and Patricia and their three children, he had acquired the unacquirable: his own canal. He had had it built, in open violation of the law, for his private use, and it drew water from the great common network. Even Arnie had been outraged. But there had been no prosecution, and today the canal, modestly named after Rockingham's eldest child, carried water eighty miles out into the desert, so that Pat Rockingham could live in a lovely spot and have a lawn, a swimming pool, and a fully irrigated flower garden. She grew especially large camellia bushes, which were the only ones that had survived the transplanting to Mars. All during the day, sprinklers revolved and sprayed her bushes, keeping them from drying up and dying.

Twelve huge camellia bushes seemed to Arnie Kott an

ostentation. He did not get along well with his sister or Ed Rockingham. What had they come to Mars for? he asked himself. To live, at incredible expense and effort, as much as possible as they had back Home on Earth. To him it was absurd. Why not remain on Earth? Mars, for Arnie, was a new place, and it meant a new life, lived with a new style. He and the other settlers, both big and small, had made in their time on Mars countless minute adjustments in a process of adaptation through so many stages that they had in fact evolved; they were new creatures, now. Their children born on Mars started out like this, novel and peculiar, in some respects enigmatic to their parents. Two of his own boys—his and Anne's—now lived in a settlement camp at the outskirts of Lewistown. When he visited them he could not make them out; they looked toward him with bleak eyes, as if waiting for him to go away. As near as he could tell, the boys had no sense of humor. And yet they were sensitive; they could talk forever about animals and plants, the landscape itself. Both boys had pets, Martian critters that struck him as horrid: praying mantis types of bugs, as large as donkeys. The damn things were called *boxers*, because they were often seen propped up erect and squaring off at one another in a ritual battle which generally ended up with one killing and eating the other. Bert and Ned had gotten their pet boxers trained to do manual chores of a low caliber, and not to eat each other. And the things were their companions; children on Mars were lonely, partly because there were still so few of them and partly because . . . Arnie did not know. The children had a large-eyed, haunted look, as if they were starved for something as yet invisible. They tended to become reclusive, if given half a chance, wandering off to poke about in the wastelands. What they brought back was worthless, to themselves and to the settlements, a few bones or relics of the old nigger civilization, perhaps. When he flew by 'copter, Arnie always spotted some isolated children, one here and another there, toiling away out in the desert, scratching at the rock and sand as if trying vaguely to pry up the surface of Mars and get underneath. . . .

Unlocking the bottom drawer of his desk, Arnie got out the little battery-powered encoding dictation machine and set it up for use. Into it he said, "Anne, I'd like to meet with you and talk. That committee has too many women on it, and it's going the wrong way. For example, the last ad in the *Times* worries me because—" He broke off, for the encoding machine had groaned to a stop. He poked at it, and the reels turned slowly and then once more settled back into silence.

Thought it was fixed, Arnie thought angrily. Can't those jerks fix nothing? Maybe he would have to go to the black market and buy, at an enormous price, another. He winced at the thought.

The not-too-good-looking secretary from the pool, who had been sitting quietly across from him waiting, now responded to his nod. She produced her pencil and pad and began as he dictated.

"Usually," Arnie Kott said, "I can understand how hard it is to keep things running, what with no parts hardly, and the way the local weather affects metal and wiring. However, I'm fed up with asking for competent repair service on a vital item like my encoding machine. I just got to have it, that's all. So if you guys can't keep it working, I'm going to disband you and withdraw your franchise to practice the craft of repairing within the settlement, and I'll rely on outside service for our maintenance." He nodded once more, and the girl ceased writing.

"Shall I take the encoder over to the repair department, Mr. Kott?" she asked. "I'd be happy to, sir."

"Naw," Arnie grumbled. "Just run along."

As she departed, Arnie once more picked up his New York *Times* and again read. Back home on Earth you could buy a new encoder for almost nothing; in fact, back home you could—hell. Look at the stuff being advertised . . . from old Roman coins to fur coats to camping equipment to diamonds to rocket ships to crabgrass poison. Jeez!

However, his immediate problem was how to contact his ex-wife without the use of his encoder. Maybe I can just drop by and see her, Arnie said to himself. Good excuse to get out of the office.

He picked up the telephone and called for a 'copter to be made ready up above him on the roof of the Union Hall, and then he finished off the remains of his breakfast, wiped his mouth hurriedly, and set off for the elevator.

"Hi, Arnie," the 'copter pilot greeted him, a pleasant-faced young man from the pilot pool.

"Hi, my boy," Arnie said, as the pilot assisted him into the special leather seat which he had had made at the settlement's fabric and upholstery shop. As the pilot got into the seat ahead of him Arnie leaned back comfortably, crossed his legs, and said, "Now you just take off and I'll direct you in flight.

And take it easy because I'm in no hurry. It looks like a nice day."

"Real nice day," the pilot said, as the blades of the 'copter began to rotate. "Except for that haze over around the F.D.R. Range."

They had hardly gotten into the air when the 'copter's loud-speaker came on. "Emergency announcement. There is a small party of Bleekmen out on the open desert at gyrocompass point 4.65003 dying from exposure and lack of water. Ships north of Lewistown are instructed to direct their flights to that point with all possible speed and give assistance. United Nations law requires all commercial and private ships to respond." The announcement was repeated in the crisp voice of the UN announcer, speaking from the UN transmitter on the artificial satellite somewhere overhead.

Feeling the 'copter alter its course, Arnie said, "Aw, come on, my boy."

"I have to respond, sir." the pilot said. "It's the law."

Chrissake, Arnie thought with disgust. He made a mental note to have the boy sacked or at least suspended as soon as they got back from their trip.

Now they were above the desert, moving at good speed toward the intersect which the UN announcer had given. Bleekmen niggers, Arnie thought. We have to drop everything we're doing to bail them out, the damn fools—can't they trot across their own desert? Haven't they been doing it without our help for five thousand years?

As Jack Bohlen started to lower his Yee Company repair-ship toward McAuliff's dairy ranch below, he heard the UN announcer come on with the emergency notification, the like of which Bohlen had heard many times before and which never failed to chill him.

". . . Party of Bleekmen out on the open desert," the matter-of-fact voice declared. ". . . Dying from exposure and lack of water. Ships north of Lewistown—"

I've got it, Jack Bohlen said to himself. He cut his mike on and said, "Yee Company repairship close by gyrocompass point 4.65003, ready to respond at once. Should reach them in two or three minutes." He swung his 'copter south, away from McAuliff's ranch, getting a golden-moment sort of satis-faction at the thought of McAuliff's indignation right now as he saw the 'copter swing away and guessed the reason. No one had less use for the Bleekmen than did the big ranchers; the poverty-stricken, nomadic natives were constantly showing up at the ranches for food, water, medical help, and sometimes just a plain old-fashioned handout, and nothing seemed to madden the prosperous dairymen more than to be used by the creatures whose land they had appropriated.

Another 'copter was responding, now. The pilot was saying, "I am just outside Lewistown at gyrocompass point 4.78995 and will respond as soon as possible. I have rations aboard including fifty gallons of water." He gave his identification and then rang off.

The dairy ranch with its cows fell away to the north, and Jack Bohlen was gazing intently down at the open desert once more, seeking to catch sight of the party of Bleekmen. Sure enough, there they were. Five of them, in the shade cast by a small hill of stone. They were not moving. Possibly they were already dead. The UN satellite, in its swing across the sky, had discovered them, and yet it could not help them. Their mentors were powerless. And we who can help them— what do we care? Jack thought. The Bleekmen were dying out anyhow, the remnants getting more tattered and despairing every year. They were wards of the UN, protected by them. Some protection, Jack thought.

But what could be done for a waning race? Time had run out for the natives of Mars long before the first Soviet ship had appeared in the sky with its television cameras grinding away, back in the '60's. No human group had conspired to exterminate them; it had not been necessary. And anyhow they had been a vast curiosity, at first. Here was a discovery worth the billions spent in the task of reaching Mars. Here was an extraterrestrial race.

He landed the 'copter on the flat sand close by the party of Bleekmen, switched off the blades, opened the door, and stepped out.

The hot morning sun beat down on him as he walked across the sand toward the unmoving Bleekmen. They were alive; they had their eyes open and were watching him.

"Rains are falling from me onto your valuable persons," he called to them, the proper Bleekman greeting in the Bleeky dialect.

Close to them now he saw that the party consisted of one wrinkled old couple, a young male and female, no doubt husband and wife, and their infant. A family, obviously, which had set out across the desert alone on foot, probably seeking water or food; perhaps the oasis at which they had been subsisting had dried up. It was typical of the plight of the Bleek-men, this conclusion to their trek. Here they lay, unable to go on any farther; they had withered away to something re-sembling heaps of dried vegetable matter and they would have died soon had not the UN satellite spotted them.

Rising to his feet slowly, the young Bleekman male genu-flected and said in a wavering, frail voice, "The rains falling from your wonderful presence envigor and restore us, Mister."

Jack Bohlen tossed his canteen to the young Bleekman, who at once knelt down, unscrewed the cap, and gave it to the supine elderly couple. The old lady seized it and drank from it.

The change in her came at once. She seemed to swell back into life, to change from the muddy gray color of death before his eyes.

"May we fill our eggshells?" the young Bleekman male asked Jack. Lying upright on the sand were several paka eggs, pale hollow shells which Jack saw were completely empty. The Bleekmen transported water in these shells; their technical ability was so slight that they did not even possess clay pots. And yet, he reflected, their ancestors had constructed the great canal system.

"Sure," he said. "There's another ship coming with plenty of water." He went back to his 'copter and got his lunch pail; returning with it, he handed it to the Bleekman male. "Food," he explained. As if they didn't know. Already the elderly cou-ple were on their feet, tottering up with their hands stretched out.

Behind Jack, the roar of a second 'copter grew louder. It was landing, a big two-person 'copter that now coasted up and halted, its blades slowly spinning.

The pilot called down, "Do you need me? If not, I'll go on."

"I don't have much water for them," Jack said.

"O.K.," the pilot said, and switched off his blades. He hopped out, lugging a five-gallon can. "They can have this."

Together, Jack and the pilot stood watching the Bleekman filling their eggshells from the can of water. Their possessions were not many—a quiver of poisoned arrows, an animal hide for each of them; the two women had their pounding blocks, their sole possessions of value: without the blocks they were not fit women, for on them they prepared either meat or grain, whatever food their hunt might bring. And they had a few cigarettes.

"My passenger," the young pilot said in a low voice in Jack's ear, "isn't too keen about the UN being able to compel us to stop like this. But what he doesn't realize is they've got that satellite up there and they can see if you fail to stop. And it's a hell of a big fine."

Jack turned and looked up into the parked 'copter. He saw seated inside it a heavy-set man with a bald head, a well-fed, self-satisfied-looking man who gazed out sourly, paying no attention to the five Bleekmen.

"You have to comply with the law," the pilot said in a defensive voice. "It'd be me who they'd sock with the fine."

Walking over to the ship, Jack called up to the big bald-headed man seated within, "Doesn't it make you feel good to know you saved the lives of five people?"

The bald-headed man looked down at him and said, "Five niggers, you mean. I don't call that saving five people. Do you?"

"Yeah, I do," Jack said. "And I intend to continue doing so."

"Go ahead, call it that," the bald-headed man said. Flushing, he glanced over at Jack's 'copter, read the markings on it. "See where it gets you."

Coming over beside Jack, the young pilot said hurriedly, "That's Arnie you're talking to. Arnie Kott." He called up, "We can leave now, Arnie." Climbing up, the pilot disappeared inside the 'copter, and once more the blades began to turn.

The 'copter rose into the air, leaving Jack standing alone by the five Bleekmen. They had now finished drinking and were eating from the lunch pail which he had given them. The empty water can lay off to one side. The paka eggshells had been filled and were now stoppered. The Bleekmen did not glance up as the 'copter left. They paid no attention to Jack, either; they murmured among themselves in their dialect.

"What's your destination?" Jack asked them.

The young Bleekman named an oasis very far to the south.

"You think you can make it?" Jack asked. He pointed to the old couple. "Can they?"

"Yes, Mister," the young Bleekman answered. "We can make it now, with the food and water yourself and the other Mister gave us."

I wonder if they can, Jack said to himself. Naturally they'd say it, even if they knew it wasn't possible. Racial pride, I guess.

"Mister," the young Bleekman said, "we have a present for you because you stopped." He held out something to Jack.

Their possessions were so meager that he could not believe they had anything to spare. He held his hand out, however, and the young Bleekman put something small and cold into it, a dark, wrinkled, dried bit of substance that looked to Jack like a section of tree root.

"It is a water witch," the Bleekman said. "Mister, it will bring you water, the source of life, any time you need."

"It didn't help you, did it?" Jack said.

With a sly smile the young Bleekman said, "Mister, it helped; it brought you."

"What'll you do without it?" Jack asked.

"We have another. Mister, we fashion water witches." The young Bleekman pointed to the old couple. "They are authorities."

More carefully examining the water witch, Jack saw that it had a face and vague limbs. It was mummified, once a living creature of some sort; he made out its drawn-up legs, its ears . . . he shivered. The face was oddly human, a wizened, suffering face, as if it had been killed while crying out.

"How does it work?" he asked the young Bleekman.

"Formerly, when one wanted water, one pissed on the water witch, and she came to life. Now we do not do that, Mister; we have learned from you Misters that to piss is wrong. So we spit on her instead, and she hears that, too, almost as well. It wakes her, and she opens her eyes and looks around, and then she opens her mouth and calls the water to her. As she did with you, Mister, and that other Mister, the big one who sat and did not come down, the Mister with no hair on his head."

"That Mister is a powerful Mister," Jack said. "He is monarch of the plumbers' union settlement, and he owns all of Lewistown."

"That may be," the young Bleekman said. "If so, we will not stop at Lewistown, because we could see that the Mister with no hair did not like us. We did not give him a water witch in return for his water, because he did not want to give us water; his heart was not with him in that deed, it came from his hands only."

Jack said goodbye to the Bleekmen and got back into his 'copter. A moment later he was ascending; below him, the Bleekmen waved solemnly.

I'll give the water witch to David, he decided. When I get home at the end of the week. He can piss on it or spit on it, whichever he prefers, to his heart's content.

three

NORBERT STEINER had a certain freedom to come and go as he pleased, because he was self-employed. In a small iron building outside of Bunchewood Park he manufactured health foods, made entirely from domestic plants and minerals, with no preservatives or chemical sprays or nonorganic attractive fertilizers. A firm at Bunchewood Park packaged his products for him in professional-type boxes, cartons, jars, and envelopes, and then Steiner drove about Mars selling them direct to the consumer.

His profit was fair, because after all he had no competition; his was the sole health food business on Mars.

And then, too, he had a sideline. He imported from Earth various gourmet food items such as truffles, goose-liver paté, caviar, kangaroo tail soup, Danish blue cheese, smoked oysters, quail eggs, rum babas, all of which were illegal on Mars, due to the attempt by the UN to force the colonies to become self-sufficient foodswise. The UN food experts claimed that it was unsafe to transport food across space, due to the chance of harmful radiation contaminating it, but Steiner knew better; the actual reason was their fear of the consequences to the colonies in case of war back Home. Food shipments would cease, and unless the colonies were self-sufficient they probably would starve themselves out of existence within a short time.

While he admired their reasoning, Steiner did not wish to acquiesce in fact. A few cans of French truffles imported on the sly would not cause the dairy ranchers to stop trying to produce milk, nor the hog, steer, and sheep ranchers from keeping on with the struggle to make their farms pay. Apple and peach and apricot trees would still be planted and tended, sprayed and watered, even if glass jars of caviar showed up in the various settlements at twenty dollars each.

31

At this moment, Steiner was inspecting a shipment of tins of halvah, a Turkish pastry, which had arrived the night before aboard the self-guiding ship which shuttled between Manila and the tiny field in the wastelands of the F.D.R. Mountains which Steiner had constructed, using Bleekmen as laborers. Halvah sold well, especially in New Israel, and Steiner, inspecting the tins for signs of damage, estimated that he could get at least five dollars for each one. And then also old Arnie Kott at Lewistown took almost anything sweet that Steiner could lay his hands on, plus cheeses and canned fish of every kind, not to mention the Canadian smoked bacon which showed up in five-pound tins, the same as Dutch hams. In fact, Arnie Kott was his best single customer.

The storage shed, where Steiner now sat, lay within sight of his small, private, illegal landing field. Upright on the field stood the rocket which had come in last night; Steiner's technician—he himself had no manual ability of any sort—was busy preparing it for its return flight to Manila. The rocket was small, only twenty feet high, but it was Swiss-made and quite stable. Above, the ruddy Martian sun cast elongated shadows from the peaks of the surrounding range, and Steiner had turned on a kerosene heater to warm his storage shed. The technician, seeing Steiner look out through the window of the shed, nodded to indicate that the rocket was ready for its return load, so Steiner put down his tins of halvah temporarily. Taking hold of the hand truck, he began pushing the load of cartons through the doorway of the shed and out onto the rocky ground.

"That looks like over a hundred pounds," his technician said critically, as Steiner came up pushing the hand truck.

"Very light cartons," Steiner said. They contained a dried grass which, back in the Philippines, was processed in such a way that the end result very much resembled hashish. It was smoked in a mixture with ordinary Virginia burley tobacco, and got a terrific price in the United States. Steiner had never tried the stuff himself; to him, physical and moral health were one—he believed in his health foods, and neither smoked nor drank.

Together he and Otto loaded the rocket with its cargo, sealed it, and then Otto set the guidance system's clock. In a few days José Pesquito back Home at Manila would be unloading the cargo, going over the order form included, and assembling Steiner's needs for the return trip.

"Will you fly me back with you?" Otto asked.

"I'm going first to New Israel," Steiner said.

"That's O.K. I've got plenty of time."

On his own, Otto Zitte had once operated a small black-market business; he dealt exclusively in electronic equipment, components of great fragility and small size, which were smuggled in aboard the common carriers operating between Earth and Mars. And at former times he had tried to import such prize black-market items as typewriters, cameras, tape recorders, furs, and whiskey, but there competition had driven him out. Trade in those necessities of life, selling on a mass basis throughout the colonies, had been taken over by the big professional black-market operators who had enormous capital to back them up and their own full-scale transportation system. And, anyhow, Otto's heart was not in it. He wanted to be a repairman; in fact, he had come to Mars for that purpose, not knowing that two or three firms monopolized the repair business, operating like exclusive guilds, such as the Yee Company, for whom Steiner's neighbor, Jack Bohlen, worked. Otto had taken the aptitude tests, but he was not good enough. Therefore, after a year or so on Mars, he had turned to working for Steiner and running his small import operation. It was humiliating for him, but at least he was not doing manual labor on one of the colonies' work gangs, out under the sun reclaiming the desert.

As Otto and Steiner walked back to the storage shed, Steiner said, "I personally can't stand those Israelis, even though I have to deal with them all the time. They're unnatural, the way they live, in those barracks, and always out trying to plant orchards, oranges or lemons, you know. They have the advantage over everybody else because back Home they lived almost like we live here, with desert and hardly any resources."

"True," Otto said. "But you have to hand it to them; they really hustle. They're not lazy."

"And not only that," Steiner said, "they're hypocrites regarding food. Look at how many cans of nonkosher meat they buy from me. None of them keep the dietary laws."

"Well, if you don't approve of them buying smoked oysters from you, don't sell to them," Otto said.

"It's their business, not mine," Steiner said.

He had another reason for visiting New Israel, a reason which even Otto did not know about. A son of Steiner's lived there, in a special camp for what were called "anomalous children." The term referred to any child who differed from the norm either physically or psychologically to the extent that

33

he could not be educated in the Public School. Steiner's son was autistic, and for three years the instructor at the camp had been working with him, trying to bring him into communication with the human culture into which he had been born.

To have an autistic child was a special shame, because the psychologists believed that the condition came from a defect in the parents, usually a schizoid temperament. Manfred Steiner, age ten, had never spoken a word. He ran about on tiptoe, avoiding people as if they were things, sharp-pointed and dangerous. Physically, he was a large healthy blond-haired boy, and for the first year or so the Steiners had rejoiced in having him. But now—even the instructor at Camp B-G could offer little hope. And the instructor was always optimistic; it was her job.

"I may be in New Israel all day," Steiner said, as he and Otto loaded the cans of halvah into the 'copter. "I have to visit every damn kibbutz in the place, and that takes hours."

"Why don't you want me along?" Otto demanded, with hot anger.

Steiner shuffled his feet, hung his head, and said guiltily, "You misunderstand. I'd love to have company, but—" For an instant he thought of telling Otto the truth. "I'll take you to the tractor-bus terminal and drop you off—O.K.?" He felt weary. When he got to Camp B-G he would find Manfred just the same, never meeting anyone's eye, always darting about on the periphery, more like a taut, wary animal than a child . . . . It was hardly worth going, but still he would go.

In his own mind, Steiner blamed it all on his wife; when Manfred was a baby, she had never talked to him or shown him any affection. Having been trained as a chemist, she had an intellectual, matter-of-fact attitude, inappropriate in a mother. She had bathed and fed the baby as if he were a laboratory animal like a white rat. She kept him clean and healthy but she had never sung to him, laughed with him, had not really used language to or with him. So naturally he had become autistic; what else could he do? Steiner, thinking about it, felt grim. So much for marrying a woman with a master's degree. When he thought of the Bohlen boy next door, yelling and playing—but look at Silvia Bohlen; she was a genuine mother and woman, vital, physical attractive, *alive.* True, she was domineering and selfish . . . she had a highly developed sense of what was hers. But he admired her for that. She was not sentimental; she was strong. For instance, consider the water

34

question, and her attitude. It was not possible to break her down, even by alleging that his own water tank had leaked out their two weeks' supply. Thinking about that, Steiner smiled ruefully. Silvia Bohlen hadn't been taken in, even for a moment.

Otto said, "Drop me off at the bus terminal, then."

With relief, Steiner said, "Good enough. And you won't have to endure those Israelis."

Eying him, Otto said, "I told you, Norbert, I don't mind them."

Together, they entered the 'copter, and Steiner seated himself at the controls and started the engine. He said nothing more to Otto.

As he set his 'copter down at Weizmann Field north of New Israel, Steiner felt guilty that he had talked badly about the Israelis. He had done it only as part of his speech designed to dissuade Otto from coming along with him, but nevertheless it was not right; it went contrary to his authentic feelings. Shame, he realized. That was why he had said it; shame because of his defective son at Camp B-G . . . what a powerful drive it was, it could make a man say anything.

Without the Israelis, his son would be uncared for. No other facilities for anomalous children existed on Mars, although there were dozens of such institutions back Home, as was every other facility one could think of. And the cost of keeping Manfred at the camp was so low as to be a mere formality. As he parked his 'copter and got out, Steiner felt his guilt grow until he wondered how he could face the Israelis. It seemed to him that, God forbid, they might be able to read his mind, might somehow intuit what he had said about them when he was elsewhere.

However, the Israeli field personnel greeted him pleasantly, and his guilt began to fade; evidently it did not show after all. Lugging his heavy suitcases, he crossed the field to the parking lot where the tractor-bus waited to take passengers into the central business district.

He had already boarded the bus and was making himself comfortable when he remembered that he had not brought any present for his son. Miss Milch, the instructor, had told him always to bring a gift, a durable object by which Manfred could recall his father after he had left. I'll just have to stop somewhere, Steiner said to himself. Buy a toy, a game perhaps. And then he remembered that one of the parents who visited her child at Camp B-G ran a gift shop in New Israel; Mrs. Esterhazy. He could stop there; Mrs. Esterhazy had seen Manfred and understood about the anomalous children in general. She would know what to give him, and there would be no embarrassing questions such as, How old is the boy?

At the stop nearest the gift shop he got off the bus and walked up the sidewalk, enjoying the sight of small, well-kept stores and offices. New Israel in many ways reminded him of Home; it was a true city, more so than Bunchewood Park itself or Lewistown. Many people could be seen, most of them hurrying as if they had business to conduct, and he drank in the atmosphere of commerce and activity.

He came to the gift shop, with its modern sign and sloping glass windows. Except for the Martian shrub growing in the windowbox, it could have been a store in downtown Berlin. He entered, and found Mrs. Esterhazy standing at the counter, smiling as she recognized him. She was an attractive matronly woman in her early forties, with dark hair, and always well-dressed, always looking fresh and intelligent. As everyone knew, Mrs. Esterhazy was terribly active in civic affairs and politics; she put out a newsletter and belonged to one committee after another.

That she had a child in Camp B-G: that was a secret, known only to a few of the other parents and of course the staff at the camp. It was a young child, only three, suffering from one of the formidable physical defects associated with exposure to gamma rays during its intrauterine existence. He had seen it only once. There were many sobering anomalies at Camp B-G, and he had come to accept them, whatever they looked like. At first it had startled him, the Esterhazy child; it was so small and shriveled, with enormous eyes like a lemur's. It had peculiar webbed fingers, as if it had been fashioned for an aquatic world. He had the feeling about it that it was astonishingly acute in its perceptions; it had studied him with deep intensity, seeming to reach some depth in him usually inaccessible, perhaps even to himself. . . . It had seemed to reach out somehow and probe his secrets and then it had withdrawn, accepting him on the basis of what it had picked up.

The child, he had surmised, was a Martian, that is, born on Mars, to Mrs. Esterhazy and some man who was not her husband, since she no longer had a husband. That fact he had picked up from her in conversation; she announced it calmly, making no bones about it. She had been divorced for a number of years. Obviously, then, the child at Camp B-G had been born out of wedlock, but Mrs. Esterhazy, like so many modern women, did not consider that a disgrace. Steiner shared her opinion.

Setting down his heavy suitcases, Steiner said, "What a nice little shop you have here, Mrs. Esterhazy."

"Thank you," she said, coming around from behind the counter. "What can I do for you, Mr. Steiner? Are you here to sell me yogurt and wheat germ?" Her dark eyes twinkled.

"I need a present for Manfred," Steiner said.

A soft, compassionate expression appeared on her face. "I see. Well—" She moved away from him, toward one of the counters. "I saw your son the other day, when I was visiting B-G. Has he shown any interest in music? Often autistic children enjoy music."

"He's fond of drawing. He paints pictures all the time."

She picked up a small wooden flutelike instrument. "This is locally made. And very well made, too." She held it out to him.

"Yes," he said. "I'll take this."

"Miss Milch is utilizing music as a method of reaching the authistic children at B-G," Mrs. Esterhazy said as she went to wrap up the wooden flute. "The dance, in particular." She hesitated, then. "Mr. Steiner, you know that I'm in constant touch with the political scene back Home. I—there's a rumor that the UN is considering—" She lowered her voice, her face pale. "I do so hate to inflict suffering on you, Mr. Steiner, but if there is any truth in this, and there certainly seems to be . . ."

"Go ahead." But he wished now that he had not come in. Yes, Mrs. Esterhazy was in touch with important happenings, and it made him uneasy just to know that, without hearing anything more.

Mrs. Esterhazy said, "There's supposed to be a measure under debate at the UN right now, having to do with anomalous children." Her voice shook. "It would require the closing of Camp B-G."

After a moment he was able to say, "But, why?" He stared at her.

"They're afraid—well, they don't want to see what they call 'defective stock' appearing on the colonial planets. They want to keep the race pure. Can you understand that? I can, and yet I—well, I can't agree. Probably because of my own child. No, I just can't agree. They're not worried about the anomalous children at Home, because they don't have the aspirations for themselves that they do for us. You have to understand the idealism and anxiety which they have about us. . . . Do you remember how you felt before you emigrated here with your family? Back Home they see the existence of anomalous children on Mars as a sign that one of Earth's major problems has been transplanted into the future, because we *are* the future, to them, and—"

Steiner interrupted her. "You're certain about this bill?"

"I feel certain." She faced him, her chin up, her intelligent eyes calm. "We can't be too careful; it would be dreadful if they closed Camp B-G and—" She did not finish. In her eyes he read something unspeakable. The anomalous children, his boy and hers, would be killed in some scientific, painless, instantaneous way. Did she mean that?

"Say it," he said.

Mrs. Esterhazy said, "The children would be put to sleep."

Revolted, he said, "Killed, you mean."

"Oh, she said, "how can you speak it like that, as if you didn't care?" She gazed at him in horror.

"Christ," he said with violent bitterness. "If there's any truth in this—" But he did not believe her. Because, perhaps, he didn't want to? Because it was too ghastly? No, he thought. Because he did not trust her instincts, her sense of reality; she had picked up some garbled hysterical rumor. Perhaps there was a bill directed toward some tangential aspect of this that might affect Camp B-G and its children in some fashion. But they—the parents of anomalous children—had always lived under that cloud. They had read of the mandatory sterilization of both parents and offspring in cases where it was proved that the gonads had been permanently altered, generally in cases of exposure to gamma radiation in unusual mass quantity.

"Who in the UN are authors of this bill?" he asked.

"There are six members of the In-planet Health and Welfare Committee who are supposed to have written the bill." She began writing. "Here are their names. Now, Mr. Steiner, what we'd like you to do is to write to these men, and have anybody you know who—"

He barely listened. He paid for his flute, thanked her, accepted the folded piece of paper, and made his way out of the gift shop.

Goddamn, how he wished he hadn't gone in there! Did she enjoy telling such stories? Wasn't there trouble enough in the world as it was, without old wives' tales being peddled by middle-aged females who should not have had anything to do with public affairs in the first place?

But in him a quiet voice said, She may be right. You have to face it. Gripping his heavy suitcases, he walked on, confused and frightened, hardly aware of the small new shops which he passed as he hurried toward Camp B-G and his waiting son.

When he entered the great glass-domed solarium of Camp Ben-Gurion, there stood young, sandy-haired Miss Milch in her work smock and sandals, with clay and paint splattered on her, a hectic expression knitting her eyebrows. She tossed her head and pushed her tousled hair back from her face as she came toward him. "Hello, Mr. Steiner. What a day we've had. Two new children, and one of them a holy terror."

"Miss Milch," he said, "I was talking to Mrs. Esterhazy at her shop just now—"

"She told you about the supposed bill at the UN?" Miss Milch looked tired. "Yes, there is such a bill. Ann gets every sort of inside piece of news, although how she does it I have no idea. Try to keep from showing any agitation around Manfred, if you possibly can; he's been upset by the new arrivals today." She started off, to lead Mr. Steiner from the solarium down the corridor to the playroom in which his son would be found, but he hurried after her, halting her.

"What can we do about this bill?" he demanded breathlessly. He set down his suitcases, holding now only the paper bag in which Mrs. Esterhazy had put the wooden flute.

"I don't know that we can do anything," Miss Milch said. She went on slowly to the door and opened it. The sound of children's voices came shrill and loud to their ears. "Naturally, the authorities at New Israel and back Home in Israel itself have made furious protests, and so have several other governments. But so much of this is secret; the bill is secret, and it all has to be done sub rosa, so they won't start a panic. It's such a touchy subject. Nobody really knows what public sentiment is, on this, or even if it should be listened to." Her voice, weary and brittle, dragged, as if she were running down. But then she seemed to perk up. She patted him on the shoulder. "I think the worst they would do, once they closed B-G, is deport the anomalous children back Home; I don't think they'd ever go so far as to destroy them."

Steiner said quickly, "To camps back on Earth."

"Let's go and find Manfred," Miss Milch said. "All right?

I think he knows this is the day you come; he was standing by the window, but of course he does that a lot."

Suddenly, to his own surprise, he burst out in a choked voice, "I wonder if maybe they might be right. What use is it to have a child that can't talk or live among people?"

Miss Milch glanced at him but said nothing.

"He'll never be able to hold a job," Steiner said. "He'll always be a burden on society, like he is now. Isn't that the truth?"

"Autistic children still baffle us," Miss Milch said. "By what they are, and how they got that way, and by their tendency to begin to evolve mentally, all at once, for no apparent reason, after years of complete failure to respond."

"I think I can't in good conscience oppose this bill," Steiner said. "Not after thinking it over. Now that the first shock is over. It would be fair. I feel it's fair." His voice shook.

"Well," Miss Milch said, "I'm glad you didn't say that to Anne Esterhazy, because she'd never let you go; she'd be after you making speeches at you until you came around to her side." She held open the door to the big playroom. "Manfred is over in the corner."

Seeing his son from a distance, Steiner thought, You would never know to look at him. The large, well-formed head, the curly hair, the handsome features . . . The boy was bent over, absorbed in some object which he held. A genuinely good-looking boy, with eyes that shone sometimes mockingly, sometimes with glee and excitement . . . and such terrific coordination. The way he sprinted about, on the tips of his toes, as if dancing to some unheard music, some tune from inside his own mind whose rhythms kept him enthralled.

We are so pedestrian, compared to him, Steiner thought. Leaden. We creep along like snails, while he dances and leaps, as if gravity does not have the same influence on him as it does on us. Could he be made from some new and different kind of atom?

"Hi, Manny," Mr. Steiner said to his son.

The boy did not raise his head or show any sign of awareness; he continued fooling with the object.

I will write to the framers of the bill, Steiner thought, and tell them I have a child in the camp. And that I agree with them.

His thoughts frightened him.

Murder, of Manfred—he recognized it. My hatred of him coming out, released by this news. I see why they're debating it in secret; many people have this hate, I bet. Unrecognized inside.

"No flute for you, Manny," Steiner said. "Why should I give it to you, I wonder? Do you give a damn? No." The boy did not look up or give any indication of hearing. "Nothing," Steiner said. "Emptiness."

While Steiner stood there, tall, slender Dr. Glaub in his white coat, carrying his clipboard, approached. Steiner became suddenly aware of him and started.

"There is a new theory about autism," Dr. Glaub said. "From Berghölzlei, in Switzerland. I wished to discuss it with you, because it seems to offer us a new avenue with your son, here."

"I doubt it," Steiner said.

Dr. Glaub did not seem to hear him, he continued, "It assumes a derangement in the sense of time in the autistic individual, so that the environment around him is so accelerated that he cannot cope with it, in fact, he is unable to perceive it properly, precisely as we would be if we faced a speeded-up television program, so that objects whizzed by so fast as to be invisible, and sound was a gobbledegook—you know? Just extremely high-pitched mishmash. Now, this new theory would place the autistic child in a closed chamber, where he faced a screen on which filmed sequences were projected slowed down—do you see? Both sound and video slowed, at last so slow that you and I would not be able to perceive motion or comprehend the sounds as human speech."

Wearily, Steiner said, "Fascinating. There's always something new, isn't there, in psychotherapy?"

"Yes," Dr. Glaub said, nodding. "Especially from the Swiss; they're ingenious in comprehending the world-views of disturbed persons, of encapsulated individuals cut off from ordinary means of communication, isolated—you know?"

"I know," Steiner said.

Dr. Glaub, still nodding, had moved on, to stop by another parent, a woman, who was seated with her small girl, both of them examining a cloth picture book.

Hope before the deluge, Steiner thought. Does Dr. Glaub know that any day the authorities back on Earth may close Camp B-G? The good doctor labors on in idiotic innocence . . . happy in his schemes.

Walking after Dr. Glaub, Steiner waited until there was a pause in the conversation and then he said, "Doctor, I'd like to discuss this new theory a little further."

"Yes, yes," Dr. Glaub said, excusing himself from the woman and her child; he led Steiner over to one side, where they could talk privately. "This concept of time-rates may open a doorway to minds so fatigued by the impossible task of communicating in a world where everything happens with such rapidity that—"

Steiner interrupted, "Suppose your theory works out. How can you help such an individual function? Did you intend for him to stay in the closed chamber with the slowed-down picture screen the rest of his life? I think, Doctor, that you're all playing games, here. You're not facing reality. All of you at Camp B-G; you're so virtuous. So without guile. But the outside world—it's not like that. This is a noble, idealistic place, in here, but you're fooling yourselves. So in my opinion you're also fooling the patients; excuse me for saying it. This sloweddown closed chamber, it epitomizes you all, here, your attitude."

Dr. Glaub listened, nodding, with an intent expression on his face. "We have practical equipment promised," he said, when Steiner had finished. "From Westinghouse, back on Earth. Rapport with others in society is achieved primarily through sound, and Westinghouse has designed for us an audio recorder which picks up the message directed at the psychotic individual—for example, your boy Manfred—then, having recorded this message on iron-oxide tape, replays it almost instantly for him at lower speed, then erases itself and records the next message and so on, with the result that a permanent contact with the outside world, at his own rate of time, is maintained. And later we hope to have in our hands here a video recorder which will present a constant but slowed-down record to him of the visual portion of reality, synchronized with the audio portion. Admittedly, he will be one step removed from contact with reality, and the problem of touch presents difficulties—but I disagree when you say this is too idealistic to be of use. Look at the widespread chemical therapy that was tried not so long ago. Stimulants speeded up the psychotic's interior time-sense so that he could comprehend the stimuli pouring in on him, but as soon as the stimulant wore off, the psychotic's cognition slowed down as his faulty metabolism reestablished itself—you know? Yet we learned a good deal from that; we learned that psychosis has a chemical basis, not a psychological basis. Sixty years of erroneous notions were upset in a single experiment, using sodium amytal—"

"Dreams," Steiner interrupted. "You will never make contact with my boy." Turning, he walked away from Dr. Glaub.

From Camp B-G he went by bus to a swanky restaurant, the Red Fox, which always bought a good deal of his wares. After he had finished his business with the owner he sat for a time at the bar, drinking a beer.

The way Dr. Glaub had babbled on—that was the kind of idiocy that had brought them to Mars in the first place. To a planet where a glass of beer cost twice what a shot of Scotch cost, because it had so much more water in it.

The owner of the Red Fox, a small, bald, portly man wearing glasses, seated himself next to Steiner and said, "Why you looking so glum, Norb?"

Steiner said, "They're going to close down Camp B-G."

"Good," the owner of the Red Fox said. "We don't need those freaks here on Mars; it's bad advertising."

"I agree," Steiner said, "at least to a certain extent."

"It's like those babies with seal flippers back in the '60's, from them using that German drug. They should have destroyed all of them; there's plenty of healthy normal children born, why spare those others? If you had a kid with extra arms or no arms, deformed in some way, you wouldn't want it kept alive, would you?"

"No," Steiner said. He did not say that his wife's brother back on Earth was a phocomelus; he had been born without arms and made use of superb artificial ones designed for him by a Canadian firm which specialized in such equipment.

In fact he said nothing to the little portly man; he drank his beer and stared at the bottles behind the bar. He did not like the man at all, and he had never told him about Manfred. He knew the man's deepseated prejudice. Nor was he unusual. Steiner could summon up no resentment toward him; he merely felt weary, and did not want to discuss it.

"That was the beginning," the owner said. "Those babies born in the early '60's—are there any of them at Camp B-G— I've never set foot inside there and I never will."

Steiner said, "How could they be at B-G? They're hardly anomalous; anomalous means one of a kind."

"Oh, yeah," the man admitted. "I see what you mean. Anyhow, if they'd destroyed them years ago we wouldn't have such places as B-G, because in my mind there's a direct link between the monsters born in the '60's and all the freaks supposedly born due to radiation ever since; I mean, it's all

43

due to substandard genes, isn't it? Now, I think that's where the Nazis were right. They saw the need of weeding out the inferior genetic strains as long ago as 1930; they saw—"

"My son," Steiner began, and then stopped. He realized what he had said. The portly man stared at him. "My son is there," Steiner at last went on, "means as much to me as your son does to you. I know that someday he will emerge into the world once more."

"Let me buy you a drink, Norbert," the portly man said, "to show you how sorry I am; I mean, about the way I talked."

Steiner said, "If they close B-G it will be a calamity too great for us to bear, we who have children in there. I can't face it."

"I see what you mean," the portly man said. "I understand your feeling."

"You are superior to me if you understand how I feel," Steiner said, "because I can make no sense out of it." He set down his empty beer glass and stepped off the stool. "I don't want another drink," he said. "Excuse me; I have to leave." He picked up his heavy suitcases.

"You've been coming in here all this time," the owner said, "and we talked about that camp a lot, and you never told me you had a son in there. That wasn't right." He looked angry, now.

"Why wasn't it right?"

"Hell, if I had known I wouldn't have said what I said; you're responsible, Norbert—you could have told me, but you deliberately didn't. I don't like that one bit." His face was red with indignation.

Carrying his suitcases, Steiner left the bar.

"This is not my day," he said aloud. Argued with everybody; I'll have to spend the next visit here making apologies ... if I come back at all. But I have to come back; my business depends on it. And I have to stop at Camp B-G; there is no other way.

Suddenly it came to him that he should kill himself. The idea appeared in his mind full blown, as if it had always been there, always a part of him. Easy to do it, just crash the 'copter. He thought, I am goddamn tired of being Norbert Steiner; I didn't ask to be Norbert Steiner or sell black-market food or anything else. What is my reason for staying alive? I'm not good with my hands, I can't fix or make anything; I can't use my mind, either, I'm just a salesman. I'm tired of my wife's scorn because I can't keep our water ma-

44

chinery going—I'm tired of Otto who I had to hire because I'm helpless even in my own business.

In fact, he thought, why wait until I can get back to the 'copter? Along the street came a huge, rumbling tractor-bus, its sides dull with sand; it had crossed the desert just now, was coming to New Israel from some other settlement. Steiner set down his suitcases and ran out into the street, directly at the tractor-bus.

The bus honked; its airbrakes screeched. Other traffic halted as Steiner ran forward with his head down, his eyes shut. Only at the last moment, with the sound of the air horn so loud in his ears that it became unbearably painful, did he open his eyes; he saw the driver of the bus gaping down at him, saw the steering wheel and the number on the driver's cap. And then—

In the solarium at Camp Ben-Gurion, Miss Milch heard the sounds of sirens, and she paused in the middle of the Dance of the Sugar Plum Fairy from Tchaikovsky's *Nutcracker Suite,* which she was playing on the piano for the children to dance to.

"Fire!" one of the little boys said, going to the window. The other children followed.

"No, it's an ambulance, Miss Milch," another boy said, at the window, "going downtown."

Miss Milch resumed playing, and the children, at the sound of the rhythms coming from the piano, straggled back to their places. They were bears at the zoo, cavorting for peanuts; that was what the music suggested to them, Miss Milch told them to go ahead and act it out.

Off to one side, Manfred stood heedless of the music, his head down, a thoughtful expression on his face. As the sirens wailed up loudly for a moment, Manfred lifted his head. Noticing that, Miss Milch gasped and breathed a prayer. The boy had heard! She thumped away at the Tchaikovsky music even more loudly than before, feeling exultation: she and the doctors had been right, for through sound there had come about a contact with the boy. Now Manfred went slowly to the window to look out; all alone he gazed down at the buildings and streets below, searching for the origin of the noise which had aroused him, attracted his attention.

Things are not so hopeless after all, Miss Milch said to herself. Wait until his father hears; it shows we must never talk of giving up.

She played on, loudly and happily.

four

DAVID BOHLEN, building a dam of wet soil at the end of his family's vegetable garden under the hot midafternoon Martian sun, saw the UN police 'copter settle down and land before the Steiners' house, and he knew instantly that something was going on.

A UN policeman in his blue uniform and shiny helmet stepped from the 'copter and walked up the path to the Steiners' front door, and when two of the little girls appeared the policeman greeted them. He then spoke to Mrs. Steiner and then he disappeared on inside, and the door shut after him.

David got to his feet and hurried from the garden, across the stretch of sand to the ditch; he leaped the ditch and crossed the patch of flat soil where Mrs. Steiner had tried unsuccessfully to raise pansies, and at the corner of the house he suddenly came upon one of the Steiner girls; she was standing inertly, picking apart a stalk of wur-weed, her face white. She looked as if she were going to be sick.

"Hey, what's wrong?" he asked her. "Why's the policeman talking to your mom?"

The Steiner girl glanced at him and then bolted off, leaving him.

I'll bet I know what it is, David thought. Mr. Steiner has been arrested because he did something illegal. He felt excited and he jumped up and down. I wonder what he did. Turning, he ran back the way he had come, hopped once more across the ditch of water, and at last threw open the door to his own house.

"Mom!" he shouted, running from room to room. "Hey, you know how you and Dad always are talking about Mr. Steiner being outside the law, I mean in his work? Well, you know what?"

46

His mother was nowhere to be found; she must have gone visiting, he realized. For instance, Mrs. Henessy who lived within walking distance north along the ditch; often his mom was gone most of the day visiting other ladies, drinking coffee with them and exchanging gossip. Well, they're really missing out, David declared to himself. He ran to the window and looked out, to be sure of not missing anything.

The policeman and Mrs. Steiner had gone outside, now, and both were walking slowly to the police 'copter. Mrs. Steiner held a big handkerchief to her face, and the policeman had hold of her shoulder, as if he was a relative or something. Fascinated, David watched the two of them get into the 'copter. The Steiner girls stood together in a small group, their faces peculiar. The policeman went over and spoke to them, and then he returned to the 'copter—and then he noticed David. He beckoned to him to come outdoors, and David, feeling fright, did so; he emerged from the house, blinking in the sunlight, and step by step approached the policeman with his shining helmet and his armband and the gun at his waist.

"What's your name, son?" the policeman asked, with an accent.

"David Bohlen." His knees shook.

"Is Mother or Father home, David?"

"No," he said, "just me."

"When your parents return, you tell them to keep watch on the Steiner children until Mrs. Steiner is back." The policeman started up the motor of the 'copter, and the blades began to turn. "You do that, David? Do you understand?"

"Yes, sir," David said, noticing that the policeman had on the blue stripe which meant he was Swedish. The boy knew all the identifying marks which the different UN units wore. He wondered how fast the police 'copter could go; it looked like a special fast job, and he wished he could ride in it: he was no longer frightened of the policeman and he wished they could talk more. But the policeman was leaving; the 'copter rose from the ground, and torrents of wind and sand blew around David, forcing him to turn away and put his arm across his face.

The four Steiner girls still stood gathered together, none of them speaking. One, the oldest, was crying; tears ran down her cheeks but she made no sound. The smallest, who was only three, smiled shyly at David.

"You want to help me with my dam?" David called to them.

47

"You can come over; the policeman told me it was O.K."

After a moment the youngest Steiner girl came toward him, and then the others followed.

"What did your dad do?" David asked the oldest girl. She was twelve, older than he. "The policeman said you could say," he added.

There was no answer; the girl merely stared at him.

"If you tell me," David said, "I won't tell anyone. I promise to keep it a secret."

Sunbathing out on June Henessy's fenced, envined patio, sipping iced tea and drowsily conversing, Silvia Bohlen heard the radio from within the Henessy house give the late afternoon news.

Beside her, June raised herself up and said, "Say, isn't he the man who lives next door to you?"

"Shh," Silvia said, intently listening to the announcer. But there was no more, only the brief mention: Norbert Steiner, a dealer in health foods, had committed suicide on a downtown New Israel street by throwing himself in the path of a bus. It was the same Steiner, all right; it was their neighbor, she knew it at once.

"How dreadful," June said, sitting up and fastening the straps of her polka-dot cotton halter. "I only saw him a couple of times, but—"

"He was a dreadful little man," Silvia said. "I'm not surprised he did it." And yet she felt horrified. She could not believe it. She got to her feet, saying, "With four children—he left her to take care of four children! Isn't that dreadful? What's going to happen to them? They're so helpless anyhow."

"I heard," June said, "that he deals on the black market. Had you heard that? Maybe they were closing in on him."

Silvia said, "I better go right home and see if there's anything I can do for Mrs. Steiner. Maybe I can take the children for a while." Could it have been my fault? she asked herself. Could he have done it because I refused them that water, this morning? It could be, because he was there; he had not gone to work yet.

So maybe it is our fault, she thought. The way we treated them—which of us has ever been really nice to them and accepted them? But they are such dreadful whining people, always asking for help, begging and borrowing . . . who could respect them?

Going into the house she changed, in the bedroom, to her slacks and t-shirt. June Henessy followed along with her.

"Yes," June said, "you're right—we all have to pitch in and help where we can. I wonder if she'll stay on or if she'll go back to Earth. I'd go back—I'm practically ready to go back anyhow, it's so dull here."

Getting her purse and cigarettes, Silvia said goodbye to June and set out on the walk back down the ditch to her own home. Breathless, she arrived in time to see the police 'copter disappearing into the sky. That was them notifying her, she decided. In the backyard she found David with the four Steiner girls; they were busy playing.

"Did they take Mrs. Steiner with them?" she called to David.

The boy scrambled at once to his feet and came up to her excitedly. "Mom," she went along with him. "I'm taking care of the girls."

That's what I was afraid of, Silvia thought. The four girls still sat at the dam, playing a slow-motion, apathetic game with the mud and water, none of them looking up or greeting her; they seemed inert, no doubt from the shock of learning about their father's death. Only the smallest one showed any signs of reviving, and she probably had not comprehended the news in the first place. Already, Silvia thought, that little man's death has reached out and touched others, and the coldness is spreading. She felt the chill in her own heart. And I did not even like him, she thought.

The sight of the four Steiner girls made her quake. Am I going to have to take on these pudding-y, plump, vapid, low-class children? she asked herself. The answering thought thrust its way up, tossing every other consideration aside: *I don't want to!* She felt panic, because it was obvious that she had no choice; even now they were playing on her land, in her garden —she had them already.

Hopefully, the smallest girl asked, "Miz Bohlen, could we have some more water for our dam?"

Water, always wanting water, Silvia thought. Always leeching on us, as if it was a trait born into them. She ignored the child and said instead to her son, "Come into the house—I want to talk to you."

Together, they went indoors, where the girls could not overhear.

"David," she said, "their father is dead, it came over the radio. That's why the police came and took her. We'll have to help out for a while." She tried to smile, but it was impossible. "However much we may dislike the Steiners—"

David burst out—"I don't dislike them, Mom. How come he died? Did he have a heart attack? Was he set on by wild Bleekmen, could that be?"

"It doesn't matter how he happened to die; what we have to think of now is what we can do for those girls." Her mind was empty; she could think of nothing. All she knew was that she did not want to have the girls near her. "What should we do?" she asked David.

"Maybe fix them lunch. They told me they didn't have any; she was just about to fix it."

Silvia went out from the house and down the path. "I'm going to fix lunch, girls, for any of you who want it. Over at your house." She waited a moment and then started toward the Steiner house. When she looked back she saw that only the smallest child was following.

The oldest girl said in a tear-choked voice, "No, thank you."

"You'd better eat," Silvia said, but she was relieved. "Come along," she said to the little girl. "What's your name?"

"Betty," the little girl said shyly. "Could I have a egg sandwich? And cocoa?"

"We'll see what there is," Silvia said.

Later, while the child ate her egg sandwich and drank her cocoa, Silvia took the opportunity to explore the Steiner house. In the bedroom she came upon something which interested her: a picture of a small boy with dark, enormous, luminous eyes and curly hair; he looked, Silvia thought, like a despairing creature from some other world, some divine and yet dreadful place beyond their own.

Carrying the picture into the kitchen she asked little Betty who the boy was.

"That's my brother Manfred," Betty answered, her mouth full of egg and bread. Then she began to giggle. Between the giggles a few hesitant words emerged, and Silvia caught the fact that the girls were not supposed to mention their brother to anyone.

"Why doesn't he live with you?" Silvia asked, full of curiosity.

"He's at camp," Betty said. "Because he can't talk."

"What a shame," Silvia said, and she thought, At that camp in New Israel, no doubt. No wonder the girls aren't supposed to mention him; he's one of those anomalous children you hear of but never see. The thought made her sad. Unglimpsed tragedy in the Steiner household; she had never guessed. And it was in New Israel that Mr. Steiner had taken his life. Undoubtedly he had been visiting his son.

Then it has nothing to do with us, she decided as she returned the picture to its place in the bedroom. Mr. Steiner's decision was based on a personal matter. So she felt relieved.

Strange, she thought, how one has the immediate reaction of guilt and responsibility when one hears of a suicide. If only I hadn't done this, or had done that . . . I could have averted it. I'm at fault. And it was not so in this situation, not at all; she was a total outsider to the Steiners, sharing no part of their actual life, only imagining, in a fit of neurotic guilt, that she did so.

"Do you ever see your brother?" she asked Betty.

"I think I saw him last year," Betty said hesitantly. "He was playing tag, and there were a lot of other boys bigger than me."

Now, silently, the three older Steiner girls filed into the kitchen and stood by the table. At last the eldest burst out, "We changed our mind, we would like lunch."

"All right, Silvia said. "You can help me crack the eggs and peel them. Why don't you go and get David, and I'll feed him at the same time? Wouldn't that be fun, to all eat together?"

They nodded mutely.

Walking up the main street of New Israel, Arnie Kott saw a crowd ahead and cars pulled to a halt at the curb, and he paused momentarily before turning in the direction of Anne Esterhazy's Contemporary Arts Gift Shop. Something up, he said to himself. Robbery? Street brawl?

However, he did not have time to investigate. He continued on his way and arrived presently at the small modern shop which his ex-wife ran; hands in his trouser pockets, he sauntered in.

"Anybody home?" he called jovially.

No one there. She must have taken off to see the excitement, Arnie said to himself. Some business sense; didn't even lock up the store.

A moment later Anne came hurrying breathlessly back into the store. "Arnie," she said in surprise, seeing him. "Oh my God, do you know what happened? I was just talking to him, just talking, not more than an hour ago. And now he's dead." Tears filled her eyes. She collapsed onto a chair, found a Kleenex, and blew her nose. "It's just terrible," she said in

51

a muffled voice. "And it wasn't an accident; he did it deliberately."

"Oh, so that's what's going on," Arnie said, wishing now
that he had gone on and taken a look. "Who do you mean?"

"You wouldn't know him. He has a child at the camp;
that's how I met him." She rubbed her eyes and sat for a
time, while Arnie meandered about the store. "Well," she
said at last, "what can I do for you? It's nice to see you."

"My goddamn encoder broke down," Arnie said. "You know
how hard it is to get decent repair service. What could I do but
come by? What do you say to having lunch with me? Lock up
the store a little while."

"Of course," she said distractedly. "Just let me go wash my
face. I feel as if it was me. I saw him, Arnie. The bus rolled
right over him; they have such mass, they just can't stop. I
would like some lunch—I want to get out of here." She hurried
into the washroom—and closed the door.

Soon afterwards the two of them were walking up the sidewalk together.

"Why do people take their own lives?" Anne asked. "I
keep thinking I could have prevented it. I sold him a flute
for his boy. He still had the flute; I saw it with his suitcases
on the curb—he never gave it to his son. Is that the reason,
something to do with the flute? I debated between the flute
and—"

"Cut it out," Arnie said. "It's not your fault. Listen, if a man
is going to take his life nothing can stop him. And you can't
cause a person to do it; it's in his bloodstream, it's his destiny.
They work themselves up to doing it years in advance, and
then it's just like a sudden inspiration; all of a sudden—wham.
They do it, see?" He wrapped his arm around her and patted
her.

She nodded.

"Now, I mean, *we've* got a kid there at Camp B-G, but it
doesn't get us down," Arnie went on. "It's not the end of the
world, right? We go on. Where do you want to eat? How's
that place across the street, that Red Fox? Any good? I'd like
some fried prawns, but hell, it's been almost a year since I
saw them. This transportation problem has got to be licked
or nobody is emigrating."

"Not the Red Fox," Anne said. "I loathe the man who runs
it. Let's try that place on the corner; it's new, I haven't ever
eaten in there. I hear it's supposed to be good."

As they sat at a table in the restaurant, waiting for their

food to come, Arnie went on and developed his point. "One thing, when you hear about a suicide, you can be sure the guy knows this: he knows he's not a useful member of society. That's the real truth he's facing about himself, that's what does it, knowing you're not important to anybody. If there's one thing I'm sure of it's that. It's nature's way—the expendable are removed, by their own hand, too. So I don't lose any sleep when I hear of a suicide, and you'd be surprised how many so-called natural deaths here on Mars are actually suicides; I mean, this is a harsh environment. This place weeds out the fit from the unfit."

Anne Esterhazy nodded but did not seem cheered up.

"Now this guy—" Arnie continued.

"Steiner," Anne said.

"Steiner!" He stared at her. "Norbert Steiner, the black-market operator?" His voice rose.

"He sold health foods."

"That's the guy!" He was flabbergasted. "Oh, no, not Steiner." Good grief, he got all his goodies from Steiner; he was utterly dependent on the man.

The waiter appeared with their food.

"This is awful," Arnie said, "I mean, really awful. What am I going to do?" Every party he threw, every time he had a cozy two-person dinner arranged for himself and some girl, for instance Marty or especially of late Doreen . . . It was just too goddamn much in one day, this and his encoder, both together.

"Don't you think," Anne said, "it might have something to do with him being German? There's been so much sorrow in Germans since that drug plague, those children born with flippers. I've talked to some who've said openly they thought it was God's punishment on them for what was done during the Nazi period. And these weren't religious men, these were businessmen, one here on Mars, the other at Home."

"That damn stupid Steiner," Arnie said. "That cabbage head."

"Eat your food, Arnie." She began to unfold her napkin. "The soup looks good."

"I can't eat," he said. "I don't want this slop." He pushed his soup bowl away.

"You're still just like a big baby," Anne said. "Still having your tantrums." Her voice was soft and compassionate.

"Hell," he said, "sometimes I feel like I've got the weight

of the entire planet on me, and you call me a baby!" He glared at her in baffled outrage.

"I didn't know that Norbert Steiner was involved in the black market," Anne said.

"Naturally you wouldn't, you and your lady-committees. What do you know about the world around you? That's why I'm here—I read that last ad you had in the *Times* and it stank. You have to stop giving out that crap like you do; it repels intelligent people—it's just for other cranks like yourself."

"Please," Anne said. "Eat your food. Calm down."

"I'm going to assign a man from my Hall to look over your material before you distribute it. A professional."

"Are you?" she said mildly.

"We've got a real problem—we're not getting the skilled people to come over from Earth any more, the people we need. We're rotting—everybody knows that. We're falling apart."

Smiling, Anne said, "Somebody will take Mr. Steiner's place; there must be other black-market opeartors."

Arnie said, "You're deliberately misunderstanding me so as to make me look greedy and small, whereas actually I'm one of the most responsible members of the entire colonization attempt here on Mars, and that's why our marriage broke down, because of your belittling me out of jealousy and competitiveness. I don't know why I came over here today—it's impossible for you to work things out on a rational basis, you have to inflict personalities into everything."

"Did you know there's a bill before the UN to shut Camp B-G?" Anne said calmly.

"No," Arnie said.

"Does it distress you to think of B-G being closed?"

"Hell, we'll give Sam private individual care."

"What about the other children there?"

"You changed the subject," Arnie said. "Listen, Anne, you have to knuckle down to what you call masculine domination and let my people edit what you write. Honest to God, it does more harm than good—I hate to say this to your face but it's the truth. You're a worse friend than you would be an enemy, the way you go about things. You're a dabbler! Like most women. You're—irresponsible." He wheezed with wrath. Her face showed no reaction; what he said had no effect on her.

"Can you bring any pressure to bear to help keep B-G

open?" she asked. "Maybe we can make a deal. I want to see it kept open."

"A *cause,*" Arnie said ferociously.

"Yes."

"You want my blunt answer?"

She nodded, facing him coolly.

"I've been sorry ever since those Jews opened that camp."

Anne said, "Bless you, honest blunt Arnie Kott, mankind's friend."

"It tells the entire world we've got nuts here on Mars, that if you travel across space to get here you're apt to damage your sexual organs and give birth to a monster that would make those German flipper-people look like your next-door neighbor."

"You and the gentleman who runs the Red Fox."

"I'm just being hard-headedly realistic. We're in a struggle for our life; we've got to keep people emigrating here or we're dead on the vine, Anne. You know that. If we didn't have Camp B-G we could advertise that away from Earth's H-bomb-testing, contaminated atmosphere there are no abnormal births. I hoped to see that, but B-G spoils it."

"Not B-G. The births themselves."

"No one would be able to check up and show our abnormal births," Arnie said, "without B-G."

"You'd say it, knowing it's not true, if you could get away with it, telling them back Home that they're safer here—"

"Sure." He nodded.

"That's—immoral."

"No. Listen. You're the immoral one, you and those other ladies. By keeping Camp B-G open you're—"

"Let's not argue, we'll never agree. Let's eat, and then you go on back to Lewistown. I can't take any more."

They ate their meal in silence.

Dr. Milton Glaub, member of the psychiatric pool at Camp B-G, on loan from the Interplan Truckers' Union settlement, sat by himself in his own office once more, back from B-G, his stint there over for today. In his hands he held a bill for roof repairs done on his home the month before. He had put off the work—it involved the use of the scraper which kept the sand from piling up—but finally the settlement building inspector had mailed him a thirty-day condemnation notice. So he had contacted the Roofing Maintenance workers, knowing that he could not pay, but seeing no alternative. He was broke. This had been the worst month so far.

If only Jean, his wife, could spend less. But the solution did not lie there, anyhow; the solution was to acquire more patients. The ITU paid him a monthly salary, but for every patient he received an additional fifty-dollar bonus: incentive, it was called. In actuality it meant the difference between debt and solvency. Nobody with a wife and children could possibly live on the salary offered to psychiatrists, and the ITU, as everyone knew, was especially parsimonious.

And yet, Dr. Glaub continued to live in the ITU settlement; it was an orderly community, in some respects much like Earth. New Israel, like the other national settlements, had a charged, explosive quality.

As a matter of fact, Dr. Glaub had once lived in another national colony, the United Arab Republic one, a particularly opulent region in which much vegetation, imported from Home, had been induced to grow. But, to him, the settlers, constant animosity toward neighboring colonies had been first irritating and then appalling. Men, at their daily jobs, brooded over wrongs committed. The most charming individuals blew up when certain topics were mentioned. And at night the hostility took practical shape; the national colonies lived for the night. Then, the research labs, which were scenes of scientific experimentation and development during the day, were thrown open to the public, and infernal machines were turned out—it was all done with much excitement and glee, and of course national pride.

The hell with them, Dr. Glaub thought. Their lives were wasted; they had simply carried over the old quarrels from Earth—and the purpose of colonization had been forgotten. For instance, in the UN newspaper that morning he had read about a fracas in the streets of the electrical workers' settlement; the newspaper account implied that the nearby Italian colony was responsible, since several of the aggressors had been wearing the long waxed mustaches popular in the Italian colony. . . .

A knock at his office door broke his line of thought. "Yes," he said, putting the roofing bill away in a desk drawer.

"Are you ready for Goodmember Purdy?" his wife asked, opening the door in the professional manner that he had taught her.

"Send Goodmember Purdy in," Dr. Glaub said. "Wait a couple of minutes, though, so I can read over his case history."

"Did you eat lunch?" Jean asked.

"Of course. Everybody eats lunch."

"You look wan," she said.

That's bad, Dr. Glaub thought. He went from his office into the bathroom, where he carefully darkened his face with the caramel-colored powder currently in fashion. It did improve his looks, although not his state of mind. The theory behind the powder was that the ruling circles in the ITU were of Spanish and Puerto Rican ancestry, and they were apt to feel intimidated if a hired person had skin lighter than their own. Of course the ads did not put it like that; the ads merely pointed out to hired men in the settlement that "the Martian climate tends to allow natural skin tone to fade to unsightly white."

It was now time to see his patient.

"Good afternoon, Goodmember Purdy."

"Afternoon, Doc."

"I see from your file that you're a baker."

"Yeah, that's right."

A pause. "What did you wish to consult with me about?"

Goodmember Purdy, staring at the floor and fooling with his cap, said, "I never been to a psychiatrist before."

"No, I can see here that you haven't."

"There's this party my brother-in-law's giving . . . I'm not much on going to parties."

"Are you compelled to attend?" Dr. Glaub had quietly set the clock on his desk; it ticked away the goodmember's half-hour.

"They're sort of throwing it for me. They, uh, want me to take on my nephew as an apprentice so he'll be in the union eventually." Purdy droned on. ". . . And I been lying awake at night trying to figure out how to get out of it—I mean, these are my relatives, and I can't hardly come out and tell them no. But I just can't go, I don't feel good enough to. So that's why I'm here."

"I see," Dr. Glaub said. "Well, you'd better give me the particulars on this party, when and where it is, the names of the persons involved, so I can do a right bang-up job while I'm there."

With relief, Purdy dug into his coat pocket and brought out a neatly typed document. "I sure appreciate your going in my place, Doc. You psychiatrists really take a load off a man's back; I'm not joking when I say I been losing sleep over this." He gazed with grateful awe at the man before him,

57

skilled in the social graces, capable of treading the narrow, hazardous path of complex interpersonal realtions which had defeated so many union members over the years.

"Don't worry any further about it," Dr. Glaub said. For after all, he thought, what's a little schizophrenia? That is, you know, what you're suffering from. I'll take the social pressure from you, and you can continue in your chronic maladaptive state, at least for another few months. Until the next overpowering social demand is made on your limited capabilities. . . .

As Goodmember Purdy left the office, Dr. Glaub reflected that this certainly was a practical form of psychotherapy which had evolved here on Mars. Instead of curing the patient of his phobias, one became in the manner of a lawyer the actual advocate in the man's place at—

Jean called into the office, "Milt, there's a call for you from New Israel. It's Bosley Touvim."

Oh, God, Dr. Glaub thought. Touvim was the President of New Israel; something was wrong. Hurriedly he picked up the phone on his desk. "Dr. Glaub here."

"Doctor," sounded the dark, stern, powerful voice, "this is Touvim. We have a death here, a patient of yours, I understand. Will you kindly fly back here and attend to this? Allow me to give you a few token details . . . Norbert Steiner, a West German—"

"He's not my patient, sir," Dr. Glaub interrupted. "However, his son is—a little autistic child at Camp B-G. What do you mean, Steiner is dead? For heaven's sake, I was just talking to him this morning—are you sure it's the same Steiner? If it is, I do have a file on him, on the entire family, because of the nature of the boy's illness. In child autism we feel that the family situation must be understood before therapy can begin. Yes, I'll be right over."

Touvim said, "This is evidently a suicide."

"I can't believe it," Dr. Glaub said.

"For the past half-hour I have been discussing this with the staff at Camp B-G; they tell me you had a long conversation with Steiner shortly before he left the camp. At the inquest our police will want to know what indications if any Steiner gave of a depressed or morbidly introspective mood, what he said that might have given you the opportunity to dissuade him or, barring that, compel him to undergo therapy. I take it the man said nothing that would alert you to his intentions."

"Absolutely nothing," Dr. Glaub said.

"Then if I were you I wouldn't worry," Touvim said. Merely be prepared to give the clinical background of the man . . . discuss possible motives which might have led him to take his life. You understand."

"Thank you, Mr. Touvim," Dr. Glaub said weakly. "I suppose it is possible he was depressed about his son, but I outlined a new therapy to him; we have very high hopes for it. However, he did seem cynical and shut in, he did not respond as I would have expected. But suicide!"

What if I lose the B-G assignment? Doctor Glaub was asking himself. I just can't. Working there once a week added enough to his income so that he could imagine—although not attain—financial security. The B-G check at least made the goal plausible.

Didn't it occur to that idiot Steiner what effect his death might have on others? Yes, it must have; he did it to get vengeance on us. Paying us back—but for what? For trying to heal his child?

This is a very serious matter, he realized. A suicide, so close on the heels of a doctor-patient interview. Thank God Mr. Touvim warned me. Even so, the newspapers will pick it up, and all those who want to see Camp B-G closed will benefit from this.

Having repaired the refrigeration equipment at McAuliff's dairy ranch, Jack Bohlen returned to his 'copter, put his tool box behind the seat, and contacted his employer, Mr. Yee.

"The school," Mr. Yee said. "You must go there, Jack; I still have no one else to take that assignment."

"O.K., Mr. Yee." He started up the motor of the 'copter, feeling resigned to it.

"A message from your wife, Jack."

"Oh?" He was surprised; his employer frowned on wives of his employees phoning in, and Silvia knew that. Maybe something had happened to David. "Can you tell me what she said?" he asked.

Mr. Yee said, "Mrs. Bohlen asked our switchboard girl to inform you that a neighbor of yours, a Mr. Steiner, has taken his own life. Mrs. Bohlen is caring for the Steiner children, she wants you to know. She also asked if it was possible for you to come home tonight, but I told her that although we regretted it we could not spare you. You must stay available on call until the end of the week, Jack."

Steiner dead, Jack said to himself. The poor ineffectual sap. Well, maybe he's better off.

"Thank you, Mr. Yee," he said into the microphone.

As the 'copter lifted from the sparse grass of the pasture, Jack thought, This is going to affect all of us, and deeply. It was a strong and acute feeling, an intuition. I don't believe I ever exchanged more than a dozen words with Steiner at any one time, and yet—there is something enormous about the dead. Death itself has such authority. A transformation as awesome as life itself, and so much harder for us to understand.

He turned the 'copter in the direction of the UN headquarters on Mars, on his way to the great self-winding entity of their lives, the unique artificial organism which was their Public School, a place he feared more than any other in his experience away from Home.

five

WHY WAS IT that the Public School unnerved him? Scrutinizing it from above, he saw the duck-egg-shaped building, white against the dark, blurred surface of the planet, apparently dropped there in haste; it did not fit into its surroundings.

As he parked in the paved lot at the entrance he discovered that the tips of his fingers had whitened and lost feeling, a sign, familiar to him, that he was under tension. And yet this place did not bother David, who was picked up and flown here three days a week, along with other children of his achievement group. Evidently it was some factor in his own personal make-up; perhaps, because his knowledge of machines was so great, he could not accept the illusion of the school, could not play the game. For him, the artifacts of the school were neither inert nor alive; they were in some way both.

Soon he sat in a waiting room, his tool box beside him.

From a magazine rack he took a copy of *Motor World,* and heard, with his trained ears, a switch click. The school had noted his presence. It noted which magazine he selected, how long he sat reading, and what he next took. It measured him.

A door opened, and a middle-aged woman wearing a tweed suit, smiling at him, said, "You must be Mr. Yee's repairman."

"Yes," he said, standing.

"So glad to see you." She beckoned him to follow her. "There's been so much fuss about this one Teacher, but it is at the output stage." Striding down a corridor, she held a door open for him as he caught up. "The Angry Janitor," she said, pointing.

He recognized it from his son's description.

"It broke down suddenly," the woman was saying in his ear. "See? Right in the middle of its cycle—it had gone down the street and shouted and then it was just about to wave its fist."

"Doesn't the master circuit know—"

"I am the master circuit," the middle-aged woman said, smiling at him cheerfully, her steel-rimmed glasses bright with the sparkle in her eyes.

"Of course," he said, chagrined.

"We think it might be this," the woman—or rather this peripatetic extension of the school—said, holding out a folded paper.

Unwadding it, he found a diagrammed congeries of self-regulating feedback valves.

"This is an authority figure, isn't it?" he said. "Teaches the child to respect property. Very righteous type, as the Teachers go."

"Yes," the woman said.

Manually, he reset the Angry Janitor and restarted it. After clicking for a few moments, it turned red in the face, raised its arm and shouted, "You boys keep out of here, you understand?" Watching the whiskery jowls tremble with indignation, the mouth open and shut, Jack Bohlen could imagine the powerful effect it would have on a child. His own reaction was one of dislike. However, this construct was the essence of the successful teaching machine; it did a good job, in conjunction with two dozen other constructs placed, like booths in an amusement park, here and there along the corridors which made up the school. He could see the next teaching machine, just around the corner; several children stood respectfully in front of it as it delivered its harangue.

" . . . And then I thought," it was telling them in an affable, informal voice, "my gosh—what is it we folks can learn from an experience like that? Do any of you know? You, Sally."

A small girl's voice: "Um, well, maybe we can learn that there is some good in everybody, no matter how bad they act."

"What do you say, Victor?" the teaching machine bumbled on. "Let's hear from Victor Plank."

A boy stammered, "I'd say about what Sally said, that most people are really good underneath if you take the trouble to really look. Is that right, Mr. Whitlock?"

So Jack was overhearing the Whitlock Teaching Machine. His son had spoken of it many times; it was a favorite of his. As he got out his tools, Jack listened to it. The Whitlock was an elderly, white-haired gentleman, with a regional accent, perhaps that of Kansas. . . . He was kindly, and he let others express themselves; he was a permissive variety of teaching machine, with none of the gruffness and authoritarian manner of the Angry Janitor; he was, in fact, as near as Jack could tell, a combination of Socrates and Dwight D. Eisenhower.

"Sheep are funny," the Whitlock said. "Now, you look at how they behave when you throw some grub over the fence to them, such as corn stalks. Why, they'll spot that from a mile away." The Whitlock chuckled. "They're smart when it comes to what concerns them. And maybe that helps us see what true smartness is; it isn't having read a lot of big books, or knowing long words . . . it's being able to spot what's to our advantage. It's got to be useful to be real smartness."

Kneeling down, Jack began unscrewing the back from the Angry Janitor. The master circuit of the school stood watching.

This machine, he knew, went through its song-and-dance in response to a reel of instruction tape, but its performance was open to modification at each stage, depending on the behavior of its audience. It was not a closed system; it compared the children's answers with its own tape, then matched, classified, and at last responded. There was no room for a unique answer because the Teaching Machine could recognize only a limited number of categories. And yet, it gave a convincing illusion of being alive and viable; it was a triumph of engineering.

Its advantage over a human teacher lay in its capacity to deal with each child individually. It tutored, rather than merely teaching. A teaching machine could handle up to a thousand pupils and yet never confuse one with the next; with each child its responses altered so that it became a subtly different entity. Mechanical, yes—but almost infinitely complex. The teaching machines demonstrated a fact that Jack Bohlen was well aware of: there was an astonishing depth to the so-called "artificial."

And yet he felt repelled by the teaching machines. For the entire Public School was geared to a task which went contrary to his grain: the school was there not to inform or educate, but to mold, and along severely limited lines. It was the link to their inherited culture, and it peddled that culture, in its entirety, to the young. It bent its pupils to it; perpetuation of the culture was the goal, and any special quirks in the children which might lead them in another direction had to be ironed out.

It was a battle, Jack realized, between the composite psyche of the school and the individual psyches of the children, and the former held all the key cards. A child who did not properly respond was assumed to be autistic—that is, oriented according to a subjective factor that took precedence over his sense of objective reality. And that child wound up by being expelled from the school; he went, after that, to another sort of school entirely, one designed to rehabilitate him: he went to Camp Ben-Gurion. He could not be taught; he could only be dealt with as *ill*.

Autism, Jack reflected, as he unscrewed the back of the Angry Janitor, had become a self-serving concept for the authorities who governed Mars. It replaced the older term "psychopath," which in its time had replaced "moral imbecile," which had replaced "criminally insane." And at Camp B-G, the child had a human teacher, or rather *therapist*.

Ever since his own son David had entered the Public School, Jack had waited to hear the bad news, that the boy could not be graded along the scale of achievement by which the teaching machines classified their pupils. However, David had responded heartily to the teaching machines, had in fact scored very high. The boy liked most of his Teachers and came home raving about them; he got along fine with even the most severe of them, and by now it was obvious that he had no problems—he was not autistic, and he would never see the inside of Camp B-G. But this had not made Jack feel better. Nothing, Silvia had pointed out, would make him feel better. Only the two possibilities lay open, the Public School and Camp B-G, and Jack distrusted both. And why was that? He did not know.

Perhaps, he had once conjectured, it was because there really was such a condition as autism. It was a childhood form of schizophrenia, which a lot of people had; schizophrenia was a major illness which touched sooner or later almost every family. It meant, simply, a person who could not live out the drives implanted in him by his society. The reality which the schizophrenic fell away from—or never incorporated in the first place—was the reality of interpersonal living, of life in a given culture with given values; it was not biological life, or any form of inherited life, but *life which was learned*. It had to be picked up bit by bit from those around one, parents and teachers, authority figures in general . . . from everyone a person came in contact with during his formative years.

The Public School, then, was right to eject a child who did not learn. Because what the child was learning was not merely facts or the basis of a money-making or even useful career. It went much deeper. The child learned that certain things in the culture around him were worth preserving at any cost. His values were fused with some objective human enterprise. And so he himself became a part of the tradition handed down to him; he maintained his heritage during his lifetime and even improved on it. He cared. True autism, Jack had decided, was in the last analysis an apathy toward public endeavor; it was a private existence carried on as if the individual person were the creator of all value, rather than merely the repository of inherited values. And Jack Bohlen, for the life of him, could not accept the Public School with its teaching machines as the sole arbiter of what was and what wasn't of value. For the values of a society were in ceaseless flux, and the Public School was an attempt to stabilize those values, to jell them at a fixed point—to embalm them.

The Public School, he had long ago decided, was neurotic. It wanted a world in which nothing new came about, in which there were no surprises. And that was the world of the compulsive-obsessive neurotic; it was not a healthy world at all.

Once, a couple of years ago, he had told his wife his theory. Silvia had listened with a reasonable amount of attention and then she had said, "But you don't see the point, Jack. Try to understand. There are things so much worse than neurosis." Her voice had been low and firm, and he had listened. "We're just beginning to find them out. You know what they are. *You've gone through them.*"

And he had nodded, because he did know what she meant. He himself had had a psychotic interlude, in his early twenties. It was common. It was natural. And, he had to admit, it was horrible. It made the fixed, rigid, compulsive-neurotic Public School seem a reference point by which one could gratefully steer one's course back to mankind and shared reality. It made him comprehend why a neurosis was a deliberate artifact, deliberately constructed by the ailing individual or by a society in crisis. It was an invention arising from necessity.

"Don't knock neurosis," Silvia had said to him and he understood. Neurosis was a deliberate stopping, a freezing somewhere along the path of life. Because beyond lay—

Every schizophrenic knew what lay there. And every ex-schizophrenic, Jack thought, as he remembered his own episode.

The two men across the room from him gazed at him queerly. What had he said? *Herbert Hoover was a much better head of the FBI than Carrington will ever be.* "I know I'm right," he added. "I'll lay you odds." His mind seemed fuzzy, and he sipped at his beer. Everything had become heavy, his arm, and the glass itself; it was easier to look down rather than up. . . . He studied the match folder on the coffee table.

"You don't mean Herbert Hoover," Lou Notting said. "You mean J. Edgar—"

Christ! Jack thought in dismay. Yes, he had said Herbert Hoover, and until they had pointed it out it seemed O.K. What's the matter with me? he wondered. I feel like I'm half asleep. And yet he had gone to bed at ten the night before, had slept almost twelve hours. "Excuse me," he said. "Of course I mean . . ." He felt his tongue stumble. With care he said, "J. Edgar Hoover." But his voice sounded blurred and slowed down, like a turntable losing its momentum. And now it was almost impossible for him to raise his head; he was falling asleep where he sat, there in Notting's living room, and yet his eyes weren't closing—he found when he tried that he couldn't close them. His attention had become riveted on the match folder. Close cover before striking, he read. Can you draw this horse? First art lesson free, no obligation. Turn over for free enrollment blank. Unblinking, he stared on and on, while Lou Notting and Fred Clarke argued about abstract ideas such as the curtailment of liberties, the democratic process . . . he heard all the words perfectly clearly, and he did not mind listening. But he felt no desire to argue, even though he knew they both were wrong. He let them argue on; it was easier. It simply happened. And he let it happen.

"Jack's not with us tonight," Clarke was saying. With a start, Jack Bohlen realized they had turned their attention on him; he had to do or say something, now.

"Sure I am," he said, and it cost him terrific effort; it was like rising up out of the sea. "Go on, I'm listening."

"God, you're like a dummy," Notting said. "Go home and go to bed, for chrissakes."

Entering the living room, Lou's wife Phyllis said. "You'll never get to Mars in the state you're in now, Jack." She turned up the hi-fi; it was a progressive jazz group, vibes and double bass, or perhaps it was an electronic instrument playing. Blonde, pert Phyllis seated herself on the couch near him and studied him. "Jack, are you sore at us? I mean, you're so withdrawn."

"It's just one of his moods," Notting said. "When we were in the service he used to get them, especially on Saturday night. Morose and silent, brooding. What are you brooding about right now, Jack?"

The question seemed odd to him; he was not brooding about

anything, his mind was empty. The match folder still filled up his range of perception. Nevertheless, it was necessary that he give them an account of what he was brooding over; they all expected it, so, dutifully, he made up a topic. "The air," he said. "On Mars. How long will it take me to adjust? Varies, among different people." A yawn, which never came out, had lodged in his chest, diffusing throughout his lungs and windpipe. It left his mouth hanging partly open; with an effort he managed to close his jaws. "Guess I better go on," he said. "Hit the sack." With the use of all his strength he managed to get to his feet.

"At nine o'clock?" Fred Clarke yelled.

Later, as he walked home to his own apartment, along the cool dark streets of Oakland, he felt fine. He wondered what had been wrong back there at Notting's. Maybe bad air or the ventilation.

But something was wrong.

Mars, he thought. He had cut the ties, in particular his job, had sold his Plymouth, given notice to the official who was his landlord. And it had taken him a year to get the apartment; the building was owned by the nonprofit West Coast Co-op, an enormous structure partly underground, with thousands of units, its own supermarket, laundries, child-care center, clinic, even its own psychiatrist, down below in the arcade of shops beneath the street level. There was an FM radio station on the top floor which broadcast classical music chosen by the building residents, and in the center of the building could be found a theater and meeting hall. This was the newest of the huge cooperative apartment buildings—and he had given it all up, suddenly. One day he had been in the building's bookstore, waiting in line to buy a book, and the idea came to him.

After he had given notice he had wandered along the corridors of the co-op arcade. When he came to the bulletin board with its tacked-up notices, he had halted automatically to read them. Children scampered past him, on their way to the playground behind the building. One notice, large and printed, attracted his attention.

HELP SPREAD THE CO-OP MOVEMENT TO NEWLY COLONIZED AREAS. EMIGRATION PREPARED BY THE CO-OP BOARD IN SACRAMENTO IN ANSWER TO BIG BUSINESS AND BIG LABOR UNION EXPLOITATION OF MINERAL-RICH AREAS OF MARS. SIGN UP NOW!

It read much like all the co-op notices, and yet—why not? A lot of young people were going. And what was left for him on Earth? He had given up his co-op apartment, but he was still a member; he still had his share of stock and his number.

Later on, when he had signed up and was in the process of being given his physical and his shots, the sequence had blurred in his mind; he remembered the decision to go to Mars *as coming first,* and then the giving up of his job and apartment. It seemed more rational that way, and he told that story to his friends. But it simply wasn't true. What was true? For almost two months he had wandered about, confused and despairing, not certain of anything except that on November 14, his group, two hundred co-op members, would leave for Mars, and then everything would be changed; the confusion would lift and he would see clearly, as he had once at some vague period in the past. He knew that: once, he had been able to establish the order of things in space and time; now, for reasons unknown to him, both space and time had shifted so that he could not find his bearings in either one.

His life had no purpose. For fourteen months he had lived with one massive goal: to acquire an apartment in the huge new co-op building, and then, when he had gotten it, there was nothing. The future had ceased to exist. He listened to the Bach suites which he requested; he bought food at the supermarket and browsed in the building bookstore . . . but what for? he asked himself. Who am I? And at his job, his ability faded away. That was the first indication, and in some ways the most ominous of all; that was what had first frightened him.

It began with a weird incident which he was never able fully to account for. Apparently, part of it had been pure hallucination. But which part? It had been dreamlike, and he had had a moment of overwhelming panic, the desire to run, to get out at any cost.

His job was with an electronics firm in Redwood City, south of San Francisco; he operated a machine which maintained quality control along the assembly line. It was his responsibility to see that his machine did not deviate from its concept of acceptable tolerances in a single component: a liquid-helium battery no larger than a match-head. One day he was summoned to the personnel manager's office, unexpectedly; he did not know why they wanted him, and as he took the elevator up he was quite nervous. Later, he remembered that; he was unusually nervous.

"Come in, Mr. Bohlen." The personnel manager, a fine-looking man with curly gray hair—perhaps a fashion wig—welcomed him into his office. "This won't take but a moment." He eyed Jack keenly. "Mr. Bohlen, why aren't you cashing your paychecks?"

There was silence.

"Aren't I?" Jack said. His heart thudded ponderously, making his body shake. He felt unsteady and tired. I thought I was, he said to himself.

"You could stand a new suit," the personnel manager said, "and you need a haircut. Of course, it's your business."

Putting his hand to his scalp, Jack felt about, puzzled; did he need a haircut? Hadn't he just had one last week? Or maybe it was longer ago than that. He said, "Thanks." He nodded. "O.K., I will. What you just said."

And then the hallucination, if it was that, happened. He saw the personnel manager in a new light. The man was dead.

He saw, through the man's skin, his skeleton. It had been wired together, the bones connected with fine copper wire. The organs, which had withered away, were replaced by artificial components, kidney, heart, lungs—everything was made of plastic and stainless steel, all working in unison but entirely without authentic life. The man's voice issued from a tape, through an amplifier and speaker system.

Possibly at some time in the past the man had been real and alive, but that was over, and the stealthy replacement had taken place, inch by inch, progressing insidiously from one organ to the next, and the entire structure was there to deceive others. To deceive him, Jack Bohlen, in fact. He was alone in this office; there was no personnel manager. No one spoke to him, and when he himself talked, no one heard; it was entirely a lifeless, mechanical room in which he stood.

He was not sure what to do; he tried not to stare too hard at the manlike structure before him. He tried to talk calmly, naturally, about his job and even his personal problems. The structure was probing; it wanted to learn something from him. Naturally, he told it as little as possible. And all the time, as he gazed down at the carpet, he saw its pipes and valves and working parts functioning away; he could not keep from seeing.

All he wanted to do was get away as soon as possible. He began to sweat; he was dripping with sweat and trembling, and his heart pounded louder and louder.

"Bohlen," the structure said, "are you sick?"

"Yes," he said. "Can I go back down to my bench now?" He turned and started toward the door.

"Just a moment," the structure said from behind him.

That was when panic overtook him, and he ran; he pulled the door open and ran out into the hall.

An hour or so later he found himself wandering along an unfamiliar street in Burlingame. He did not remember the intervening time and he did not know how he had gotten where he was. His legs ached. Evidently he had walked, mile after mile.

His head was much clearer. I'm schizophrenic, he said to himself. I know it. Everyone knows the symptoms; it's catatonic excitement with paranoid coloring: the mental health people drill it into us, even into the school kids. I'm another one of those. That was what the personnel manager was probing.

I need medical help.

As Jack removed the power supply of the Angry Janitor and laid it on the floor, the master circuit of the school said, "You are very skillful."

Jack glanced up at the middle-aged female figure and thought to himself, It's obvious why this place unnerves me. It's like my psychotic experience of years ago. *Did I, at that time, look into the future?*

There had been no schools of this kind, then. Or if there had, he had not seen them or known about them.

"Thank you," he said.

What had tormented him ever since the psychotic episode with the personnel manager at Corona Corporation was this: suppose it was not a hallucination? Suppose the so-called personnel manager was as he had seen him, an artificial construct, a machine like these teaching machines?

If that had been the case, *then there was no psychosis.*

Instead of a psychosis, he had thought again and again, it was more on the order of a vision, a glimpse of absolute reality, with the façade stripped away. And it was so crushing, so radical an idea, that it could not be meshed with his ordinary views. And the mental disturbance had come out of that.

Reaching into the exposed wiring of the Angry Janitor, Jack felt expertly with his long fingers until at last he touched what he knew to be there: a broken lead. "I think I've got hold of it," he said to the master circuit of the school. Thank God, he thought, these aren't the old-fashioned printed circuits;

were that that the case, he would have to replace the unit. Repair would be impossible.

"My understanding," the master circuit said, "is that much effort went into the designing of the Teachers re problems of repair. We have been fortunate so far; no prolonged interruption of service has taken place. However, I believe that preventive maintenance is indicated wherever possible; therefore I would like you to inspect one additional Teacher which has as yet shown no signs of a breakdown. It is uniquely vital to the total functioning of the school." The master circuit paused politely as Jack struggled to get the long tip of the soldering gun past the layers of wiring. "It is Kindly Dad which I want you to inspect."

Jack said, "Kindly Dad." And he thought acidly, I wonder if there's an Aunt Mom in here somewhere. Aunt Mom's delicious home-baked tall tales for little tots to imbibe. He felt nauseated.

"You are familiar with that Teacher?"

As a matter of fact he was not; David hadn't mentioned it.

From farther down the corridor he could hear the children still discussing life with the Whitlock; their voices reached him as he lay on his back, holding the soldering gun above his head and reaching into the works of the Angry Janitor to keep the tip in place.

"Yes," the Whitlock was saying in its never-ruffled, absolutely placid voice, "the raccoon is an amazing fellow, ol' Jimmy Raccoon is. Many times I've seen him. And he's quite a large fellow, by the way, with powerful, long arms which are really quite agile."

"I saw a raccoon once," a child piped excitedly. "Mr. Whitlock, I saw one, and he was this close to me!"

Jack thought, You saw a raccoon on Mars?

The Whitlock chuckled. "No, Don, I'm afraid not. There aren't any raccoons around here. You'd have to go all the way across over to old mother Earth to see one of those amazing fellows. But the point I'd like to make is this, boys and girls. You know how ol' Jimmy Raccoon takes his food, and carries it oh so stealthily to the water, and washes it? And how we laughed at ol' Jimmy when the lump of sugar dissolved and he had nothing at all left to eat? Well, boys and girls, do you know that we've got Jimmy Raccoons right here in this very—"

"I think I'm finished," Jack said, withdrawing the gun. "Do you want to help me put this back together?"

The master circuit said, "Are you in a rush?"

"I don't like that thing talking away in there," Jack said. It made him tense and shaky, so much so that he could hardly do his work.

A door rolled shut, down the corridor from them; the sound of the Whitlock's voice ceased. "Is that better?" the master circuit asked.

"Thanks," Jack said. But his hands were still shaking. The master circuit noted that; he was aware of her precise scrutiny. He wondered what she made of it.

The chamber in which Kindly Dad sat consisted of one end of a living room with fireplace, couch, coffee table, curtained picture window, and an easy chair in which Kindly Dad himself sat, a newspaper open on his lap. Several children sat attentively on the couch as Jack Bohlen and the master circuit entered; they were listening to the expostulations of the teaching machine and did not seem aware that anyone had come in. The master circuit dismissed the children, and then she started to leave, too.

"I'm not sure what you want me to do," Jack said.

"Put it through its cycle. It seems to me that it repeats portions of the cycle or stays stuck; in any case, too much time is consumed. It should return to its starting stage in about three hours." A door opened for the master circuit, and she was gone; he was alone with Kindly Dad and he was not glad of it.

"Hi, Kindly Dad, he said without enthusiasm. Setting down his tool case he began unscrewing the back plate of the Teacher.

Kindly Dad said in a warm, sympathetic voice, "What's your name, young fellow?"

"My name," Jack said, as he unfastened the plate and laid it down beside him, "is Jack Bohlen, and I'm a kindly dad, too, just like you, Kindly Dad. My boy is ten years old, Kindly Dad. So don't call me young fellow, O.K.?" Again he was trembling hard, and sweating.

"Ohh," Kindly Dad said. "I see!"

"What do you see?" Jack said, and discovered that he was almost shouting. "Look," he said. "Go through your goddamn cycle, O.K.? If it makes it easier for you, go ahead and pretend I'm a little boy." I just want to get this done and get out of here, he said to himself, with as little trouble as possible. He could feel the swelling, complicated emotions inside him. Three hours! he thought dismally.

Kindly Dad said, "Little Jackie, it seems to me you've got a mighty heavy weight on your chest today. Am I right?"

"Today and every day." Jack clicked on his trouble-light and shone it up into the works of the Teacher. The mechanism seemed to be moving along its cycle properly so far.

"Maybe I can help you," Kindly Dad said. "Often it helps if an older, more experienced person can sort of listen in on your troubles, can sort of share them and make them lighter."

"O.K.," Jack agreed, sitting back on his haunches. "I'll play along; I'm stuck here for three hours anyhow. You want me to go all the way back to the beginning? To the episode back on Earth when I worked for Corona Corporation and had the occlusion?"

"Start wherever you like," Kindly Dad said graciously.

"Do you know what schizophrenia is, Kindly Dad?"

"I believe I've got a pretty good idea, Jackie," Kindly Dad said.

"Well, Kindly Dad, it's the most mysterious malady in all medicine, that's what it is. And it shows up in one out of every six people, which is a lot of people."

"Yes, that certainly is," Kindly Dad said.

"At one time," Jack said, as he watched the machinery moving, "I had what they call situational polymorphous schizophrenia simplex. And, Kindly Dad, it was rough."

"I just bet it was," Kindly Dad said.

"Now, I know what you're supposed to be for," Jack said, "I know your purpose, Kindly Dad. We're a long way from Home. Millions of miles away. Our connection with our civilization back Home is tenuous. And a lot of folks are mighty scared, Kindly Dad, because with each passing year that link gets weaker. So this Public School was set up to present a fixed milieu to the children born here, an Earthlike environment. For instance, this fireplace. We don't have fireplaces here on Mars; we heat by small atomic furnaces. That picture window with all that glass—sandstorms would make it opaque. In fact there's not one thing about you that's derived from our actual world here. Do you know what a Bleekman is, Kindly Dad?"

"Can't say that I do, Little Jackie. What is a Bleekman?"

"It's one of the indigenous races of Mars. You do know you're on Mars, don't you?"

Kindly Dad nodded.

"Schizophrenia," Jack said, "is one of the most pressing problems human civilization has ever faced. Frankly, Kindly Dad, I emigrated to Mars because of my schizophrenic episode when I was twenty-two and worked for Corona Corporation. I was cracking up. I had to move out of a complex urban environment and into a simpler one, a primitive frontier environment with more freedom. The pressure was too great for me; it was emigrate or go mad. That co-op building; can you imagine a thing going down level after level and up like a skyscraper, with enough people living there for them to have their own supermarket? I went mad standing in line at the bookstore. Everybody else, Kindly Dad, every single person in that bookstore and in that supermarket—all of them lived in the same building I did. It was a society, Kindly Dad, that one building. And today it's small by comparison with some that have been built. What do you say to that?"

"My, my," Kindly Dad said, shaking his head.

"Now here's what I think," Jack said. "I think this Public School and you teaching machines are going to rear another generation of schizophrenics, the descendents of people like me who are making a fine adaptation to this new planet. You're going to split the psyches of these children because you're teaching them to expect an environment which doesn't exist for them. It doesn't even exist back on Earth, now; it's obsolete. Ask that Whitlock Teacher if intelligence doesn't have to be practical to be true intelligence. I heard it say so, it has to be a tool for adaptation. Right, Kindly Dad?"

"Yes, Little Jackie, it has to be."

"What you ought to be teaching," Jack said, "is, how do we—"

"Yes, Little Jackie," Kindly Dad interrupted him, "it has to be." And as it said this, a gear-tooth slipped in the glare of Jack's trouble-light, and a phase of the cycle repeated itself.

"You're stuck," Jack said. "Kindly Dad, you're got a worn gear-tooth."

"Yes, Little Jackie," Kindly Dad said, "it has to be."

"You're right," Jack said. "It does have to be. Everything wears out eventually; nothing is permanent. Change is the one constant of life. Right, Kindly Dad?"

"Yes, Little Jackie," Kindly Dad said, "it has to be."

Shutting off the teaching machine at its power supply, Jack began to disassemble its main-shaft, preparatory to removing the worn gear.

74

"So you found it," the master circuit said, when Jack emerged a half-hour later, wiping his face with his sleeve.

"Yes," he said. He was exhausted. His wrist watch told him that it was only four o'clock; an hour more of work lay ahead of him.

The master circuit accompanied him to the parking lot. "I am quite pleased with the promptness with which you attended to our needs," she said. "I will telephone Mr. Yee and thank him."

He nodded and climbed into his 'copter, too worn out even to say goodbye. Soon he was ascending; the duck egg which was the UN-operated Public School became small and far away below him. Its stifling presence vanished, and he could breathe again.

Flipping on his transmitter he said, "Mr. Yee. This is Jack; I'm done at the school. What next?"

After a pause Mr. Yee's pragmatic voice answered. "Jack, Mr. Arnie Kott at Lewistown called us. He requested that we service an encoding dictation machine in which he places great trust. Since all others of our crew are tied up, I am sending you."

six

ARNIE KOTT owned the only harpsichord on Mars. However, it was out of tune, and he could find no one to service it. No matter which way you cut it, there were no harpsichord tuners on Mars.

For a month now he had been training his tame Bleekman to tackle this task; Bleekmen had a fine ear for music, and his particular one seemed to understand what Arnie wanted. Heliogabalus had been provided with a translation into the Bleeky dialect of a manual on keyboard instrument maintenance, and Arnie expected results any day now. But meanwhile the harpsichord was virtually unplayable.

Back in Lewistown from his visit to Anne Esterhazy, Arnie Kott felt glum. The death of the black-market goodies man, Norbert Steiner, was a solid blow below the belt, and Arnie knew that he would have to make a move, probably a drastic and unprecedented one, to compensate for it. It was now three o'clock in the afternoon. What had he gotten out of his trip to New Israel? Only a piece of bad news. Anne, as usual, could not be talked into anything; she intended to go right on with her amateurish campaigns and causes, and if she were the laughingstock of Mars it did not matter to her.

"Goddamn you, Heliogabalus," Arnie said with fury, "you get that goddamn instrument playing right or I'm kicking you out of Lewistown. You can go back to eating beetles and roots in the desert with the rest of your kind."

Seated on the floor beside the harpsichord, the Bleekman winced, glanced up acutely at Arnie Kott, then lowered his eyes to the manual once more.

"Nothing ever gets fixed around here," Arnie grumbled.

All Mars, he decided, was a sort of Humpty Dumpty; the original state had been one of perfection, and they and their property had all fallen from that state into rusty bits and useless debris. He felt sometimes as if he presided over an enormous junkyard. And then, once more, he thought about the Yee Company repair 'copter which he had run into in the desert, and the zwepp piloting it. Independent bastards, Arnie said to himself. Ought to be taken down a peg or two. But they knew their worth. Vital to the economy of the planet; it was written on their faces. We bow to no man, etcetera. Arnie paced about the big front room of the Lewistown house which he maintained in addition to his apartment at Union Hall, hands in his pockets, scowling.

Imagine: that guy talked back to me just like that, Arnie reflected. He must be a hell of a good repairman to be so confident.

And Arnie also thought, I'm going to get that guy if it's the last thing I do. Nobody talks to me like that and gets away with it.

But of the two thoughts about the Yee Company uppity repairman, the former slowly began to dominate his mind, because he was a practical man and he knew that things had to be kept running. Codes of conduct had to come second. We're not running a medieval society here, Arnie said to himself. If the guy's really good he can say what he wants to me; all I care about is results.

With that in mind, he telephoned the Yee Company at Bunchewood Park, and soon had Mr. Yee himself on the line.

"Listen," Arnie said, "I got a sick encoder over here, and if you fellows can get it working maybe I can use you on a permanent contract basis; you follow me?"

There was no doubt of it; Mr. Yee followed him, all right. He saw the entire picture. "Our best man, sir. Right away. And I know we'll give absolute satisfaction, any hour of the day or night."

"I want one particular man," Arnie said, and he thereupon described the repairman he had met in the desert.

"Young, dark-haired, slender," Mr. Yee repeated. "Glasses, and with a nervous manner. That would be Mr. Jack Bohlen. Our finest."

"Let me tell you," Arnie said, "that this Bohlen guy talked to me in a way I don't let nobody talk to me, but after I thought it over I realized he was in the right, and when I see him I'm going to tell him that to his face." However, in actuality Arnie Kott no longer could recall what the issue had been. "That guy Bohlen seems to have a good head on him," he wound up. "Can he get over here today?"

Without hesitation Mr. Yee promised service by five o'clock. "I appreciate that," Arnie said. "And be sure and tell him that Arnie holds no grudges. Sure, I was taken aback at the time; but that's all over. Tell him—" He pondered. "Tell Bohlen he's got absolutely nothing to worry about regarding me." He rang off, then, and sat back with a feeling of grim, honest accomplishment.

So the day after all wasn't a total waste. And, too, he had gotten an interesting bit of information from Anne, while over at New Israel. He had brought up the topic of the rumored goings-on in the F.D.R. Mountains, and as usual Anne knew a few inside yarns emanating from Home, accounts no doubt garbled in the chain of oral tellings . . . yet the nugget of veracity was there. The UN back Home was in the process of staging one of its periodic coups. It was going to descend on the F.D.R. Mountains in another couple of weeks and lay claim to them as public domain land belonging to no one— which was palpably true. But why was it that the UN wanted a big hunk of worthless real estate? There, Anne's tale got perplexing. One story noised about back at Geneva was that the UN intended to build an enormous supernational park, a sort of Garden of Eden, to lure emigrants out of Earth. Another had it that the UN engineers were going to make a vast final attack on the problem of beefing up the power sources on Mars; they were going to set up a huge hydrogen atomic energy power plant, unique in both size and scope. The water system would be revitalized. And, with adequate sources of power, heavy industry could at last move over to Mars, taking advantage of free land, light gravity, low taxation.

And then another rumor had it that the UN was going to set up a military base in the F.D.R. Mountains to offset United States and Soviet plans along the same general lines.

Whichever rumor was true, one fact stuck out: certain parcels of land in the F.D.R. range were going to be acutely valuable, pretty soon. The entire range was up for sale right now, in pieces varying from half an acre to a hundred thousand acres, and at a staggeringly low price. Once speculators got wind of the UN's plans, this would change . . . no doubt the speculators were already beginning to act. To claim land on Mars they had to be on the spot; it could not be done from Home—that was the law. So one could expect the speculators to start coming over any time now, if Anne's rumors were correct. It would be like the first year of colonization, when speculators were active everywhere.

Seating himself at his out-of-tune harpsichord, Arnie opened a book of Scarlatti sonatas and began to bang away at one of his favorites, a cross-hand one on which he had been practicing for months. It was strong, rhythmic, vigorous music, and he pounded the keys with delight, ignoring the distorted sound itself. Heliogabalus moved further off to study his manual; the sound hurt his ears.

"I've got a long-playing record of this," he said to Heliogabalus as he played. "So goddamn old and valuable that I don't dare play it."

"What is a long-playing record?" the Bleekman asked.

"You wouldn't understand if I told you. Glenn Gould playing. It's forty years old; my family passed it down to me. It was my mother's. That guy could really hammer these cross-hand sonatas out." His own playing discouraged him, and he gave up. I could never be any good, he decided, even if this instrument were in peak condition like it was before I had it shipped here from Home.

Seated on the bench but not playing, Arnie ruminated once more on the golden opportunities involved in the F.D.R. Mountains land. I could buy in any time, he thought, with Union funds. But *where?* It's a big range; I can't buy it *all.*

Who knows that range? he asked himself. That Steiner probably did, because as I understand it his base of operations is—or rather was—someplace near there. And there are prospectors coming and going. And Bleekmen live there, too.

"Helio," he said, "do you know the F.D.R. range?"

"Mister, I do know them," the Bleekman said. "I shun them. They are cold and empty and have no life."

"Is it true," Arnie said, "that you Bleekmen have an oracular rock that you go to when you want to know the future?"

"Yes, Mister. The uncivilized Bleekmen have that. But it is vain superstition. Dirty Knobby, the rock is called."

"You never consult it, yourself."

"No, Mister."

"Could you find that rock, if necessary?"

"Yes, Mister."

"I'll give you a dollar," Arnie said, "if you take a question to your goddamn Dirty Knobby rock for me."

"Thank you, Mister, but I cannot do it."

"Why not, Helio?"

"It would proclaim my ignorance, to consult with such fraudulency."

79

"Christ," Arnie said, disgusted. "Just as a game—can't you do that? For a joke."

The Bleekman said nothing, but his dark face was tight with resentment. He pretended to resume his reading of the manual.

"You fellows were stupid to give up your native religion," Arnie said. "You showed how weak you are. I wouldn't have. Tell me how to find Dirty Knobby and I'll ask it myself. I know goddamn well that your religion teaches that you can foretell the future, and what's so peculiar about that? We've got extrasensory individuals back Home, and some of them have precognition, can read the future. Of course we have to lock them up with the other nuts, because that's a symptom of schizophrenia, if you happen to know what that means."

"Yes, Mister," Heliogabalus said. "I know schizophrenia; it is the savage within the man."

"Sure, it's the reversion to primitive ways of thought, but so what, if you can read the future? In those mental health camps back Home there must be hundreds of precogs—" And then a thought struck Arnie Kott. Maybe there're a couple here on Mars, at Camp B-G.

The hell with Dirty Knobby rock, then, Arnie thought. I'll drop by B-G one day before they close it and get me a precog nut; I'll bail him out of the camp and put him on the payroll, right here in Lewistown.

Going to his telephone, he called the Union steward, Edward L. Goggins. "Eddy," he said, when he had hold of the steward, "you trot over to our psychiatric clinic and collar those doctors, and you bring back a description of what a precog nut is like, I mean, what symptoms, and if they know one at Camp B-G we could nab."

"O.K., Arnie. Will do."

"Who's the best psychiatrist on Mars, Eddy?"

"Gosh, Arnie, I'd have to check into it. The Truckers have a good one, Milton Glaub. Reason I know that is, my wife's brother is a Trucker and got analysis from Glaub last year, plus naturally effective representation."

"I suppose this Glaub knows B-G pretty good."

"Oh, yeah, Arnie; he's over there once a week, they all take turns. The Jews pay pretty good, they've got so much dough to spend. They get the dough from Israel back on Earth, you know."

"Well, get hold of this Glaub and tell him to rustle up a precog schizophrenic for me as soon as possible. Put Glaub on the payroll, but only if you have to; most of those psychiatrists are aching for regular money, they see so little of it. Understand, Eddy?"

"Right, Arnie." The steward rang off.

"You ever been psychoanalyzed, Helio?" Arnie said to him, feeling cheerful, now.

"No, Mister. Entire psychoanalysis is a vainglorious foolishness."

"How zat, Helio?"

"Question they never deal with is, what to remold sick person like. There is no what, Mister."

"I don't get you, Helio."

"Purpose of life is unknown, and hence way to be is hidden from the eyes of living critters. Who can say if perhaps the schizophrenics are not correct? Mister, they take a brave journey. They turn away from mere things, which one may handle and turn to practical use; they turn inward to *meaning*. There, the black-night-without-bottom lies, the pit. Who can say if they will return? And if so, what will they be like, having glimpsed meaning? I admire them."

"Kee-rist," Arnie said, with derision, "you half-educated freak— I'll bet if human civilization disappeared from Mars you'd be right back there among those savages in ten seconds flat, worshipping idols and all the rest of it. Why do you pretend you want to be like us? Why are you reading that manual?"

Heliogabalus said, "Human civilization will never leave Mars, Mister; that is why I study this book."

"Out of that book," Arnie said, "you better be able to tune up my goddamn harpsichord, or you will be back in the desert, whether human civilization stays on Mars or not."

"Yes sir," his tame Bleekman said.

Ever since he had lost his union card and could not then legally perform his job, Otto Zitte's life had been a continual mess. With a card he would be by now a first-class repairman. It was his secret that he had once held such a card and had managed to lose it; even his employer, Norb Steiner, did not know it. For reasons he himself did not understand, Otto preferred others to believe he had simply failed the aptitude tests. Perhaps it was easier to think of himself as a failure; after all, the repair business was almost impossible to get into . . . and after having gotten into it, to be booted out—

It was his own fault. There he had been, three years ago, a paid-up member of the union in good standing, in other words a bona fide Goodmember. The future was wide open for him; he was young, he had a girl friend and his own 'copter—the latter, leased; the former, although he had not known it at the time, shared—and what could hold him back? What, except possibly his own stupidity.

He had broken a union ruling which was a basic law. In his opinion it was a foolish ruling, but nonetheless . . . vengeance is mine, sayeth the Extraterrestrial Repairmen's Union, Martian Branch. Wow, how he hated the bastards; his hatred had warped his life and he recognized that—and he did nothing about it: he wanted it to warp him. He wanted to keep on hating them, the vast monolithic structure, wherever it existed.

They had caught him for giving socialized repair.

And the hell of it was that it wasn't actually socialized, because he expected to get back a profit. It was just a new way of charging his customers, and in a sense not so new, anyhow. It was actually the oldest way in the world, a barter system. But his revenue could not be divvied up so that the union got its cut. His trade had been with certain housewives living out in remote tracts, very lonely women whose husbands stayed in the city five days a week, coming home only on weekends. Otto, who was good-looking, slender, with long, combed-back black hair (in his account of himself, anyhow), had made time with one woman after another; and an outraged husband, on finding out, had, instead of shooting Otto to death, gone instead to the Union Hiring Hall and lodged a formal charge: repairs without compensation at scale.

Well, it certainly was not scale; he admitted that.

And so now this job with Norb Steiner, which meant that he had practically to live in the wastelands of the F.D.R. Mountains, alienated from society for weeks on end, growing more and more lonely, more embittered all the time. It had been his need for intimate personal contact that had gotten him into trouble in the first place, and now look at him. As he sat in the storage shed waiting for the next rocket to show up, he looked back on his life and reflected that even the Bleekmen wouldn't be willing or able to live as he lived, cut off from everyone like this. If only his own black-market operations had succeeded! He, like Norb Steiner, had been able to swing around the planet daily, visiting one person after another. Was it his fault that the items he chose to import were hot enough to interest the big boys? His judgment had been too good; his line had sold too well.

He hated the big racketeers, too, same as he hated the big

unions. He hated bigness per se; bigness had destroyed the American system of free enterprise, the small businessman had been ruined—in fact, he himself had been perhaps the last authentic small businessman in the solar system. That was his real crime: he had tried to live the American way of life, instead of just talking about it.

"Screw them," he said to himself, seated on a crate, surrounded by boxes and cartons and packages and the workings of several dismantled rocketships which he had been revamping. Outside the shed window . . . silent, desolate rock hills, with only a few shrubs, dried up and dying, as far as the eye could see.

And where was Norb Steiner right now? No doubt ensconced in some bar or restaurant or some woman's cheery living room, prattling his line, handing over tins of smoked salmon and getting in return—

"Screw them all," Otto mumbled, getting up to pace back and forth. "If that's what they want, let 'em have it. Bunch of animals."

Those Israeli girls . . . that's where Steiner was, with a kibbutzful of them, those hot, black-eyed, heavy-lipped, big-breasted, sexy ones who got tanned working out in the fields in shorts and cotton shirts clinging to them, no bras, just those big solid breasts—you could actually see their nipples, because the damp fabric stuck to them.

That's why he wouldn't let me go with him, Otto decided.

The only women he ever saw out here in the F.D.R. range were those stunted, black, dried-out Bleekman women, not even human, at least not to him. He wasn't taken in by those anthropologists saying that the Bleekmen were from the same stock as homo sapiens, that probably both planets were colonized a million years ago from one interplanetary race. Those toads, human? Sleep with one of those? Christ, better to chop it off, first.

As a matter of fact, here came a party of Bleekmen right now, stepping gingerly with bare feet down the irregular rock surface of a northern hill. On their way here, Otto observed. As usual.

He opened the door of the shed, waiting until they had reached him. Four bucks, two of them elderly, one elderly woman, several skinny kids, carrying their bows, their pounding blocks, their paka eggshells.

Halting, they regarded him silently, and then one of the

bucks said, "Rains are falling from me onto your valuable person."

"Likewise," Otto said, leaning against the shed and feeling dull, weighed down with hopelessness. "What do you want?"

The Bleekman buck held out a small bit of paper, and Otto, taking it, saw that it was a label from a can of turtle soup. The Bleekmen had eaten the soup, retaining the label for this purpose; they could not tell him what they wanted because they did not know what it was called.

"O.K.," he said. "How many?" He held up fingers. At five they nodded. Five cans. "Whatcha got?" Otto demanded, not stirring.

One of the young Bleekman women stepped forward and pointed to that part of herself which had been so much in Otto's thoughts for so long.

"Oh Christ," Otto said in despair. "No, go on. Beat it. Not any more; I don't want any more." He turned his back on them, made his way into the storage shed and slammed the door so hard that the shed walls trembled; he threw himself down on a packing crate, his head in his hands. "I'm going crazy," he said to himself, his jaw stiff, his tongue swelling up so that he could hardly talk. His chest ached. And then, to his amazement, he began to cry. Jesus, he thought in fright, I really am going crazy; I'm breaking down. Why? Tears rolled down his cheeks. He hadn't cried in years. What's this all about? he wondered. His mind had no concept in it; it was only his body bawling away, and he was a spectator to it.

But it brought him relief. With his handkerchief he wiped his eyes, his face, and cursed as he saw that his hands were clawlike with rigidity, the fingers writhing.

Outside the window of the shed the Bleekmen remained, perhaps seeing him; he could not tell. Their faces showed no expression, but he felt sure they must have seen, and probably were as perplexed as he. It sure is a mystery, he thought. I agree with you.

The Bleekmen gathered together in a huddle and conferred, and then one of them detached himself from the group and approached the shed. Otto heard a rap on the door. Going over to it and opening it, he found the young Bleekman standing there holding out something.

"This, then," the young Bleekman said.

Otto took it, but for the life of him he could not make out what it was. It had glass and metal to it, and calibrations.

And then he realized that it was an instrument used in surveying. On its side was stamped: UN PROPERTY.

"I don't want it," he said irritably, turning it over and over. The Bleekmen must have stolen it, he realized. He handed it back; the young buck accepted it stoically and returned to his group. Otto shut the door.

This time they went off; he watched them through the window as they trailed away up the side of the hill. Steal you blind, he said to himself. Anyhow, what was a UN survey company doing in the F.D.R. range?

To cheer himself up he rummaged around until he found a can of smoked frogs' legs; opening it, he sat eating morosely, not getting from the dainty anything at all, and yet methodically finishing the can.

Into the microphone Jack Bohlen said, "Don't send me, Mr. Yee—I already ran into Kott today and offended him." Weariness settled over him. Naturally I ran into Kott, for the first time in my life, and naturally I insulted him, he thought to himself. And just as naturally, because that's how my life works, it's the same day that Arnie Kott decides to call up Yee Company and ask for service. It's typical of the little game I play with the powerful, inanimate forces of life.

"Mr. Kott mentioned meeting you on the desert," Mr. Yee said. "In fact, his decision to call us was based on that meeting."

"The hell you say." He was dumbfounded.

"I do not know what the issue was, Jack, but no harm has been done. Direct your ship to Lewistown. If you run over beyond five o'clock you will be paid time and a half. And Mr. Kott, who is known as a generous man, is so anxious to have his encoder working that he promises to see that you receive a bountiful meal."

"All right," Jack said. It was too much for him to dope out. After all, he knew nothing of what went on in Arnie Kott's mind.

Not long thereafter, he was lowering his 'copter to the roof parking lot of the Water Workers' Union Hall at Lewistown.

A slavey sauntered out and regarded him suspiciously.

"Yee Company repairman," Jack said. "Call put in by Arnie Kott."

"O.K., buddy," the slavey said, and led him to the elevator.

He found Arnie Kott in a well-furnished, Earth-type living room; the big, bald-headed man was on the telephone, and he nodded his head at Jack's appearance. The nod indicated the desk, on which a portable encoding dictation machine sat. Jack walked over to it, removed the lid, turned it on. Meanwhile, Arnie Kott continued his phone conversation.

"Sure I know it's a tricky talent. Sure, there's a good reason why nobody's been able to make use of it—but what am I supposed to do, give up and pretend it don't exist just because people have been too damn dumb for fifty thousand years to take it seriously? I still want to try it." A long pause. "O.K., Doctor. Thanks." Arnie hung up. To Jack he said, "You ever been to Camp B-G?"

"No," Jack said. He was busy opening up the encoder.

Arnie strolled over and stood beside him. As he worked, Jack could feel the astute gaze fixed on him; it made him nervous, but there was nothing he could do except try to ignore the man and go on. A little like the master circuit, he thought to himself. And then he wondered, as he often did, if he was going to have another one of his spells; true, it had been a long time, but here was a powerful figure looming close to him, scrutinizing him, and it did feel somewhat like that old interview with Corona's personnel manager.

"That was Glaub on the phone," Arnie Kott said. "The psychiatrist. You ever heard of him?"

"No," Jack said.

"What do you do, live your life entirely with your head stuck in the back of machines?"

Jack looked up, met the man's gaze. "I've got a wife and son. That's my life. What I'm doing right now is a means of keeping my family going." He spoke calmly. Arnie did not seem to take offense; he even smiled.

"Something to drink?" Arnie asked.

"Coffee, if you have it."

"I've got authentic Home coffee," Arnie said. "Black?"

"Black."

"Yeah, you look like a black coffee man. You think you can fix that machine right here and now, or are you going to have to take it with you?"

"I can fix it here."

Arnie beamed. "That's swell! I really depend on that machine."

"Where's the coffee?"

Turning, Arnie went off dutifully; he rustled about in another room and then returned with a ceramic coffee mug, which he set down on the desk near Jack. "Listen, Bohlen.

I have a person coming here any minute now. A girl. It won't interfere with your work, will it?"

Jack glanced up, supposing the man was being sarcastic. But evidently not; Arnie was eyeing him and then the partly disassembled machine, obviously concerned with how the repair was progressing. He certainly is dependent on this, Jack decided. Strange, how people cling to their possessions, as if they're extensions of their bodies, a sort of hypochondria of the machine. You'd think a man like Arnie Kott could scrap this encoder and shell out the money for a new one.

There sounded a knock on the door, and Arnie hurried to open it. "Oh, hi." His voice came to Jack. "Come on in. Hey, I'm getting my doodad fixed."

A girl's voice said, "Arnie, you'll never get your doodad fixed."

Arnie laughed nervously. "Hey, meet my new repairman, Jack Bohlen. Bohlen, this is Doreen Anderton, our Union treasurer."

"Hi," Jack said. Out of the corner of his eye—he did not stop working—he could see that she had red hair and extremely white skin and large, wonderful eyes. Everybody's on the payroll, he thought tartly. What a great world. What a great union you've got going here for yourself, Arnie.

"Busy, isn't he?" the girl said.

"Oh, yeah," Arnie agreed, "these repair guys are bugs on getting the job done right, I mean these outside guys, not our own—ours are a bunch of slobs that sit around playing with themselves at our expense. I'm through with them, Dor. I mean, this guy Bohlen is a whiz; he's going to have the encoder working any minute now, aren't you, Jack?"

"Yeah," Jack said.

The girl said, "Don't you say hello, Jack?"

Halting his work he turned his attention on her; he faced her levelly. Her expression was cool and intelligent, with a faintly mocking quality which was peculiarly rewarding and annoying. "Hello," Jack said.

"I saw your 'copter on the roof," the girl said.

"Let him work," Arnie said peevishly. "Gimme your coat." He stood behind her, helping her out of her coat. The girl wore a dark wool suit, obviously an import from Earth and therefore expensive to an appalling degree. I'll bet that set the Union pension fund back plenty, Jack decided.

Observing the girl, he saw in her a vindication of a piece of old wisdom. Nice eyes, hair, and skin produced a pretty woman, but a truly excellent nose created a beautiful woman. This girl had such a nose: strong, straight, dominating her features, forming a basis for her other features. Mediterranean women reach the level of beauty much more easily than, say, Irish or English women, he realized, because genetically speaking the Mediterranean nose, whether Spanish or Hebrew or Turkish or Italian, played a naturally greater part in physiognomic organization. His own wife Silvia had a gay, turned-up Irish nose; she was pretty enough by any standard. But—there was a difference.

He guessed that Doreen was in her early thirties. And yet she possessed a freshness that gave her a stable quality. He had seen such clear coloration in high-school girls approaching nubility, and once in a long while one saw it in fifty-year-old women who had perfect gray hair and wide, lovely eyes. This girl would still be attractive twenty years from now, and probably had always been so; he could not imagine her any other way. Arnie, by investing in her, had perhaps done well with the funds entrusted to him; she would not wear out. Even now he saw maturity in her face, and that among women was rare.

Arnie said to him, "We're going out and have a drink. If you get that machine fixed in time—"

"It's fixed now." He had found the broken belt and had replaced it with one from his tool kit.

"Good deal," Arnie said, grinning like a happy child. "Then come on along with us." To the girl he explained, "We're meeting Milton Glaub, the famous psychiatrist; you probably heard of him. He promised to have a drink with me. I was talking to him on the phone just now, and he sounds like a topnotch sort of guy." He whacked Jack loudly on the shoulder. "I bet when you landed your 'copter on the roof you didn't think you'd be having a drink with one of the solar system's best-known psychoanalysts, did you?"

I wonder if I should go along, Jack thought. But why not? He said, "O.K., Arnie."

Arnie said, "Doc Glaub is going to scare up a schizophrenic for me; I need one, I need its professional services." He laughed, eyes twinkling, finding his own utterance outstandingly funny.

"Do you?" Jack said. "I'm a schizophrenic."

Arnie stopped laughing. "No kidding. I never would have guessed; what I mean is, you look all right."

Finishing up the task of putting the encoder back together, Jack said, "I am all right. I'm cured."

Doreen said, "No one is ever cured of schizophrenia." Her tone was dispassionate; she was simply stating a fact.

"They can be," Jack said, "if it's what is called situational schizophrenia."

Arnie eyed him with great interest, even suspicion. "You're pulling my leg. You're just trying to worm your way into my confidence."

Jack shrugged, feeling himself flush. He turned his attention back, completely, to his work.

"No offense," Arnie said. "You really are, no kidding? Listen, Jack, let me ask you; do you have any sort of ability or power to read the future?"

After a long pause, Jack said, "No."

"You sure?" Arnie said, with suspicion.

"I'm sure." He wished now that he had turned down flat that invitation to accompany them. The intent questioning made him feel exposed; Arnie was nudging too close, encroaching on him—it was difficult to breathe, and Jack moved around to the far side of the desk, to put more distance between himself and the plumber.

"Whatzamatter?" Arnie asked acutely.

"Nothing." Jack continued working, not looking at either Arnie or the girl. Both of them were watching him, and his hands shook.

Presently Arnie said, "Jack, let me tell you how I got where I am. One talent got me up here. I can judge people and tell what they're like down inside, what they really are, not just what they do and say. I don't believe you; I bet you're lying to me about your precognition. Isn't that right? You don't even have to answer." Turning to the girl, Arnie said, "Let's get balling; I want that drink." He beckoned to Jack to follow.

Laying down his tools, Jack reluctantly did so.

seven

On his journey by 'copter to Lewistown to meet Arnie Kott and have a drink with him, Dr. Milton Glaub asked himself if his good luck were true. I can't believe it, he thought, a turning point in my life like this.

He was not certain what Arnie wanted; the phone call had been so unexpected and Arnie had talked so fast that Dr. Glaub had wound up perplexed, knowing only that it had to do with parapsychological aspects of the mentally ill. Well, he could tell Arnie practically all there was to know on that topic. And yet Glaub sensed that there was something deeper in the inquiry.

Generally, a concern with schizophrenia was a symptom of the person's own inner struggle in that area. Now, it was a fact that often the first signs of the insidious growth of the schizophrenic process in a person was an inability to eat in public. Arnie had noisily gabbed on about his desire to meet Glaub—not in his own home or in the doctor's office—but at a well-known bar and restaurant in Lewistown, the Willows. Was this perhaps a reaction-formation? Mysteriously made tense by public situations, and especially by those involving the nutritive function, Arnie Kott was leaning over backward to regain the normalcy which was beginning to abandon him.

Piloting his 'copter, Glaub thought about this, but then, by slow and stealthy stages, his thinking returned to the topic of his own problems.

Arnie Kott, a man controlling a multimillion-dollar union fund; a prominent person in the colonial world, although virtually unknown back Home. A feudal baron, virtually. If Kott were to put me on his staff, Glaub speculated, I could pay off all the debts we've piled up, those hideous charge-account bills at twenty per cent interest that just seem to loom there always, never getting smaller or going away. And then we could start over, not go into debt, live within our means . . . and a highly expanded means, at that.

Then, too, old Arnie was a Swede or a Dane, something like that and so it wouldn't be necessary for Glaub to season his skin-color before receiving each patient. Plus the fact that Arnie had a reputation for informality. Milt and Arnie, it would be. Dr. Glaub smiled.

What he had to be sure to do in this initial interview was to ratify Arnie's concepts, sort of play along and not dash cold water on things, even if, say, old Arnie's notions were way out of line. A hell of a thing it would be to discourage the man! That wasn't right.

I see your point, Arnie, Dr. Glaub said to himself, practicing away as he piloted his 'copter closer and closer to Lewistown. Yes, there is a good deal to be said for that world-view.

He had handled so many types of social situations for his patients, appearing in public for them, representing those timid, shut-in schizoid personalities who shrank from interpersonal exposure, that this would undoubtedly be a snap. And—if the schizophrenic process in Arnie were beginning to bring up its heavy artillery—Arnie might need to lean on him for his very survival.

Hot dog, Dr. Glaub said to himself, and increased the velocity of the 'copter to its maximum.

Around the Willows ran a moat of cold blue water. Fountains sprayed water into the air, and bougainvillaea, purple and amber and rusty-red, grew to great heights, encircling the single-story glass structure. As he descended the black wrought-iron staircase from the parking lot, Dr. Glaub perceived his party within: Arnie Kott seated with a stunning redhead and nondescript male companion wearing repairman's overalls and canvas shirt.

True classless society, here, Dr. Glaub reflected.

A rainbow-style bridge assisted him in his crossing of the moat. Doors opened before him; he entered the lounge, passed by the bar, halted to sniff in the sight of the jazz combo composing meditatively, and then hailed Arnie. "Hi, Arnie!"

"Hi, Doc." Arnie rose to introduce him. "Dor, this is Doc Glaub. Doreen Anderton. This is my repairman, Jack Bohlen, a real fireballer. Jack, this is the foremost living psychiatrist, Milt Glaub."

They all nodded and shook hands.

"Hardly foremost," Glaub murmured, as they sat down. "It's still the Swiss at Berghölzlei, the existential psychiatrists, who dominate the field." But he was deeply gratified, untrue as Arnie's announcement had been. He could feel his face flushing with pleasure. "Sorry it took me so long to get here— I had to dash over to New Israel. Bo—Bosley Touvim—needed my advice on a medical matter which he considered pressing."

"Quite a guy, that Bos," Arnie said. He had lit a cigar, a genuine Earth-rolled Optimo Admiral. "A real go-getter. But let's get down to business. Wait, I'll get you a drink." He looked inquiringly at Glaub, while waving the cocktail waitress over.

"Scotch, if you have it," Glaub said.

"Cutty Sark, sir," the waitress said.

"Oh, fine. No ice, please."

"O.K.," Arnie said impatiently. "Now look, Doc. You got the name of a really advanced schizo for me, or not?" He scrutinized Glaub.

"Uh," said Glaub, and then he recalled his visit to New Israel not more than a short while ago. "Manfred Steiner," he said.

"Any relation to Norbert Steiner?"

"As a mater of fact, his boy. At Camp B-G—I imagine there's no breach of confidence in telling you. Totally autistic, from birth. Mother, the cold, intellectual schizoid personality, doing it by the rulebook. Father—"

"Father dead," Arnie said shortly.

"Right. Very regrettable. Nice chap, but depressive. It was suicide, you know. Typical impulse during his low-swing. A wonder he didn't do it years ago."

Arnie said, "You told me on the phone you've got a theory about the schizophrenic being out of phase in time."

"Yes, it's a derangement in the interior time-sense." Dr. Glaub had all three of them listening, and he warmed to his topic; it was his favorite. "We have yet to get total experimental verification, but that will come." And then, without hesitation or shame, he passed off the Berghölzlei theory as his own.

Evidently much impressed, Arnie said, "Very interesting." To the repairman, Jack Bohlen, he said, "Could such slow-motion chambers be built?"

"No doubt," Jack murmured.

"And sensors," Glaub said. "To get the patient out of the chamber and into the real world. Sight, hearing—"

"It could be done," Bohlen said.

"How about this," Arnie said impatiently and enthusiastically. "Could the schizophrenic be running so fast, compared to us, in time, that he's actually in what to us is the future? Would that account for his precognition?" His light-colored eyes glittered excitedly.

Glaub shrugged in a manner indicating agreement.

Turning to Bohlen, Arnie stuttered, "Hey, Jack, that's it! Goddamn it, I ought to be a psychiatrist. Slow him down, hell. Speed him up, I say. Let him live out of phase in time, if he wants to. But let's get him to share his perceptions with us—right, Bohlen?"

Glaub said, "Now, there is the rub. In autism, especially, the faculty of interpersonal communication is drastically impaired."

"I see," Arnie said, but he was not daunted. "Hell, I know enough about that to see a way out. Didn't that early guy, Carl Jung—didn't he manage to decode the schizophrenic's language years ago?"

"Yes," Glaub said, "decades ago Jung cracked the private language of the schizophrenic. But in child autism, as with Manfred, there is no language at all, at least no spoken language. Possibly totally personal private thoughts . . . but no words."

"Shit," Arnie said.

The girl glanced at him admonishingly.

"This is a serious matter," Arnie said to her. "We've got to get these unfortunates, these autistic kids, to talk to us and tell us what they knew; isn't that right, Doc?"

"Yes," Glaub said.

"That kid's an orphan now," Arnie said, "that Manfred."

"Well, he has the mother, still," Glaub said.

Waving his hand excitedly, Arnie said, "But they don't care enough about the kid to have him at home; they junked him in that camp. Hell, I'll spring him and bring him here. And, Jack, you get on this and engineer a machine to make contact with him—you see the picture?"

After a moment Bohlen said, "I don't know what to say." He laughed briefly.

"Sure you know what to say—hell, it ought to be easy for you, you're a schizophrenic yourself, like you said."

Glaub, interested, said to Bohlen, "Is that the case?" He had already noted, automatically, the repairman's skeletal tension as he sat sipping his drink, and the rigid musculature, not to mention the asthenic build. "But you appear to have made enormous strides toward recovery."

Raising his head, Bohlen met his glance, saying, "I'm totally recovered. For many years, now." His face was affect-laden.

No one makes a total recovery, Glaub thought. But he did not say it; instead he said, "Perhaps Arnie is right. You could empathize with the autistic, whereas that is our basic problem; the autistic can't take our roles, see the world as we do, and we can't take his role either. So a gulf separates us."

"Bridge that gulf, Jack!" Arnie cried. He whacked Bohlen on the back. "That's your job; I'm putting you on the payroll."

Envy filled Dr. Glaub. He glared down at his drink, hiding his reaction. The girl, however, saw it and smiled at him. He did not smile back.

Contemplating Dr. Glaub sitting opposite him, Jack Bohlen felt the gradual diffusion of his perception which he so dreaded, the change in his awareness which had attacked him this way years ago in the personnel manager's office at Corona Corporation, and which always seemed still with him, just on the edge.

He saw the psychiatrist under the aspect of absolute reality: a thing composed of cold wires and switches, not a human at all, not made of flesh. The fleshy trappings melted and became transparent, and Jack Bohlen saw the mechanical device beyond. Yet he did not let his terrible state of awareness show; he continued to nurse his drink; he went on listening to the conversation and nodding occasionally. Neither Dr. Glaub nor Arnie Kott noticed.

But the girl did. She leaned over and said softly in Jack's ear, "Aren't you feeling well?"

He shook his head. No, he was saying, I'm not feeling well.

"Let's get away from them," the girl whispered. "I can't stand it either." Aloud, to Arnie, she said, "Jack and I are going to leave you two alone. Come on." She tapped Jack on the arm and rose to her feet; he felt her light, strong fingers, and he, too, rose.

Arnie said, "Don't be gone long," and resumed his earnest conversation with Dr. Glaub.

"Thanks," Jack said, as they walked up the aisle, between tables.

Doreen said, "Did you see how jealous he was, when Arnie said he was putting you on the payroll?"

"No. Glaub?" But he was not surprised. "I get this way," he said to the girl, by way of apology. "Something to do with my eyes; it may be astigmatism. Due to tension."

The girl said, "Do you want to sit at the bar? Or go outside?"

"Outside," Jack said.

Presently they stood on the rainbow bridge, over the water. In the water fish slid about, luminous and vague, half-real beings, as rare on Mars as any form of matter conceivable. They were a miracle in this world, and Jack and the girl, gazing down, both felt it. And both knew they felt this same thought without having to speak it aloud.

"It's nice out here," Doreen said finally.

"Yeah." He did not want to talk.

"Everybody," Doreen said. "Has at one time or another known a schizophrenic . . . if they're not one themselves. It was my brother, back Home, my younger brother."

"I'll be O.K.," Jack said. "I'm O.K. now."

"But you're not," Doreen said.

"No," he admitted, "but what the hell can I do? You said it yourself. Once a schizophrenic, always a schizophrenic." He was silent, then, concentrating on the gliding, pale fish.

"Arnie thinks a lot of you," the girl said. "When he says his talent is judging the value of people he's telling the truth. He can see already that that Glaub is desperately eager to sell himself and get on the staff, here in Lewistown. I guess psychiatry doesn't pay any more, as it did once; too many in the business. There are twenty of them here in this settlement already, and none do a genuinely good traffic. Didn't your—condition cause you trouble when you applied for permission to emigrate?"

He said, "I don't want to talk about it. Please."

"Let's walk," the girl said.

They walked along the street, past the shops, most of which had closed for the day.

"What was it you saw," the girl said, "when you looked at Dr. Glaub, there at the table?"

Jack said, "Nothing."

"You'd rather not say about that, either."

"That's right."

"Do you think if you tell me things will get worse?"

"It's not things; it's me."

95

"Maybe it is the things," Doreen said. "Maybe there is something in your vision, however distorted and garbled it's become. I don't know. I used to try like hell to comprehend what it was Clay—my brother—saw and heard. He couldn't say. I know that his world was absolutely different from the rest of ours in the family. He killed himself, like Steiner did." She had paused at a newsstand, to look over the item, on page one, about Norbert Steiner. "The existential psychiatrists often say to let them go ahead and take their lives; it's the only way, for some of them . . . the vision becomes too awful to bear."

Jack said nothing.

"Is it awful?" Doreen asked.

"No. Just—disconcerting." He struggled to explain. "There's no way you can work it in with what you're supposed to see and know; it makes it impossible to go on, in the accustomed way."

"Don't you very often try to pretend, and sort of—go along with it, by acting? Like an actor?" When he did not answer, she said, "You tried to do that in there, just now."

"I'd love to fool everybody," he conceded. "I'd give anything if I could go on acting it out, playing a role. But that's a real split—there's no split up until then; they're wrong when they say it's a split in the mind. If I wanted to keep going entire, without a split, I'd have to lean over and say to Dr. Glaub—" He broke off.

"Tell me," the girl said.

"Well," he said, taking a deep breath, "I'd say, Doc, I can see y‸ ‸nder the aspect of eternity and you're dead. That's the ‸‸‸‸‸ the sick, morbid vision. I don't want it; I di‸‸‸ ‸‸."

Th‸ ‸‸‸ put her arm within his.

"I ‸‸‸ ‸ told anybody before," Jack said, "not even Silvia, my wife, or my son David. You know, I watch him; I look every day to be sure it isn't showing up in him too. It's so easy for this stuff to get passed along as with the Steiners. I didn't know they had a boy at B-G until Glaub said so. And they're neighbors of ours for years back. Steiner never let it out."

Doreen said "We're supposed to go back to the Willows for dinner. Do you want to? I think it would be a good idea. You know, you don't have to join Arnie's staff; you can stay with Mr. Yee. That's a nice 'copter you have. You don't have

96

to give all that up just because Arnie decides he can use you; maybe you can't use him."

Shrugging, he said, "It's an interesting challenge, building a conduit for communication between an autistic child and our world. I think there's a lot in what Arnie says. I could be the intermediary—I could do a useful job there." It doesn't really matter why Arnie wants to bring out the Steiner boy, he realized. Probably he's got some solid selfish motive, something that will bring him a profit in cold hard cash. I certainly couldn't care less.

In fact I can have it both ways, he realized. Mr. Yee can lease me to the Water Workers' Union; I'd be paid by Mr. Yee and he'd be paid by Arnie. Everyone would be happy, and why not? Tinkering with the broken, malfunctioning mind of a child certainly has more to recommend it than tinkering with refrigerators and encoders; if the child is suffering some of the visions that I know—

He knew of the time-theory which Glaub had trotted out as his own. He had read about it in *Scientific American;* naturally, he read anything on schizophrenia that he could get his hands on. He knew that it had orginated with the Swiss, that Glaub hadn't invented it. What an odd theory it is, he thought to himself. And yet, it rings true.

"Let's go back to the Willows," he said. He was very hungry, and it would no doubt be a bang-up meal.

Doreen said, "You're a brave person, Jack Bohlen."

"Why?" he asked.

"Because you're going back to the place that troubled you, to the people that brought on your vision of, as you said, eternity. I wouldn't do that, I'd flee."

"But," he said, "that's the whole point; it's designed to make you flee—the vision's for that purpose, to nullify your relations with other people, to isolate you. If it's successful, your life with human beings is over. That's what they mean when they say the term schizophrenia isn't a diagnosis; it's a prognosis—it doesn't say anything about what you have, only about how you'll wind up." *And I'm not going to wind up like that,* he said to himself. Like Manfred Steiner, mute and in an institution; I intend to keep my job, my wife and son, my friendships—he glanced at the girl holding on to his arm. Yes, and even love affairs, if such there be.

I intend to keep trying.

Putting his hands in his pockets as he walked along, he touched something small, cold and hard; lifting it out in surprise, he saw it was a wrinkled little object like a tree root.

"What in the world's that?" Doreen asked him.

It was the water witch which the Bleekmen had given him that morning, out in the desert; he had forgotten all about it.

"A good luck charm," Jack said to the girl.

Shivering, she said, "It's awfully ugly."

"Yes," he agreed, "but it's friendly. And we do have this problem, we schizophrenics; we do pick up other people's unconscious hostility."

"I know. The telepathic factor. Clay had it worse and worse until—" She glanced at him. "The paranoid outcome."

"It's the worst thing about our condition, this awareness of the buried, repressed sadism and aggression in others around us, even strangers. I wish to hell we didn't have it; we even pick it up from people in restaurants—" He thought of Glaub. "In buses, in a theater. Crowds."

Doreen said, "Do you have any idea what Arnie wants to learn from the Steiner boy?"

"Well, this theory about precognition—"

"But what does Arnie want to know about the future? You have no idea, do you? And it would never occur to you to try to find out."

That was so. He had not even been curious.

"You're content," she said slowly, scrutinizing him, "merely to do your technical task of rigging up the essential machinery. That's not right, Jack Bohlen; that's not a good sign at all."

"Oh," he said. He nodded. "It's very schizophrenic, I guess . . . to be content with a purely technical relationship."

"Will you ask Arnie?"

He felt uncomfortable. "It's his business, not mine. It's an interesting job, and I like Arnie, I prefer him to Mr. Yee. I just—haven't got it in me to pry. That's the way I am."

"I think you're afraid. But I don't see why—you're brave, and yet in some deep way you're terribly, terribly frightened."

"Maybe so," he said, feeling sad.

Together, they walked on back to the Willows.

That night, after everyone had gone. Including Doreen Anderton, Arnie Kott sat alone in his living room gloating. What a day it had been.

He had snared a good repairman who had already repaired his invaluable encoder and who was going to build an electronic wing-ding to tap the precog faculties of an autistic child.

He had milked, for nothing, the information he needed from a psychiatrist, and then managed to get rid of the psychiatrist.

So all in all it had been an exceptional day. It left only two problems: his harpsichord was still untuned and—what the hell else? It had slipped his mind. He pondered as he sat before his TV set, watching the fights from America the Beautiful, the U.S.A. colony on Mars.

Then he remembered. Norb Steiner's death. There was no source of goodies any more.

"I'll fix that," Arnie said aloud. He shut off the TV and got his encoder out; seated before it, mike in hand, he delivered a message. It was to Scott Temple, with whom he had worked on countless important business ventures; Temple was a cousin of Ed Rockingham, and a good egg to know—he had managed, through a charter arrangement with the UN, to gain control of most of the medical supplies entering Mars, and what a top-notch monopoly that amounted to.

The drums of the encoder turned encouragingly.

"Scott!" Arnie said, "how are you. Hey, you know that poor guy Norb Steiner? Too bad, I mean, his dying and all. I understand he was mentally you-know-what. Like the rest of us." Arnie laughed at that long and hard. "So anyhow, it leaves us with a little problem—I mean, one of procurement. Right? So listen, Scott, old man. I'd like to talk it over with you. I'm in. You get me? Stop by here in around a day or two, so we can work out the exact arrangements. I think we should forget the gear that Steiner was using; we'll start out fresh, get our own little bitty field in an out-of-the-way place, our own slave rockets, whatever else we need. Keep those smoked oysters rolling in, like they ought to." He shut the machine off and tried to think if there was more. No, he had said it all; between him and a man like Scott Temple, no more had to be said; it was a deal then and there. "O.K., Scott, boy," he said. "I'll expect to see you."

After he had removed the spool it occurred to him to play it back just to be sure it had gone into code. God, what a calamity if by some freak chance it came out in clear!

But it was in code, all right, and his dearest: the machine had put the semantic units into a catfight-like parody of contemporary electronic music. Arnie, hearing the whistles, growls, beeps, hoots, hums, laughed until tears ran down his cheeks; he had to go off to the bathroom and slap cold water on his face to stop himself.

Then, back at the encoder, he carefully marked the box into which the spool went:

Song of the Wind Spirit, A Cantata
by Karl William Dittershand

That composer, Karl William Dittershand, was the current favorite back on Earth among the intellectuals, and Arnie detested the man's electronic so-called music; he was a purist, himself: his tastes stopped firmly at Brahms. Arnie had a good laugh at that—marking his encoded message proposing his and Scott's going into the black-market importation of foodstuffs as a cantata by Dittershand—and then rang up a union Goodmember to convey the spool up north to Nova Britannica, the U.K. colony on Mars.

That, at eight-thirty in the evening, wound up the business of the day, and Arnie returned to his TV set to see the finish of the fights. He lit himself another Optimo extra-mild Admiral, leaned back, broke wind, relaxed.

I wish all days could be like this, he said to himself. I could live forever, if they were; days like this made him younger, not older. He felt as if he could see forty come by again.

Imagine me going into the black market, he said to himself. And for little stuff, little tins of wild blackberry jelly and slices of pickled eel and lox. But that was vital, too; for him especially. Nobody is going to rob me of my treats, he thought grimly. If that Steiner thought by killing himself he could cut me off where it hurts—

"Come on," he urged the colored boy taking a licking on the TV screen. "Gut up, you bugger, and give it to him."

As if he had heard, the Negro fighter scrambled back up, and Arnie Kott chuckled with deep, keen pleasure.

In the small hotel room, where he traditionally stayed weekend nights in Bunchewood Park when on call, Jack Bohlen sat by the window smoking a cigarette and pondering.

It had returned, after all these years, that which he dreaded; he had to face it. Now it was not anguished anticipation, it was actuality. Christ, he thought miserably, they're right—once you have it you've got it for keeps. The visit to the Public

School had set him up for it, and at the Willows it had appeared and smitten him, as intact and full as if he were in his twenties again, back on Earth, working for Corona Corporation down in Redwood City.

And I know, he thought, that Norbert Steiner's death figured into it. Death upsets everyone, makes them do peculiar things; it sets a radiating process of action and emotion going that works its way out, farther and farther, to embrace more people and things.

Better call Silvia, he thought, and see how she's making out with Frau Steiner and the children.

But he shrank from it. There's nothing I can do to help anyhow, he decided. I have to be on twenty-four-hour call here in town, where Mr. Yee's switchboard can get hold of me. And now, too, he had to be available to Arnie Kott at Lewistown.

There had been, however, compensation. A fine, deep, subtle, highly envigorating compensation. In his wallet he had Doreen Anderton's address and phone number.

Should he call her tonight? Imagine, he thought, finding someone, a woman, too, with whom he could talk freely, who understood about his situation, who genuinely wanted to hear and was not frightened.

It helped a lot.

His wife was the last person in the world he could talk to about his schizophrenia; on the few occasions he had tried she had simply collapsed with fear. Like everybody else, Silvia was terrified at the idea of it entering her life; she herself warded it off with the magic charms of drugs . . . as if phenobarbital could halt the most pervasive, ominous psychic process known to man. God knew how many pills he himself had swallowed during the last decade, enough to pave a road from his home to this hotel and possibly back.

He decided after some reflection not to call Doreen. Better to leave it as a way out when the going got exceptionally rough. Right now he felt fairly placid. There would be plenty of time in the future, and plenty of need, to seek out Doreen Anderton.

Of course, he would have to be incredibly careful; obviously Doreen was Arnie Kott's mistress. But she seemed to know what she was doing, and certainly she knew Arnie; she must have taken him into account when she gave out her phone number and address, and, for that matter, when she got up and left the restaurant.

I trust her, Jack said to himself. And for someone with a streak of schizophrenia, that is something.

Pondering that, Jack Bohlen put out his cigarette, went and got his pajamas, and prepared to go to bed.

He was just getting under the covers when the phone in his room rang. A service call, he thought, leaping up automatically to get it.

But it was not. A woman's voice said softly in his ear, "Jack?"

"Yes," he said.

"This is Doreen. I just wondered—if you were O.K."

"I'm fine," he said, seating himself on the edge of the bed.

"Do you think you'd want to come over tonight? To my place?"

He hesitated. "Umm," he said.

"We could play records and talk. Arnie lent me a lot of rare old stereophonic LP records from his collection . . . some of them are awfully scratchy, but some are terrific. He's quite a collector, you know; he has the largest collection of Bach on Mars. And you saw his harpsichord."

So that's what that had been, there in Arnie's living room.

"Is it safe?" he asked.

"Yes. Don't worry about Arnie; he's not possessive, if you know what I mean."

Jack said, "O.K. I'll be over." And then he realized that he couldn't, because he had to be available for service calls. Unless he could switch it through her phone.

"That's no problem," she said, when he explained it to her. "I'll call Arnie and tell him."

Dumbfounded, he said, "But—"

"Jack, you're out of your mind if you think we can do it any other way—Arnie knows everything that goes on in the settlement. Leave it to me, dear. I'll call him right now. And you come right on over here. If any calls come through while you're on your way I'll write them down, but I don't think there will be any; Arnie doesn't want you out fixing people's toasters, he wants you for his own jobs, for making that machine for talking to the Steiner boy."

"O.K.," he said, "I'll be over. Goodbye." He hung up the phone.

Ten minutes later he was on his way, flying the bright and shiny Yee Company repairship through the night sky of Mars, to Lewistown and Arnie Kott's mistress.

eight

DAVID BOHLEN KNEW that his grandfather Leo had a lot of money and didn't mind spending it. For instance, before they had even left the rocket terminal building, the old man in his stiff suit with his vest and gold cuff links—it was the suit that the boy had watched to catch sight of, along the ramp from where the passengers appeared—stopped at the flower counter and bought the boy's mother a bunch of large blue Earth flowers. And he wanted to buy something for David, too, but they didn't have any toys, only candy, which Grandfather Leo bought: a two-pound box.

Under his arm Grandfather Leo had a white carton tied with string: he hadn't let the rocketship officials take it and put it with the luggage. When they had left the terminal building and were in his dad's 'copter, Grandfather Leo opened the package. It was full of Jewish bread and pickles and thin-sliced corned beef wrapped in protective plastic, three pounds of corned beef in all.

"My gosh," Jack exclaimed in delight. "All the way from New York. You can't get that out here in the colonies, Dad."

"I know that, Jack," Grandfather Leo said. "A Jewish fella told me where to get it, and I like it so much I knew you'd like it, you and I have the same tastes." He chuckled, pleased to see how happy he had made them. "I'm gonna make you a sandwich when we get to the house. First thing we get there."

The 'copter rose now above the rocketship terminal and passed on over the dark desert.

"How's the weather you been having here?" Grandfather Leo asked.

"Lots of storms," Jack said. "Practically buried us, a week or so ago. We had to rent power equipment to dig out."

103

"Bad," Grandfather Leo said. "You ought to get that cement wall up you were talking about in your letters."

"It costs a fortune to have construction work done out here," Silvia said, "it's not like back on Earth."

"I know that," Grandfather Leo said, "but you got to protect your investment—that house is worth a lot, and the land, you have water nearby; don't forget that."

"How could we forget that?" Silvia said. "Good Lord, without the ditch we'd die."

"That canal any wider this year?" Grandfather Leo asked.

"Just the same," Jack said.

David spoke up. "They dredged it, Grandfather Leo. I watched them; the UN men, they used a big machine that sucked up the sand from the bottom, and the water's a lot cleaner. So my dad shut off the filter system, and now when the rider comes and opens the gate our way, we can pump it so fast that my dad let me put in a whole new vegetable garden I can water with overflow, and I have corn and squash and a couple of carrots, but something ate all the beets. We had corn last night from it. We put up a fence to keep those little animals from getting in—what are they called, Dad?"

"Sand rats, Leo," Jack said. "As soon as David's garden started to bear, the sand rats moved in. They're yay long." He held up his hands to show. "Harmless, except that they can eat their weight in ten minutes. The older settlers warned us, but we had to try."

"Good to grow your own produce," Grandfather Leo said. "Yeah, you wrote me about the garden, David: I like to see it tomorrow. Tonight I'm tired; that's a long trip I took, even with the new ships they got, what do they call it? Fast as light, but it really isn't; still a lot of time taking off and landing and a lot of concussion. I had a woman next to me, she was terrified, thought we'd burn up, it got so hot inside there, even with the air conditioning. I don't know why they let it get so hot, they certainly charge enough. But it's a big improvement over—remember the ship you took when you emigrated years ago? Two months!"

Jack said, "Leo, you brought your oxygen mask, I hope. Ours is too old now, unreliable."

"Sure, I got it in my brown suitcase. Don't worry about me, I can take this atmosphere—I got a different heart pill, really improved. Everything's improving back Home. Of course, it's overcrowded. But more and more people going to be emigrating over here—take my word for that. Smog's so bad back Home it nearly kills you."

David spoke up, "Grandfather Leo, the man next door, Mr. Steiner, he took his own life, and now his son Manfred is home from the camp for anomalous children, and my dad is building a mechanism so he can talk to us."

"Well," Grandfather Leo said, in a kindly way. He beamed at the boy. "That's interesting David. How old is this boy?"

"Ten," David said, "but he can't talk at all to us, yet. But my dad is going to fix that up with his mechanism, and you know who my dad is working for right now? Mr. Kott, who runs the Water Workers' Union and their settlement; he's really a big important man."

"I believe I heard about him," Grandfather Leo said, with a wink at Jack which the boy caught.

Jack said to his father, "Dad, are you still going ahead with this business of buying land in the F.D.R. range?"

"Oh, certainly," Grandfather Leo said. "You bet your life, Jack. Naturally, I came out on this trip sociably, to see you all, but I couldn't have taken off so much time as this unless it was business, too."

"I hoped you'd given that up," Jack said.

"Now Jack," Grandfather Leo said, "don't you worry; you let me worry if I'm doing the right thing; I been in land investment for many years now. Listen. You going to pilot me out there to that mountain range so I can take a first-hand look? I got a lot of maps; I want to see with my own eyes, though."

"You're going to be disappointed when you see it," Silvia said. "It's so desolate there, no water, scarcely anything living."

"Let's not worry about it right now," Grandfather Leo said, with a smile at David. He nudged the boy in the ribs. "Good to see a young man straight and healthy and out here away from the polluted air we have back Home."

"Well, Mars has its drawbacks," Silvia said. "Try living with bad water or no water at all for a while and you'll see."

"I know," Grandfather Leo said soberly. "You people sure have guts to live out here. But it's healthy; don't forget that."

Below, them now, the lights of Bunchewood Park glittered. Jack turned the 'copter toward the north and their home.

As he piloted the Yee Company 'copter, Jack Bohlen glanced at his father and marveled at how little he had aged, how vigorous and well knit Leo looked, for a man in his late seventies. And still at his job, fulltime, getting as much enjoyment out of speculating as ever.

And yet, although it did not show, he was certain that the long trip from Earth had tired Leo out more than he admitted. In any case, they were almost at the house, now. The gyrocompass reading was point 7.08054; they were only minutes away.

When they had parked on the roof of the house, and had gone downstairs, Leo at once fulfilled his promise; in the kitchen he set to work, joyfully making each of them a kosher corned-beef sandwich on Jewish bread. Soon they were all seated in the living room, eating. Everyone was peaceful and relaxed.

"You just don't know how we're starved for food of this sort," Silvia said finally. "Even on the black market—" She glanced at Jack.

"Sometimes you can pick up delicatessen foods on the black market," Jack said, "although lately it's gotten harder. We don't, personally. No moral reason: it's just too expensive."

They talked for a while, finding out about Leo's trip and about conditions back Home. David was sent to bed at ten-thirty, and then, at eleven, Silvia excused herself and went to bed, too. Leo and Jack were left in the living room, still sitting, just the two of them.

Leo said, "Can we step outside and take a glance at the boy's garden? You got a big flashlight?"

Finding his trouble-lantern, Jack led the way out of the house and into the cold night air.

As they stood at the edge of the patch of corn, Leo said to him in a low voice, "How are you and Silvia getting along these days?"

"Fine," Jack said, a little taken aback by the question.

"Seems to me there's a coolness between the two of you," Leo said. "It sure would be terrible, Jack, if you grew apart. That's a fine woman you got, there—one in a million."

"I recognize that," Jack said uncomfortably.

"Back Home," Leo said, "when you were a young fellow, you always played around a lot. But I know you're settled down, now."

"I am," Jack said. "And I think you're imagining things."

"You do seem withdrawn, Jack," his father said. "I hope that old trouble of yours, you know what I mean, isn't bothering you. I'm talking about—"

"I know what you're talking about."

Relentlessly, Leo went on, "When I was a boy there was no mental illness like there is now. It's a sign of the times; too many people, too much overcrowding. I remember when you first got sick, and a long time before that, say from when you were seventeen on, you were cold toward other people, uninterested in them. Moody, too. Seems to me you're like that, now."

Jack glared at his father. This was the trouble with having one's folks visit; they could never resist the temptation to resume their old roles as the All-wise, the All-knowing. To Leo, Jack was not a grown man with a wife and child; he was simply his son Jack.

"Look, Leo," Jack said. "Out here there are very few people; this is a sparsely settled planet, as yet. Naturally, people here are less gregarious; they have to be more inner-directed than back Home where it's like you said, just a mob-scene day after day."

Leo nodded. "Hmm. But that should make you more glad to see fellow humans."

"If you're referring to yourself, I'm very glad to see you."

"Sure, Jack," Leo said, "I know. Maybe I'm just tired. But you don't seem to say much; you're preoccupied."

"My work," Jack said. "This boy Manfred, this autistic child—I have that on my mind all the time."

But, as in the old days, his father could see through his pretexts effortlessly, with true parental instinct. "Come on, boy," Leo said. "You got a lot on your mind, but I know how you work; your job is with your hands, and I'm talking about your mind, it's your mind that's turned inward. Can you get that psychotherapy business here on Mars? Don't tell me no, because I know better."

"I'm not going to tell you no," Jack said, "but I will tell you that it's none of you goddamn business."

Beside him in the darkness his father seemed to shrink, to settle. "O.K., boy," he murmured. "Sorry I butted in."

They were both uncomfortably silent.

"Hell," Jack said, "let's not quarrel, Dad. Let's go back inside and have a drink or something and then turn in. Silvia fixed up a good soft bed for you in the other bedroom; I know you'll have a good rest."

"Silvia's very attentive to a person's needs," Leo said, with a faint note of accusation toward his son. Then his voice softened as he said, "Jack, I always worry about you. Maybe I'm old-fashioned and don't understand about this—mental

107

illness business; everybody seems to have it nowadays; it's common, like flu and polio used to be, like when we were kids and almost everybody caught measles. Now you have this. One out of every three, I heard on TV, one time. Skizo—whatever. I mean, Jack, with so much to live for, why would anyone turn his back on life, like these skizo people do. It doesn't make sense. You got a whole planet to conquer, here. Tomorrow, for instance, I'm going with you to the F.D.R. Mountains, and you can show me around all over, and then I've got all the details on legal procedure here; I'm going to be buying. Listen: You buy in, too, you hear me? I'll advance you the money." He grinned hopefully at Jack, showing his stainless-steel teeth.

"It's not my cup of tea," Jack said. "But thanks."

"I'll pick out the parcel for you," Leo offered.

"No. I'm just not interested."

"You—enjoying your job, now, Jack? Making this machine to talk to the little boy who can't speak? Sounds like a worthy occupation; I'm proud to hear about it. David is a swell kid, and boy, is he proud of his dad."

"I know he is," Jack said.

"David doesn't show any signs of that skizo thing, does he?"

"No," Jack said.

Leo said, "I don't know where you got yours, certainly not from me—I love people."

"I do, too," Jack said. He wondered how his father would act if he knew about Doreen. Probably Leo would be grief-stricken; he came from a strait-laced generation—born in 1924, a long, long time ago. It was a different world, then. Amazing, how his father had adapted to this world, now; a miracle. Leo, born in the boom period following World War One, and now standing here on the edge of the Martian desert . . . but he still would not understand about Doreen, about how vital it was for him to maintain an intimate contact of this sort, at any cost; or rather, almost any cost.

"What's her name?" Leo said.

"W-what?" Jack stammered.

"I got a little of that telepathic sense," Leo said in a toneless voice. "Don't I?"

After a pause, Jack said, "Evidently."

"Does Silvia know?"

"No."

"I could tell because you didn't look me in the eye."

"Balls," Jack said fiercely.

"Is she married, too? She got kids, too, this other woman you're mixed up with?"

Jack said in as level a voice as possible, "Why don't you use your telepathic sense and find out?"

"I just don't want to see Silvia hurt," Leo said.

"She won't be," Jack said.

"Too bad," Leo said, "to come all this way and find out something like this. Well—" He sighed. "I got my business, anyhow. Tomorrow you and I'll get up good and early and get started."

Jack said, "Don't be too harsh a judge, Dad."

"All right," Leo agreed. "I know, it's modern times. You think by this playing around you keep yourself well—right? Maybe so. Maybe it's a way to sanity. I don't mean you're not sane—"

"Just tainted," Jack said, with violent bitterness. Christ, your own father, he thought. What an ordeal. What a miserable tragedy.

"I know you'll come out O.K.," Leo said. "I can see now that you're struggling; it's not just playing around. I can tell by your voice—you got troubles. Same ones you always had, only as you get older you wear out, and it's harder—right? Yeah, I see that. This planet is lonely. It's a wonder all you emigrants didn't go crazy right off the bat. I can see why you would value love anywhere you can find it. What you need is something like what I've got, this land thing of mine; maybe you can find it in building your machine for that poor mute kid. I'd like to see him."

"You will," Jack said. "Possibly tomorrow."

They stood for a moment longer, and then they walked back into the house. "Does Silvia still take dope?" Leo asked.

"Dope!" He laughed. "Phenobarbital. Yes, she does."

"Such a nice girl," Leo said. "Too bad she's so tense and worries so much. And helping that unfortunate widow next door, like you were telling me." In the living room, Leo seated himself in Jack's easy chair, crossed his legs and leaned back, sighing, making himself comfortable so that he could continue talking . . . he definitely had much more to say, on a variety of subjects, and he intended to say it.

In bed, Silvia lay almost lost in sleep, her faculties doused by the 100 miligram tablet of phenobarbital which she had taken, as usual, upon retiring. Vaguely, she had heard the murmur of her husband's and her father-in-law's voices from the yard; once, their tone became sharp and she had sat up, alarmed.

Are they going to bicker? she asked herself. God, I hope not; I hope Leo's stay isn't going to disrupt things. However, their voices had sunk back down, and now she rested easily once more.

He certainly is a fine old man, she thought. Much like Jack, only more set in his ways.

Lately, since he had started working for Arnie Kott, her husband had changed. No doubt it was the eerie job which he had been given; the mute, autistic Steiner boy upset her, and she had been sorry from the first to see him appear. Life was complicated enough already. The boy flitted in and out of the house, always running on his toes, his eyes always darting as if he saw objects not present, heard sounds beyond the normal range. If only time could be turned back and Norbert Steiner could be somehow restored to life! If only . . .

In her drugged mind she saw, in a flash, that ineffectual little man setting out in the morning with his suitcases of wares, salesman off on his rounds, yogurt and blackstrap molasses.

Is he still alive somewhere? Perhaps Manfred saw him, lost as the boy was—according to Jack—in disfigured time. What a surprise is in store for them when they make contact with the boy and find they have rekindled that sad little specter . . . but more likely their theory is right, and it is the next, he sees the next. They will have what they want. Why is it Jack? What do you want it for, Jack? Affinity between you and that ill child. That it? Oh . . . Her thoughts gave way to darkness.

And then what? Will you care about me again?

No affinity between the sick and the sound. You are different; it weighs me down. Leo knows it, I know it. Do you? Care?

She slept.

High in the sky circled meat-eating birds. At the base of the windowed building lay their excrement. He picked up the wads until he held several. They twisted and swelled like dough, and he knew there were living creatures within; he carried them carefully into the empty corridor of the building. One wad opened, parted with a split in its woven, hairlike side; it became too large to hold, and he saw it now in the wall. A compartment where it lay on its side, the rent so wide that he perceived the creature within.

Gubbish! A worm, coiled up, made of wet, bony-white pleats, the inside gubbish worm, from a person's body. If only the high-flying birds could find it and eat it down, like that. He ran down the steps, which gave beneath his feet. Boards missing. He saw down through the sieve of wood to the soil beneath, the cavity, dark, cold, full of wood so rotten that it lay in damp powder, destroyed by gubbish-rot.

Arms lifted up, tossed him to the circling birds; he floated up, falling at the same time. They ate his head off. And then he stood on a bridge over the sea. Sharks showed in the water, their sharp, cutting fins. He caught one on his line and it came sliding up from the water, mouth open, to swallow him. He stepped back, but the bridge caved in and sagged so that the water reached his middle.

It rained gubbish, now; all was gubbish, wherever he looked. A group of those who didn't like him appeared at the end of the bridge and held up a loop of shark teeth. He was emperor. They crowned him with the loop, and he tried to thank them. But they forced the loop down past his head to his neck, and they began to strangle him. They knotted the loop and the shark teeth cut his head off. Once more he sat in the dark, damp basement with the powdery rot around him, listening to the tidal water lap-lapping everywhere. A world where gubbish ruled, and he had no voice; the shark teeth had cut his voice out.

I am Manfred, he said.

"I tell you," Arnie Kott said to the girl beside him in the wide bed, "you're really going to be delighted when we make contact with him—I mean, we got an inside track, there: we got the future, and where else do you think things happen except in the future?"

Stirring, Doreen Anderton murmured.

"Don't go to sleep," Arnie said, leaning over to light another cigarette. "Listen, guess what—a big-time land speculator came over from Earth, today; we had a union guy at the rocket terminal, and he recognized him, although naturally the speculator registered under an assumed name. We checked with the carrier, and he got right out of there, eluding our guy. I predicted they'd be showing up! Listen, when we hear from that Steiner kid, it'll blow the lid off this whole thing. Right?"

He shook the sleeping girl. "If you don't wake up," Arnie said, "I'm gonna shove you right out of bed on your ass, and you can walk home to your apartment."

Doreen groaned, turned over, sat up. In the dim light of Arnie Kott's master bedroom, she sat palely translucent, tucking her hair back from her eyes and yawning. One strap of her nightgown slipped down her arm, and Arnie saw with appreciation her high, hard left breast with its gem of a nipple set dead-center.

Gosh, I really got a gal, Arnie said to himself. She's really something. And she's done a terrific job in keeping that Bohlen from shucking it all and wandering off, the way those hebephrenic schizophrenics do—I mean, it's almost impossible to keep them at the grindstone, they're so moody and irresponsible. That guy Bohlen; he's an idiot savant, an idiot who can fix things, and we have to cater to his idiocy, we have to yield. You can't force a guy like that; he don't force. Arnie took hold of the covers and tossed them aside, off Doreen; he smiled at her bare legs, smiled to see her draw her nightgown down to her knees.

"How can you be tired?" he asked her. "You ain't done nothin' but lie. Isn't that so? Is lying there so hard?"

She eyed him narrowly. "No more," she said.

"What?" he said. "You kidding? We just begun. Take off that nightgown." Catching it by the hem he whisked it back up once more; he put his arm beneath her, lifted her up, and in an instant had it off over her head. He deposited it on the chair by the bed.

"I'm going to sleep," Doreen said, closing her eyes. "If you don't mind."

"Why should I mind?" Arnie said. "You're still there, aren't you? Awake or asleep—you're plenty there in the flesh, and how."

"Ouch," she protested.

"Sorry." He kissed her on the mouth. "Didn't mean to hurt you."

Her head lolled; she actually was going to sleep. Arnie felt offended. But what the hell—she never did much anyhow.

"Put my nightgown back on me," Doreen murmured, "when you're through."

"Yeah, well I'm not through." I'm good for an hour more, Arnie said to himself. Maybe even two. I sort of like it this way, too. A woman asleep don't talk. That's what spoils it, when they start to talk. Or make those moans. He could never stand the moans.

He thought, I'm dying to get results on that project of Bohlen's. I can't wait; I know we're going to hear something really downright wonderful when we do start hearing. The closed-up mind of that kid; think of all the treasures it contains. Must be like fairyland, in there, all beautiful and pure and real innocent.

In her half-sleep Doreen moaned.

nine

Into LEO BOHLEN's hand his son Jack put a large green seed. Leo examined it, handed it back.

"What did you see?" Jack asked.

"I saw it, the seed."

"Did anything happen?"

Leo pondered, but he could not think of anything he had seen happen, so at last he said, "No."

Seated at the movie projector, Jack said, "Now watch." He snapped off the lights in the room, and then, on the screen, an image appeared as the projector whirred. It was a seed, embedded in soil. As Leo watched, the seed split open. Two probing feelers appeared; one started upward, the other divided into fine hairs and groped down. Meanwhile, the seed revolved in the soil. Enormous projections unfolded from the upward moving feeler, and Leo gasped.

"Say, Jack," he said, "some seeds you got here on Mars; look at it go. My gosh, it's working away like mad."

Jack said, "That's a plain ordinary lima bean, the same as I gave you just now. This film is speeded up, five days compressed into seconds. We can now see the motion that goes on in a germinating seed; normally, the process takes place too slowly for us to see any motion at all."

"Say, Jack," Leo said, "that's really something. So this kid's time-rate is like this seed. I understand. Things that we can see move would whiz around him so darn fast they'd be practically invisible, and I bet he sees slow processes like this seed here; I bet he can go out in the yard and sit down and watch the plants growing, and five days for him is like say ten minutes for us."

Jack said, "That's the theory, anyhow." He went on, then, to explain to Leo how the chamber worked. The explanation was filled with technical terms, however, which Leo did not understand, and he felt a little irritable as Jack droned on. The time was eleven A.M., and still Jack showed no sign of taking him on his trip over the F.D.R. Mountains; he seemed completely immersed in this.

"Very interesting," Leo murmured, at one point.

"We take a tape recording, done at fifteen inches per second, and run it off for Manfred at three and three-fourths inches per second. A single word, such as 'tree.' And at the same time we flash up a picture of a tree and the word beneath it, a still, which we keep in sight for fifteen or twenty minutes. Then what Manfred says is recorded at three and three-fourths inches per second, and for our own listening we speed it up and replay at fifteen."

Leo said, "Listen, Jack, we just gotta get going on that trip."

"Christ," Jack said, "this is my job." He gestured angrily. "I thought you wanted to meet him—he'll be over here any time now. She sends him over—"

Breaking in, Leo said, "Look, son, I came millions of miles to have a look at that land. Now are we going to fly there or not?"

Jack said, "We'll wait until the boy comes, and we'll take him with us."

"O.K.," Leo said. He wanted to avoid friction; he was willing to compromise, at least as much as was humanly possible.

"My God, here you are for the first time in your life on the surface of another planet. I should think you'd want to walk around, take a look at the canal, the ditch." Jack gestured over toward the right. "You haven't even glanced at it, and people have been wanting to see the canals—they've argued about their existence—for centuries!"

Feeling chagrined, Leo nodded dutifully. "Show me, then." He followed Jack from the workshop, outdoors into the dull ruddy sunlight. "Cold," Leo observed, sniffing the air. "Say, it's sure easy to walk around; I noticed that last night I felt like I weighed only fifty or sixty pounds. Must be because Mars is so small—right? Must be good for people with cardiac conditions, except the air's so thin. I thought last night it was the corned beef that made me—"

"Leo," his son said, "be quiet and look around, will you?"

Leo looked around. He saw a flat desert with meager mountains in the far distance. He saw a deep ditch of sluggish brown water, and, beside the ditch, a mosslike vegetation, green. That was all, except for Jack's house and the Steiner house a little farther on. He saw the garden, but he had seen that last night.

"Well?" Jack said.

Being obliging, Leo said, "Very impressive, Jack. You've got a nice place here; a nice little modern place. A little more planting, landscaping, and I'd say it was perfect."

Grinning at him crookedly, Jack said, "This is the dream of a million years, to stand here and see this."

"I know that, son, and I'm exceptionally proud of what you've accomplished, you and that fine woman." Leo nodded solemnly. "Now can we get started? Maybe you could go over to that other house where that boy is and get him, or did David go over? Maybe David's getting him; I don't see him around."

"David's at school. He was picked up while you were sleeping."

Leo said, "I don't mind going over and getting that boy, Manfred or whatever his name is, if it's O.K. with you."

"Go ahead," Jack said. "I'll come along."

They walked past a small ditch of water, crossed an open field of sand and sparse fernlike plants, and arrived at the other house. Leo heard from within the sound of small girls' voices. Without hesitation he ascended the steps to the porch and rang the bell.

The door opened and there stood a big, blond-haired woman with tired, pain-filled eyes. "Good morning," Leo said, "I'm Jack Bohlen's dad; I guess you're the lady of the house. Say, we'll take your boy with us on a trip and bring him back safe and sound."

The big blonde woman looked past him to Jack, who had come up on the porch; she said nothing, but turned and went off back into the interior of her house. When she returned she had a small boy with her. So this is the skizo little fellow, Leo thought. Nice-looking, you'd never know in a million years.

"We're going on a ride, young man," Leo said to him. "How does that sound?" Then, remembering what Jack had said about the boy's timesense, he repeated what he had said very slowly, dragging each word out.

The boy darted past him and shot down the steps and off toward the canal; he moved in a blur of speed and disappeared from sight behind the Bohlen house.

"Mrs. Steiner," Jack said, "I want you to meet my father."

The big blonde woman put out her had vaguely; she did

not seem to be all there herself, Leo observed. However, he shook hands with her. "Glad to meet you," he said politely. "Sorry to hear about the loss of your husband; it's a terrible thing, something striking like that, without any warning. I knew a fella back in Detroit, good friend of mine, did the same thing one weekend; went out of the shop and said goodbye and that was the last anybody saw of him."

Mrs. Steiner said, "How do you do, Mr. Bohlen."

"We'll go round up Manfred," Jack said to her. "We should be home late this afternoon."

As Leo and his son walked back, the woman remained where she was on the porch, looking after them.

"Pretty odd herself," Leo murmured. Jack said nothing.

They located the boy, standing off by himself in David's overflow garden, and presently the three of them were in the Yee Company 'copter, flying above the desert in the direction of the line of mountains to the north. Leo unfolded a great map which he had brought with him and began to make marks on it.

"I guess we can talk freely," he said to Jack, nodding his head toward the boy. "He won't—" He hesitated. "You know."

"If he understands us," Jack said drily, "It'll be—"

"O.K., O.K.," Leo said, "I just wanted to be sure." He carefully refrained from marking the place on the map that he had heard would be the UN site. But he did mark their route, using the gyrocompass reading visible on the dashboard of the 'copter. "What rumors have you heard, son?" he asked. "About UN interest in the F.D.R. range?"

Jack said, "Something about a park or a power station."

"Want to know exactly what it is?"

"Sure."

Leo reached into his inside coat pocket and brought out an envelope. From it he took a photograph, which he handed to Jack. "Does this remind you of anything?"

Glancing at it, Jack saw that it was a picture of a long, thin building. He stared at it a long time.

"The UN," Leo said, "is going to build these. Multiple-unit dwellings. Whole tracts of them, mile after mile, with shopping centers, complete—supermarkets, hardware stores, drugstores, laundries, ice cream parlors. All built by slave equipment, those construction automatons that feed themselves their own instructions."

Presently, Jack said, "It looks like the co-op apartment house I lived in years ago when I had my breakdown."

117

"Exactly. The co-op movement will be in with the UN on this. These F.D.R. Mountains were once fertile, as everybody knows; there was plenty of water here. The UN hydraulic engineers believe they can bring enormous quantities of water up to the surface from the table below. The water table is closer to the surface in these mountains than anywhere else on Mars; this is the original water source for the canal network, the UN engineers believe."

"The co-op," Jack said in a strange voice, "here on Mars."

"They'll be fine modern structures," Leo said. "It's quite an ambitious project. The UN will be transporting people here free, providing their passage right to their new homes, and the cost of buying each unit will be small. It will take quite a big slice of these mountains, as you might guess, and as I heard it, they expect it to be ten to fifteen years before the project is completed."

Jack said nothing.

"Mass emigration," Leo said. "This will ensure it."

"I guess so," Jack said.

"The appropriations for this are fantastic," Leo said. "The co-op alone is putting up almost a trillion dollars. It has huge reserves of cash, you know; it's one of the richest groups on Earth—it has greater assets than the insurance group or any of the big banking systems. There's not a chance in the world that with them in on it the thing could fail." He added, "The UN has been negotiating with them for six years on this matter."

Finally, Jack said, "What a change it will mean for Mars. Just to have the F.D.R. range fertile—that alone."

"And densely populated," Leo reminded him.

"It's hard to believe," Jack said.

"Yeah, I know, boy, but there's no doubt of it; within another few weeks it'll be generally known. I knew it a month ago. I've been getting investors I know to put up risk capital . . . I represent them, Jack. Alone, I just don't have the money."

Jack said, "You mean, your whole idea is to get here before the UN actually takes the land. You're going to buy if for very little and then resell it to the UN for much more."

"We're going to buy it in great pieces," Leo said, "and then at once subdivide. Cut it up into lots, say, one hunderd feet by eighty. Title will be in the hands of a fairly large number of individuals: wives, cousins, employees, friends of the members of my group."

"Of your syndicate," Jack said.

"Yes, that's what it is," Leo said, pleased. "A syndicate."

After a time Jack said in a hoarse voice, "And you don't feel there's anything wrong with doing this?"

"Wrong in what sense? I don't get you, son."

"Christ," Jack said. "It's obvious."

"Not to me. Explain."

"You're gypping the entire population of Earth—they're the ones who'll have to put up all the money. You're increasing the costs of this project in order to make a killing."

"But Jack, that's what's meant by land speculation." Leo was puzzled. "What did you think land speculation was? It's been going on for centuries; you buy land cheap when nobody wants it because you believe for one reason or another that one day it will be worth a lot more. And it's inside tips that you go on. That's about all there is to go on, when you get down to it. Every land speculator in the world will be trying to buy in, when they get word; in fact they're doing that right now. I beat them here by a matter of days. It's this regulation that you have to actually be on Mars that gets them; they're not prepared at the drop of a hat to come here. So—they've missed out. Because by nightfall I expect to have put our deposit down on the land we want." He pointed ahead of them. "It's in there. I've got all sorts of maps; I won't have any trouble locating it. The location of the piece is in a vast canyon area called the Henry Wallace. To comply with the law, I have to actually set foot on the piece I intend to buy, and place some permanent marker, fully identifiable, in an exposed spot. I have such a marker with me, a regulation steel stake which bears my name. We'll land in the Henry Wallace and you can help me drive the stake in. It's just a formality; it won't take more than a few minutes." He smiled at his son.

Looking at his father, Jack thought, *He's insane.* But Leo smiled calmly at him, and Jack knew that his father was not insane, that it was exactly as he said: land speculators did this, it was their way of going about their business, and there really was such a mammoth UN-co-op project about to start. As shrewd and experienced a businessman as his father could not be wrong. Leo Bohlen, and the men with him, did not act on the basis of a rumor. They had top connections. There had been a leak, either at the co-op or the UN or both, and Leo was putting all his resources to work to take advantage of it.

"It's—the biggest news so far," Jack said, "regarding the development of Mars." He could still hardly believe it.

"Long overdue," Leo said. "Should have taken place right from the start. But they expected private capital to be put up; they waited for the other fella to do it."

"This will change the lives of everybody who lives on Mars," Jack said. It would alter the balance of power, create a totally new ruling class: Arnie Kott, Bosley Touvim—the union settlements and the national settlements—would be small fry, once the co-op, in conjunction with the UN, had moved in.

Poor Arnie, he thought. He won't survive this. Time, progress, and civilization, all will have passed him by, Arnie and his steam baths that waste water, his tiny symbol of pomp.

"Now listen, Jack," his father said, "don't spread this information around, because it's confidential. What we want to watch is crooked business at the abstract company—that's the outfit that records your title. I mean, we put up our deposit, and then other speculators, especially local ones here, get tipped off and then have pull at the abstract company, so it turns out—"

"I see," Jack said. The abstract company would predate the deposit of a local speculator, giving him seeming priority over Leo. There must be many tricks that can be played in a game like this, Jack said to himself; no wonder Leo works carefully.

"We've investigated the abstract company here, and it appears to be honest. But you never know, when there's so much involved."

Suddenly Manfred Steiner gave a hoarse grunt.

Both Jack and Leo glanced up, startled. They had both forgotten about him; he was at the rear of the cab of the 'copter, his face pressed to the glass, staring down. He pointed excitedly.

Far below, Jack saw a party of Bleekmen threading its way along a mountain trail. "That's right," Jack said to the boy, "people down there, probably hunting." It occurred to him that very possibly Manfred had never seen a Bleekman. I wonder what his reaction would be, Jack mused, if he found himself facing them, all at once. How easy it would be to arrange it; all he had to do, really, was land the 'copter ahead of this particular party.

"What are those?" Leo asked, looking down. "Martians?"

"That's what they are," Jack said.

"I'll be darned." Leo laughed. "So those are Martians . . .

they look more like aboriginal Negroes, like the African Bushmen."

'They're closely related to them," Jack said.

Manfred had become quite excited; his eyes shone and he ran back and forth from window to window, peering down and muttering.

What would happen if Manfred lived with a family of Bleekmen for a time? Jack wondered. They move slower then we do; their lives are less complex and hectic. Possibly their sense of time is close to his . . . to the Bleekmen, we Earthmen may very well be hypomanic types, whizzing about at enormous velocity, expending huge amounts of energy over nothing at all.

But it would not bring Manfred into his own society, to put him with the Bleekmen. In fact, he realized, it might draw him so far away form us that there would be no chance of our ever communicating with him.

Thinking that, he decided not to land the 'copter.

"Do those fellas do any work?" Leo asked. "Those Martians?"

"A few have been tamed," Jack said, "as the phrase goes. But most of them continue to exist as they always have, as hunters and fruit-gatherers. They haven't reached the farming stage yet."

When they reached the Henry Wallace, Jack set the 'copter down, and he and his father and Manfred stepped out onto the parched, rocky soil. Manfred was given paper and crayons to amuse himself, and then the two men set out to search for a suitable spot at which to drive the stake.

The spot, a low plateau, was found, and the stake was driven, mostly by Jack; his father wandered about, inspecting rock formations and plants, with a clearly irritated and impatient frown. He did not seem to enjoy it here in this uninhabited region— however, he said nothing; he politely took note of a fossil formation which Jack pointed out to him.

They took photographs of the stake and the surrounding area, and then, their business done, they returned to the 'copter. There sat Manfred, on the ground, busily drawing with the crayons. The desolation of the area did not seem to bother him, Jack decided. The boy, wrapped up in his inner world, drew and ignored them; he glanced up now and then, but not at the two men. His eyes were blank.

What's he drawing? Jack wondered, and walked around behind the boy to see.

Manfred, glancing up now and then to peer sightlessly at the landscape around him, had drawn great, flat apartment buildings.

"Look at this, Dad," Jack said, and he managed to keep his voice calm and steady.

Together, the two of them stood behind the boy, watching him draw, watching the buildings become more and more distinct on the paper.

Well, there's no mistaking it, Jack thought. The boy is drawing the buildings that will be here. He is drawing the landscape which will come, not the landscape visible to our eyes.

"I wonder if he saw the photo I showed you," Leo said. "That one of the models.".

"Maybe so," Jack said. It would provide an explanation; the boy had understood their conversation, seen the papers, gotten his inspiration from that. But the photo had shown the buildings from above; it was a different perspective from this. The boy had sketched the buildings as they would appear to an observer on the ground. As they would appear, Jack realized, to someone seated where we are right now.

"I wouldn't be surprised if you've got something in this time theory," Leo said. He glanced at his wrist watch. "Now, speaking of time, I'd say—"

"Yes," Jack agreed thoughtfully, "we'll get started back."

There was something more in the child's drawing which he had noticed. He wondered if his father had seen it. The buildings, the enormous co-op apartments, which the boy was sketching, were developing in an ominous direction before their eyes. As they watched, they saw some final details which made Leo glare; he snorted and glanced at his son.

The buildings were old, sagging with age. Their foundations showed great cracks radiating upward. Windows were broken. And what looked like stiff tall weeds grew in the land around. It was a scene of ruin and despair, and of a ponderous, timeless, inertial heaviness.

"Jack, he's drawing a slum!" Leo exclaimed.

That was it, a decaying slum. Buildings that had stood for years, perhaps even decades, which had passed their prime and dwindled into their twilight, into senility and partial abandonment.

Pointing at a yawning crack which he had just drawn, Manfred said, "Bubbish." His hand traced the weeds, the broken windows. Again he said, "Gubbish." He glanced at them, smiling in a frightened way.

"What does that mean, Manfred?" Jack asked.

There was no answer. The boy continued to sketch. And as he sketched, the buildings, before their eyes, grew older and older, more in ruins with each passing moment.

"Let's go," Leo said hoarsely.

Jack took the boy's paper and crayons and got him on his feet. The three of them re-entered the 'copter.

"Look, Jack," Leo said. He was intently examining the boy's drawing. "What he's written over the entrance of the building."

In twisted, wavering letters Manfred had written:

AM-WEB

"Must be the name of the building." Leo said.

"It is," Jack said, recognizing the word; it was a contraction of a co-op slogan "Alle Menschen werden Brüder." "All men become brothers," he said under his breath. "It's on co-op stationery." He remembered it well.

Now, taking his crayons once more, Manfred resumed his work. As the two men watched, the boy began to draw something at the top of the picture. Dark birds, Jack saw. Enormous, dusky, vulture-like birds.

At a broken window of the building, Manfred drew a round face with eyes, nose, a turned-down, despairing mouth. Someone within the building, gazing out silently and hopelessly, as if trapped within.

"Well," Leo said. "Interesting." His expression was one of grim outrage. "Now, why would he want to draw that? I don't think that's a very wholesome or positive attitude; why can't he draw it like it's going to be, new and immaculate, with children playing and pets and contented people?"

Jack said, "Maybe he draws what he sees."

"Well, if he sees that, he's ill," Leo said. "There are so many bright, wonderful things he could see instead; why would he want to see that?"

"Perhaps he has no choice," Jack said. *Gubbish*, he thought. I wonder; could *gubbish* mean time? The force that to the boy means decay, deterioration, destruction, and, at last, death? The force at work everywhere, on everything in the universe.

And is that all he sees?

If so, Jack thought, no wonder he's autistic; no wonder he can't communicate with us. A view of the universe that partial—it isn't even a complete view of time. Because time also brings new things into existence; it's also the process of maturation and growth. And evidently Manfred does not perceive time in that aspect.

Is he sick because he sees this? Or does he see this because he is sick? A meaningless question, perhaps, or anyhow one that can't be answered. This is Manfred's view of reality, and according to us, he is desperately ill; he does not perceive the rest of reality, which we do. And it is a dreadful section which he does see: reality in its most repellent aspect.

Jack thought, *And people talk about mental illness as an escape!* He shuddered. It was no escape; it was a narrowing, a contracting of life into, at last, a moldering, dank tomb, a place where nothing came or went; a place of total death.

The poor damned kid, he thought. How can he live from one day to the next, having to face the reality he does?

Somberly, Jack returned to the job of piloting the 'copter. Leo looked out the window, contemplating the desert below. Manfred, with the taut, frightened expression on his face, continued to draw.

They gubbled and gubbled. He put his hands to his ears, but the product crept up through his nose. Then he saw the place. It was where he wore out. They threw him away there, and gubbish lay in heaps up to his waist; gubbish filled the air.

"What is your name?"

"Steiner, Manfred."

"Age."

"Eighty-three."

"Vaccinated against small pox?"

"Yes."

"Any venereal diseases?"

"Well, a little clap, that's all."

"V.D. clinic for this man."

"Sir, my teeth. They're in the bag, along with my eyes."

"Your eyes, oh yes. Give this man his teeth and eyes before you take him to the V.D. clinic. How about your ears, Steiner?"

"Got 'em on, sir. Thank you, sir."

They tied his hands with gauze to the sides of the bed because he tried to pull out the catheter. He lay facing the window, seeing through the dusty, cracked glass.

Outside, a bug on tall legs picked through the heaps. It ate, and then something squashed it and went on, leaving it squashed with its dead teeth sunk into what it had wanted to eat. Finally its dead teeth got up and crawled out of its mouth in different directions.

He lay there for a hundred and twenty-three years and then his artificial liver gave out and he fainted and died. By that time they had removed both his arms and legs up to the pelvis because those parts of him had decayed.

He didn't use them anyhow. And without arms he didn't try to pull the catheter out, and that pleased them.

I been at AM-WEB for a long time, he said. Maybe you can get me a transistor radio so I can tune in Friendly Fred's Breakfast Club; I like to hear the tunes, they play a lot of the old-time favorites.

Something outside gives me hayfever. Must be those yellow flowering weeds, why do they let them get so tall?

I once saw a ballgame.

For two days he lay on the floor, in a big puddle, and then the landlady found him and called for the truck to bring him here. He snored all the way, it woke him up. When they tried to give him grapefruit juice he could only work one arm, the other never worked again ever. He wished he could still make those leather belts, they were fun and took lots of time. Sometimes he sold them to people who came by on the weekend.

"Do you know who I am, Manfred?"

"No."

"I'm Arnie Kott. Why don't you laugh or smile sometimes, Manfred? Don't you like to run around and play?"

As he spoke Mr. Kott gubbled from both his eyes.

"Obviously he doesn't, Arnie, but that's not what concerns us here anyhow."

"What do you see, Manfred? Let us in on what you see. All those people, are they going to live there, is that it? Is that right, Manfred? Can you see lots of people living there?"

He put his hands over his face, and the gubble stopped.

"I don't see why this kid never laughs."

Gubble, gubble.

ten

INSIDE MR. KOTT'S SKIN were dead bones, shiny and wet. Mr. Kott was a sack of bones, dirty and yet shiny-wet. His head was a skull that took in greens and bit them; inside him the greens became rotten things as something ate them to make them dead.

He could see everything that went on inside Mr. Kott, the teeming gubbish life. Meanwhile, the outside said, "I love Mozart. I'll put this tape on." The box read: "Symphony 40 in G mol., K. 550." Mr. Kott fiddled with the knobs of the amplifier. "Bruno Walter conducting," Mr. Kott told his guests. "A great rarity from the golden age of recordings."

A hideous racket of screeches and shrieks issued from the speakers, like the convulsions of corpses. Mr. Kott shut off the tape transport.

"Sorry," he muttered. It was an old coded message, from Rockingham or Scott Temple or Anne, from someone, anyhow; Mr. Kott, he knew that. He knew that by accident it had found its way into his library of music.

Sipping her drink, Doreen Anderton said, "What a shock. You should spare us, Arnie. Your sense of humor—"

"An accident," Arnie Kott said angrily. He rummaged for another tape. Aw, the hell with it, he thought. "Listen, Jack," he said, turning. "I'm sorry to make you come here when I know your dad's visiting, but I'm running out of time; show me your progress with the Steiner boy, O.K.?" His anticipation and concern made him stutter. He looked at Jack expectantly.

But Jack Bohlen hadn't heard him; he was saying something to Doreen there on the couch where the two of them sat together.

"We're out of booze," Jack said, setting down his empty glass.

"God sake," Arnie said, "I got to hear how you've done, Jack. Can't you give me anything? Are you two just going to sit there necking and whispering? I don't feel good." He went unsteadily into the kitchen, where Heliogabalus sat on a

126

tall stool, like a dunce, reading a magazine. "Fix me a glass of warm water and baking soda," Arnie said.

"Yes, Mister." Heliogabalus closed his magazine and stepped down from the stool. "I overheard. Why don't you send them out? They are no good, no good at all, Mister." From the cabinet over the sink he took the package of bicarbonate of soda; he spooned out a teaspoonful.

"Who cares about your opinion?" Arnie said.

Doreen entered the kitchen, her face drawn and tired. "Arnie, I think I'll go home. I really can't take much of Manfred; he never stops moving around, never sits still. I can't stand it." Going up to Arnie she kissed him on the ear. "Goodnight, dear."

"I read about a kid who thought he was a machine," Arnie said. "He had to be plugged in, he said, to work. I mean, you have to be able to stand these fruits. Don't go. Stay for my sake. Manfred's a lot quieter when a woman's around, I don't know why. I have the feeling that Bohlen's accomplished nothing; I'm going out there and tell him to his face." A glass of warm water and baking soda was put into his right hand by his tame Bleekman. "Thanks." He drank it gratefully.

"Jack Bohlen," Doreen said, "has done a fine job under difficult conditions. I don't want to hear anything said against him." She swayed slightly, smiling. "I'm a little drunk."

"Who isn't?" Arnie said. He put his arm around her waist and hugged her. "I'm so drunk I'm sick. O.K., that kid gets me, too. Look, I put on that old coded tape; I must be nuts." Setting down his glass he unbuttoned the top buttons of her blouse. "Look away, Helio. Read your book." The Bleekman looked away. Holding Doreen against him, Arnie unbuttoned all the buttons of her blouse and began on her skirt. "I know they're ahead of me, those Earth bastards coming in everywhere you look. My man at the terminal can't even count them any more; they been coming in all day long. Let's go to bed." He kissed her on the collar bone, nuzzled lower and lower until she raised his head with the strength of her hands.

In the living room, his hotshot repairman hired away from Mr. Yee fiddled with the tape recorder, clumsily putting on a fresh reel. He had knocked over his empty glass.

What happens if they get there before me? Arnie Kott asked himself as he clung to Doreen, wheeling slowly about the kitchen with her as Heliogabalus read to himself. What if I can't buy in at all? Might as well be dead. He bent Doreen backwards, but all the time thinking, There has to be a place for me. I love this planet.

Music bleared; Jack Bohlen had gotten the tape going.

Doreen pinched him savagely, and he let go of her; he walked from the kitchen, back into the living room, turned down the volume, and said, "Jack, let's get down to business."

"Right," Jack Bohlen agreed.

Coming from the kitchen after him, buttoning her blouse, Doreen made a wide circuit to avoid Manfred, who was down on his hands and knees; the boy had spread out a length of butcher paper and was pasting bits cut from magazines onto it with library paste. Patches of white showed on the rug where he had slopped.

Going up to the boy, Arnie bent down close to him and said, "Do you know who I am, Manfred?"

There was no answer from the boy, nothing to show he had even heard.

"I'm Arnie Kott," Arnie said. "Why don't you laugh or smile sometimes, Manfred? Don't you like to run around and play?" He felt sorry for the boy, sorry and distressed.

Jack Bohlen said in an unsteady, thick voice, "Obviously he doesn't, Arnie, but that's not what concerns us here, anyhow." His gaze was befuddled; the hand that held the glass shook.

But Arnie continued. "What do you see, Manfred? Let us in on what you see." He waited, but there was only silence. The boy concentrated on his pasting. He had created a collage on the paper: a jagged strip of green, then a perpendicular rise, gray and dense, forbidding.

"What's it mean?" Arnie said.

"It's a place," Jack said. "A building. I brought it along." He went off, returning with a manila envelope; from it he brought a large crumpled child's crayon drawing, which he held up for Arnie to examine. "There," Jack said. "That's it. You wanted me to establish communication with him; well, I established it." He had some trouble with the two long words; his tongue seemed to catch.

Arnie, however, did not care how drunk his repairman was. He was accustomed to having his guests tank up; hard liquor was rare on Mars, and when people came upon it, as they did at Arnie's place, they generally reacted as Jack Bohlen had. What mattered was the task which Jack had been given. Arnie picked up the picture and studied it.

"This it?" he asked Jack. "What else?"

"Nothing else."

"What about that chamber that slows things down?"

"Nothing," Jack said.

"Can the boy read the future?"

"Absolutely," Jack said. "There's no doubt of it. That picture is proof right there, unless he heard us talking." Turning to Doreen he said, in a slow, thick voice, "did he hear us, do you think? No, you weren't there. It was my dad. I don't think he heard. Listen, Arnie. You aren't supposed to see this, but I guess it's O.K. It's too late now. This is a picture nobody is supposed to see; this is the way it's going to be a century from now, when it's in ruins."

"What the hell is it?" Arnie said "I can't read a kids's nutty drawing; explain it to me."

"This is AM-WEB," Jack said. "A big, big housing tract. Thousands of people living there. Biggest on Mars. Only, it's crumbling into rubble, according to the picture."

There was silence. Arnie was baffled.

"Maybe you're not interested," Jack said.

"Sure I am," Arnie said angrily. He appealed to Doreen, who stood off to one side, looking pensive. "Do you understand this?"

"No, dear," she said.

"Jack," Arnie said," I called you here for your report. And all I get is this dim-witted drawing. Where is this big housing tract?"

"In the F.D.R. Mountains," Jack said.

Arnie felt his pulse slow, then with difficulty labor on. "Oh, yeah, I see," he said. "I understand."

Grinning, Jack said, "I thought you would. You're interested in that. You know, Arnie, you think I'm a schizophrenic, and Doreen thinks so, and my father thinks so . . . but I *do* care what your motives are. I can get you plenty of information about the UN project in the F.D.R. Mountains. What else do you want to know about it? It's not a power station and it's not a park. It's in conjunction with the co-op. It's a multiple-unit, infinitely large structure with supermarkets and bakeries, dead center in the Henry Wallace."

"You got all this from this kid?"

"No," Jack said. "From my dad."

They looked at each other a long time.

"Your dad is a speculator?" Arnie said.

"Yes," Jack said.

"He just arrived from Earth the other day?"

129

"Yes," Jack said.

"Jesus," Arnie said to Doreen. "Jesus, it's this guy's father. And he's already bought in."

"Yes," Jack said.

"Is there anything left?" Arnie said.

Jack shook his head.

"Oh, Jesus Christ," Arnie said. "And he's on my payroll. I never had such bad luck."

Jack said, "I didn't know until just now that this was what you wanted to find out, Arnie."

"Yeah, that's true," Arnie said. Speaking to Doreen, he said, "I never told him, so it's not his fault." He aimlessly picked up the boy's drawing. "And this is what it'll look like."

"Eventually," Jack said. "Not at first."

To Manfred, Arnie said, "You did have the information, but we got it from you too late."

"Too late," Jack echoed. He seemed to understand; he looked stricken. "Sorry, Arnie. I really am sorry. You should have told me."

"I don't blame you," Arnie said. "We're still friends, Bohlen. It's just a case of bad luck. You've been completely honest with me; I can see that. Goddamn, it sure is too bad. He's already filed his claim, your dad? Well, that's the way it goes."

"He represents a group of investors," Jack said hoarsely.

"Naturally," Arnie said. "With unlimited capital. What could I do anyhow? I can't compete. I'm just one guy." To Manfred he said, "All these people—" He pointed to the drawing. "Are they going to live there, is that it? Is that right, Manfred? Can you see lots of people living there?" His voice rose, out of control.

"Please, Arnie," Doreen said. "Calm down; I can see how upset you are, and you shouldn't be."

Raising his head, Arnie said to her in a low voice, "I don't see why this kid never laughs."

The boy suddenly said, "Gubble, gubble."

"Yeah," Arnie said, with bitterness. "That's right. That's real good communication, kid. Gubble, gubble. To Jack he said, "You have a fine communication established; I can see that."

Jack said nothing. Now he looked grim and uneasy.

"I can see it's going to take a long time more." Arnie said, "to bring this kid out so we can talk to him. Right? Too bad we can't continue. I'm not going any further with it."

"No reason why you should," Jack said in a leaden voice.

"Right," Arnie said. "So that's it. The end of your job."

Doreen said, "But you can still use him for—"

"Oh, of course," Arnie said. "I need a skilled repairman anyhow, for stuff like that encoder; I got a thousand items busting down every goddamn day. I just mean this one particular job, here. Send him back to B-G, this kid. AM-WEB. Yeah, the co-op buildings get funny names like that. The co-op coming over to Mars! That's a big outfit, that co-op. They'll pay high for their land; they've got the loot. Tell your dad from me that he's a shrewd businessman."

"Can we shake hands, Arnie?" Jack asked.

"Sure, Jack." Arnie stuck out his hand and the two of them shook, hard and long, looking each other in the eye. "I expect to see a lot of you, Jack. This isn't the end between you and me; it's just the beginning." He let go of Jack Bohlen's hand, walked back into the kitchen, and stood by himself, thinking.

Presently Doreen joined him. "That was dreadful news for you, wasn't it?" she said, putting her arm around him.

"Very bad," Arnie said. "Worst I had in a long time. But I'll be O.K.; I'm not scared of the co-op movement. Lewistown and the Water Workers were here first, and they'll be here a lot longer. If I had gotten this project with the Steiner boy started sooner, it would have worked out differently, and I sure don't blame Jack for that." But inside him, in his heart, he thought, You were working against me, Jack. All the time. You we're working with your father. From the start, too; from the day I hired you.

He returned to the living room. At the tape transport, Jack stood morose and silent, fooling with the knobs.

"Don't take it hard," Arnie said to him.

"Thanks, Arnie," Jack said. His eyes were dull. "I feel I've let you down."

"Not me," Arnie assured him. "You haven't let me down, Jack. Because nobody lets me down."

On the floor, Manfred Steiner pasted away, ignoring them all.

As he flew his father back to the house, leaving the F.D.R. range behind them, Jack thought, Should I show the boy's picture to Arnie? Should I take it to Lewistown and hand it over to him? It's so little . . . it just doesn't look like what I ought to have produced, by now.

He knew that tonight he would have to see Arnie, in any case.

"Very desolate down there," his dad said, nodding toward the desert below. "Amazing you people have done so much reclamation work; you should all be proud." But his attention was actually on his maps. He spoke in a perfunctory manner; it was a formality.

Jack snapped on his radio transmitter and called Arnie, at Lewistown. "Excuse me, dad; I have to talk to my boss."

The radio made a series of noises, which attracted Manfred momentarily; he ceased poring over his drawing and raised his head.

"I'll take you along," Jack said to the boy.

Presently he had Arnie. "Hi, Jack." Arnie's voice came boomingly. "I been trying to get hold of you. Can you—"

"I'll be over to see you tonight," Jack said.

"Not before? How about this afternoon?"

"Afraid tonight is as soon as I can make it," Jack said. "There—" He hesitated. "Nothing to show you until tonight." If I get near him, he thought, I'll tell him about the UN—co-op project; he'll get everything out of me. I'll wait until after my dad's claim has been filed, and then it won't matter.

"Tonight, then," Arnie agreed. "And I'll be on pins, Jack. Sitting on pins. I know you're going to come up with something; I got a lot of confidence in you."

Jack thanked him, said goodbye, and rang off.

"Your boss sounds like a gentleman," his dad said, after the connection had been broken. "And he certainly looks up to you. I expect you're of priceless value to his organization, a man with your ability."

Jack said nothing. Already he felt guilty.

"Draw me a picture," he said to Manfred, "of how it's going to go tonight, between me and Mr. Kott." He took away the paper on which the boy was drawing and handed him a blank piece. "Will you Manfred? You can see ahead to tonight. You, me, Mr. Kott, at Mr. Kott's place."

The boy took a blue crayon and began to draw. As he piloted the 'copter, Jack watched.

With great care, Manfred drew. At first Jack could not make it out. Then he grasped what the scene showed. Two men. One was hitting the other in the eye.

Manfred laughed, a long, high-pitched, nervous laugh, and suddenly hugged the picture against himself.

Feeling cold, Jack turned his attention back to the controls before him. He felt himself perspire, the damp sweat of anxiety. Is that how it's going to be? he asked, silently, within himself. A fight between me and Arnie? And you will witness it, perhaps . . . or at least know of it, one day.

"Jack," Leo was saying, "you'll take me to the abstract company, won't you? And let me off there? I want to get my papers filed. Can we go right there, instead of back to the house? I have to admit I'm uneasy. There must be local operators who're watching all this, and I can't be too careful."

Jack said, "I can only repeat:, it's immoral, what you're doing."

"Just let me handle it," his father said. "It's my way of doing business, Jack. I don't intend to change."

"Profiteering," Jack said.

"I won't argue it with you," his father said. "It's none of your concern. If you don't feel like assisting me, after I've come millions of miles from Earth, I guess I can manage to round up public transportation." His tone was mild, but he had turned red.

"I'll take you there," Jack said.

"I can't stand to be moralized at," his father said.

Jack said nothing. He turned the 'copter south, toward the UN buildings at Pax Grove.

Drawing away with his blue crayon, Manfred made one of the two men in his picture, the one who had been hit in the eye, fall down and become dead. Jack saw that, saw the figure become supine and then still. Is that me? he wondered. Or is it Arnie?

Someday—perhaps soon—I will know.

Inside Mr. Kott's skin were dead bones, shiny and wet. Mr. Kott was a sack of bones, dirty and yet shiny-wet. His head was a skull that took in greens and bit them; inside him the greens became rotten things as something ate them to make them dead.

Jack Bohlen, too, was a dead sack, teeming with gubbish. The outside that fooled almost everyone, it was painted pretty and smelled good, bent down over Miss Anderton, and he saw that; he saw it wanting her in an awful fashion. It poured its wet, sticky self nearer to her and the dead bug words popped from its mouth.

"I love Mozart," Mr. Kott was saying. "I'll put this tape on."

He fiddled with the knobs of the amplifier. "Bruno Walter conducting. A great rarity from the golden age of recordings."

A hideous racket of screeches and shrieks issued from the speakers, like the convulsions of corpses. He shut off the tape transport.

"Sorry," Arnie Kott muttered.

Wincing at the sound, Jack Bohlen sniffed the woman's body beside him, saw shiny perspiration on her upper lip where a faint smear of her lipstick made her mouth look cut. He wanted to bite her lips, he wanted to make blood, there. His thumbs wanted to dig into her armpits and make an upward circle so that he worked her breasts, then he would feel they belonged to him to do with what he wanted. He had made them move already; it was fun.

"What a shock," she said. "You should spare us, Arnie. Your sense of humor—"

"An accident," Arnie said. He rummaged for another tape.

Reaching out his hand Jack Bohlen touched the woman's lap. There was no underwear there beneath her skirt. He rubbed her legs and she drew her legs up and turned toward him so that her knees pressed into him; she sat like an animal, crouching in expectation. I can't wait to get you and me out of here and where we can be alone, Jack thought. God, how I want to feel you, and not through clothing. He closed his fingers around her bare ankle and she yapped with pain, smiling at him.

"Listen, Jack," Arnie Kott said, turning toward him. "I'm sorry—" His words were cut off. Jack did not hear the rest. The woman beside him was telling him something. Hurry, she was saying. I can't wait either. Her breath came in short, brisk hisses from her mouth, and she gazed at him fixedly, her face close to his, her eyes huge, as if she were impaled. Neither of them heard Arnie. The room, now, was silent.

Had he missed something Arnie had said? Jack reached out and took hold of his glass, but there was nothing in it. "We're out of booze," he said, setting it back down on the coffee table.

"God sake," Arnie said. "I got to hear how you've done, Jack. Can't you give me anything?" Talking still, he moved away, from the living room into the kitchen; his voice dimmed. Beside Jack the woman still stared up at him, her mouth weak, as if he were holding her tightly to him, as if she could hardly breathe. We have to get out of this place and be by ourselves, Jack realized. Then, looking around, he saw that they were alone; Arnie had gone out of the room and could no longer see them. In the kitchen he was conversing with his tame Bleekman. And so he was already alone with her.

"Not here," Doreen said. But her body fluttered, it did not resist him as he squeezed her about the waist; she did not mind being squashed because she wanted to, too. She could not hold back either. "Yes," she said. "But hurry." Her nails dug into his shoulders and she shut her eyes tight, moaning and shuddering. "At the side," she said. "It unbuttons, my skirt."

Bending over her he saw her lanquid, almost rotting beauty fall away. Yellow cracks spread through her teeth, and the teeth split and sank into her gums, which in turn became green and dry like leather, and then she coughed and spat up into his face quantities of dust. The Gubbler had gotten her, he realized, before he had been able to. So he let her go. She settled backward, her breaking bones making little sharp splintering sounds.

Her eyes fused over, opaque, and from behind one eye the lashes became the furry, probing feet of a thick-haired insect stuck back there wanting to get out. It's tiny pin-head red eye peeped past the loose rim of her unseeing eye, and then withdrew; after that the insect squirmed, making the dead eye of the woman bulge, and then, for an instant, the insect peered through the lens of her eye, looked this way and that, saw him but was unable to make out who or what he was; it could not fully make use of the decayed mechanism behind which it lived.

Like over ripe puffballs, her boobies wheezed as they deflated into flatness, and from their day interiors, through the web of cracks spreading across them, a cloud of spores arose and drifted up into his face, the smell of mold and age of the Gubbler, who had come and inhabited the inside long ago and was now working his way out to the surface.

The dead mouth twitched and then from deep inside at the bottom of the pipe which was the throat a voice muttered, "You weren't fast enough." And then the head fell off entirely, leaving the white pointed stick-like end of the neck projecting.

Jack released her and she folded up into a little dried-up heap of flat, almost transparent plates, like the discarded skin of a snake, almost without weight; he brushed them away from him with his hand. And at the same time, to his surprise, he heard her voice from the kitchen.

"Arnie, I think I'll go home. I really can't take much of Manfred; he never stops moving around, never sits still." Turning his head he saw her in there, with Arnie, standing very close to him. She kissed him on the ear. "Good night, dear," she said.

"I read about a kid who thought he was a machine," Arnie said, and then the kitchen door shut; Jack could neither hear nor see them.

Rubbing his forehead he thought, I really am drunk. *What's wrong with me?* My mind, splitting . . . he blinked, tried to gather his faculties. On the rug, not far from the couch, Manfred Steiner cut out a picture from a magazine with blunt scissors, smiling to himself; the paper rustled as he cut it, a sound that distracted Jack and made it even more difficult for him to put in focus his wandering attention.

From beyond the kitchen door he heard heavy breathing and then labored, prolonged grunts. What are they doing? he asked himself. The three of them, she and Arnie and the tame Bleekman, together . . . the grunts became slower and then ceased. There was no sound at all.

I wish I was home, Jack said to himself with desperate, utter confusion. I want to get out of here, but how? He felt weak and terribly sick and he remained on the couch, where he was, unable to break away, to move or think.

A voice in his mind said, Gubble gubble gubble, I am gubble gubble gubble gubble.

Stop, he said to it.

Gubble, gubble, gubble, gubble, it answered.

Dust fell on him from the walls. The room creaked with age and dust, rotting around him. Gubble, gubble gubble, the room said. The Gubbler is here to gubble gubble you and make you into gubbish.

Getting unsteadily to his feet he managed to walk, step by step, over to Arnie's amplifier and tape recorder. He picked up a reel of tape and got the box open. After several faulty, feeble efforts he succeeded in putting it on the spindle of the transport.

The door to the kitchen opened a crack, and an eye watched him; he could not tell whose it was.

I have to get out of here, Jack Bohlen said to himself. Or fight it off; I have to break this, throw it away from me or be eaten.

It is eating me up.

He twisted the volume control convulsively so that the music blared up and deafened him, roared through the room, spilling over the walls, the furniture, lashing at the ajar kitchen door, attacking everyone and everything in sight.

The kitchen door fell forward, its hinges breaking; it crashed over and a thing came hurriedly sideways from the kitchen, dislodged into belated activity by the roar of the music. The thing scrabbled up to him and past him, feeling for the volume control knob. The music ebbed.

But he felt better. He felt sane, once more, thank God.

Jack Bohlen dropped his father off at the abstract office and then, with Manfred, flew on to Lewistown, to Doreen Anderton's apartment.

When she opened the door and saw him she said, "What is it, Jack?" She quickly held the door open and he and Manfred went on inside.

"It's going to be very bad tonight," he told her.

"Are you sure?" She seated herself across from him. "Do you have to go at all? Yes, I suppose so. But maybe you're wrong."

Jack said, "Manfred has already told me. He's already seen it."

"Don't be scared," Doreen said softly.

"But I am," he said.

"Why will it be bad?"

"I don't know. Manfred couldn't tell me that."

"But—" She gestured. "You've made contact with him; that's wonderful. That's what Arnie wants."

"I hope you'll be there," Jack said.

"Yes, I'll be there. But—there's not much I can do. Is my opinion worth anything? Because I'm positve that Arnie will be pleased; I think you're having an anxiety attack for no reason."

"It's the end," Jack said, "between me and Arnie—tonight. I know it, and I don't know why." He felt sick to his stomach. "It almost seems to me that Manfred does more than know the future; in some way he *controls* it, he can make it come out the worst possible way because that's what seems natural to him, that's how he sees reality. It's as if by being around him we're sinking into his reality. It's starting to seep over us and replace our own way of viewing things, and the kind of events we're accustomed to see come about now somehow *don't* come about. It's not natural for me to feel this way; I've never had this feeling about the future before."

He was silent, then.

"You've been around him too much," Doreen said. "Tendencies in you that are—" She hesitated. "Unstable tendencies, Jack. Allied to his; you were supposed to draw him into our world, the shared reality of our society . . . instead, hasn't he drawn you into his own? I don't think there's any precognition; I think it's been a mistake from the start. It would be better if you got out of it, if you left that boy—" She glanced toward Manfred, who had gone to the window of her apartment to stare out at the street below. "If you didn't have anything more to do with him."

"It's too late for that," Jack said.

"You're not a psychotherapist or a doctor," Doreen said. "It's one thing for Milton Glaub to be in close contact day after day with autistic and schizophrenic persons, but you—you're a repairman who blundered into this because of a crazy impulse on Arnie's part; you just happened to be there in the same room with him fixing his encoder and so you wound up with this. You shouldn't be so passive, Jack. You're letting your life be shaped by chance, and for God's sake—don't you recognize that passivity for what it is?"

After a pause he said, "I suppose I do."

"Say it."

He said, "there's a tendency for a schizophrenic individual to be passive; I know that."

"Be decisive; don't go any further with this. Call Arnie and tell him you're simply not competent to handle Manfred. He should be back at Camp B-G where Milton Glaub can work with him. They can build that slowed-down chamber there; they were starting to, weren't they?"

"They'll never get around to it. They're talking about importing the equipment from Home; you know what that means."

"And you'll never get around to it," Doreen said, "because, long before you do, you'll have cracked up mentally. I can look into the future too; you know what I see? I see you having a much more serious collapse than ever before; I see—total psychological collapse for you, Jack, if you keep working on this. Already you're being mauled by acute schizophrenic anixiety, by *panic*—isn't that so? Isn't it?"

He nodded.

"I saw that in my brother," Doreen said. "Schizophrenic

panic, and once you see it break out in a person, you can never forget it. The collapse of their reality around them . . . the collapse of their perceptions of time and space, cause and effect . . . and isn't that what's happening to you? You're talking as if this meeting with Arnie can't be altered by anything you do—and that's a deep regression on your part from adult responsibility and maturity; that's not like you at all." Breathing deeply, her chest rising and falling painfully, she went on, "I'll call Arnie and tell him your pulling out, and he'll have to get someone else to finish with Manfred. And I'll tell him that you've made no progress, that it's pointless for you and for him to continue with this. I've seen Arnie get these whims before; he keeps them percolating for a few days or weeks, and then he forgets them. He can forget this."

Jack said, "He won't forget this one."

"Try," she said.

"No," he said. "I have to go there tonight and give him my progress report. I said I would; I owe it to him."

"You're a damn fool," Doreen said.

"I know it, Jack said. "But not for the reason you think. I'm a fool because I took on a job without looking ahead to its consequences. I—" He broke off. "Maybe it is what you said. I'm not competent to work with Manfred. That's it, period."

"But you're still going ahead. What do you have to show Arnie tonight? Show it to me, right now."

Getting out a manila envelope, Jack reached into it and drew out the picture of the buildings which Manfred had drawn. For a long time Doreen studied it. And then she handed it back to him.

"That's an evil and sick drawing," she said in a voice almost inaudible. "I know what it is. It's the Tomb World, isn't it? That's what he's drawn. The world after death. And that's what he sees, and through him, that's what you're beginning to see. You want to take that to Arnie? You have lost your grip on reality; do you think Arnie wants to see an abomination like that? Burn it."

"It's not that bad," he said, deeply perturbed by her reaction.

"Yes, it is," Doreen said. "And it's a dreadful sign that it doesn't strike you that way. Did it at first?"

He had to nod yes.

"Then you know I'm right," she said.

"I have to go on," he said. "I'll see you at his place tonight."

Going over to the window, he tapped Manfred on the shoulder. "We have to go, now. We'll see this lady tonight, and Mr. Kott, too."

"Goodbye, Jack," Doreen said, accompanying him to the door. Her large dark eyes were heavy with despair. "There's nothing I can say to stop you; I can see that. You've changed. You're so less—alive—now than you were just a day or so ago . . . do you know that?"

"No," he said. "I didn't realize that." But he was not surprised to hear it; he could feel it, hanging heavy over his limbs, choking his heart. Leaning toward her, he kissed her on her full, good-tasting lips. "I'll see you tonight."

She stood at the doorway, silently watching him and the boy go.

In the time remaining before evening, Jack Bohlen decided to drop by the Public School and pick up his son. There, in that place which he dreaded before any other, he would find out if Doreen were right; he would learn if his morale and ability to distinguish reality from the projections of his own unconscious had been impaired or not. For him, the Public School was the crucial location. And, as he directed his Yee Company 'copter toward it, he felt deep within himself that he would be capable of handling a second visit there.

He was violently curious, too, to see Manfred's reaction to the place, and to its simulacra, the teaching machines. For some time now he had had an abiding hunch that Manfred, confronted by the School's Teachers, would show a significant response, perhaps similar to his own, perhaps totally opposite. In any case the reaction would be there; he was positive of that.

But then he thought resignedly, Isn't it too late? Isn't the job over, hasn't Arnie cancelled it because it doesn't matter? Haven't I already been to his place tonight? What time is it?

He thought in fright, I've lost all sense of time.

"We're going to the Public School," he murmured to Manfred. "Do you like that idea? See the school where David goes."

The boy's eyes gleamed with anticipation. Yes, he seemed to be saying. I'd like that. Let's go.

"O.K.," Jack said, only with great difficulty managing to operate the controls of the 'copter; he felt as if he were at the bottom of a great stagnant sea, struggling merely to breathe, almost unable to move. But why?

He did not know. He went on, as best he could.

eleven

INSIDE MR. KOTT's skin were dead bones, shiny and wet. Mr. Kott was a sack of bones, dirty and yet shiny-wet. His head was a skull that took in greens and bit them; inside him the greens became rotten things as something ate them to make them dead. Jack Bohlen, too, was a dead sack, teeming with gubbish. The outside that fooled almost everyone, it was painted pretty and smelled good, bent down over Miss Anderton, and he saw that; he saw it wanting her in a filthy fashion. It poured its wet, sticky self nearer and nearer to her, and the dead bug words popped from its mouth and fell on her. The dead bug words scampered off into the folds of her clothing, and some squeezed into her skin and entered her body.

"I love Mozart," Mr. Kott said. "I'll put this tape on."

Her clothing itched her, it was full of hair and dust and the droppings of the bug words. She scratched at it and the clothing tore in strips. Digging her teeth into the strips, she chewed them away.

Fiddling with the knobs of the amplifier, Mr. Kott said, "Bruno Walter conducting. A great rarity from the golden age of recordings."

A hideous racket of screeches and shrieks issued from somewhere in the room, and after a time she realized that it was her; she was convulsed from within, all the corpse-things in her were heaving and crawling, struggling out into the light of the room. God, how could she stop them? They emerged from her pores and scuttled off, dropping from strands of gummy web to the floor, to disappear into the cracks between the boards.

"Sorry," Arnie Kott muttered.

"What a shock," she said. "You should spare us, Arnie." Getting up from the couch she pushed away the dark, bad-

141

smelling object that clung to her. "Your sense of humor—" she said.

He turned and saw her as she stripped herself of the last of her clothing. He had put down the reel of tape, and now he came toward her, reaching out.

"Do it," she said, and then they were both on the floor, together; he used his feet to remove his own clothing, hooking his toes into the fabric and tearing until it was away. Arms locked around each other, they rolled into the darkness beneath the stove and lay there, sweating and thumping, gulping in the dust and the heat and the damp of their own bodies. "Do it more," she said, digging her knees into his sides to hurt him.

"An accident," he said, squashing her against the floor, breathing into her face.

Eyes appeared beyone the edge of the stove; something peeped in at them as they lay together in the darkness—something watched. It had put away its paste and scissors and magazines, dropped all that to watch this and gloat and savor each thump they made.

"Go away," she gasped at it. But it did not go away. "More," she said, then, and it laughed at her. It laughed and laughed, as she and the weight squashing her kept on. They could not stop.

Gubble me more, she said. Gubble gubble gubble me, put your gubbish into me, into my gubbish, you Gubbler. Gubble gubble, I like gubble! Don't stop. Gubble, gubble gubble gubble, *gubble!*

As Jack Bohlen lowered the Yee Company 'copter toward the landing field of the Public School directly below, he glanced at Manfred and wondered what the boy was thinking. Wrapped up in his thoughts, Manfred Steiner stared sightlessly out, his features twisted into a grimace that repelled Jack and made him instantly look away.

Why did he have anything to do with this boy? Jack wondered. Doreen was right; he was in over his head, and the unstable, schizophrenic aspects of his own personality were being stirred into life by the presence beside him. And yet he did not know how to get out; somehow it was too late, as if time had collapsed and left him here, for eternity, caught in a symbiosis with this unfortunate, mute creature who did nothing but rake over and inspect his own private world, again and again.

He had imbibed, on some level, of Manfred's world-view, and it was obviously bringing about the stealthy disintegration of his own.

Tonight, he thought. I have to keep going until tonight: somehow I must hold out until I can see Arnie Kott. Then I can jettison all this and return to my own space, my own world; I will never have to look at Manfred Steiner again.

Arnie, for Christ's sake, save me, he thought.

"We're here," he said as the 'copter bumped to a halt on the roof field. He switched off the motor.

At once Manfred moved to the door, eager to get out.

So you want to see this place, Jack thought. I wonder why. He got to his feet and went to unlock the door of the 'copter; at once Manfred hopped out onto the roof and scampered toward the descent ramp, almost as if he knew the way by heart.

As Jack stepped from the ship the boy disappeared from sight. On his own he had hurried down the ramp and plunged into the school.

Doreen Anderton and Arnie Kott, Jack said to himself. The two people who mean the most to me, the friends with whom my contacts, my intimacy with life itself, is the strongest. And yet it's right there that the boy has managed to infiltrate; he has unfastened me from my relationships where they are the strongest.

What's left? he asked himself. Once I have been isolated there, the rest—my son, my wife, my father, Mr. Yee—all follow almost automatically, without a fight.

I can see what lies ahead for me if I continue to lose, step by step, to this completely psychotic boy. Now I can see what psychosis is: the utter alienation of perception from the objects of the outside world, especially the objects which matter: the warmhearted people there. And what takes their place? A dreadful preoccupation with—the endless ebb and flow of one's own self. The changes emanating from within which affect only the inside world. It is a splitting apart of the two worlds, inner and outer, so that neither registers on the other. Both still exist, but each goes its own way.

It is the stopping of time. The end of exeperience, of anything new. Once the person becomes psychotic, nothing ever happens to him again.

And, he realized, I stand on the threshold of that. Perhaps I always did; it was impilcit in me from the start. But this boy has led me a long way. Or, rather, because of him I have gone a long way.

A coagulated self, fixed and immense, which effaces everything else and occupies the entire field. Then the most minute change is examined with the greatest attention. That is Manfred's state now; has been, from the beginning. The ultimate stage of the schizophrenic process.

"Manfred, wait," he called, and followed slowly after the boy, down the ramp and into the Public School building.

Seated in June Henessy's kitchen, sipping coffee, Silvia Bohlen discoursed on her problems of late.

"What's so awful about them," she said, meaning Erna Steiner and the Steiner children, "is that, let's face it, they're vulgar. We're not supposed to talk in terms like that, but I've been forced to see so much of them that I can't ignore it; my face has been rubbed in it every day."

June Henessy, wearing white shorts and a skimpy halter, padded barefoot here and there in the house, watering from a glass pitcher her various indoor plants. "That's really a weird boy. He's the worst of all, isn't he?"

Shuddering, Silvia said, "And he's over all day long. Jack is working with him, you know, trying to make him part of the human race. I think myself they ought to just wipe out freaks and sports like that; it's terribly destructive in the long run to let them live; it's a false mercy to them and to us. That boy will have to be cared for for the rest of his life; he'll never be out of an institution."

Returning to the kitchen with the empty pitcher, June said, "I want to tell you what Tony did the other day." Tony was her current lover; she had been having an affair with him for six months now, and she kept the other ladies, especially Silvia, up to date. "We had lunch together over at Geneva II, at a French restaurant he knows; we had escargots—you know, snails. They serve them to you in the shells and you get them out with a horrible-looking fork that has tines a foot long. Of course, that's all black-market food; did you know that? That there're restaurants serving exclusively black-market delicacies? I didn't until Tony took me there. I can't tell you the name of it, of course."

"Snails," Silvia said with aversion, thinking of all the wonderful dishes she herself would have ordered, if she had a lover and he had taken her out.

How would it be to have an affair? Difficult, but surely

144

worth it, if she could keep it from her husband. The problem, of course, was David. And now Jack worked a good deal of the time at home, and her father-in-law was visiting as well. And she could never have him, her lover, at the house, because of Erna Steiner next door; the big baggy hausfrau would see, comprehend, and probably at once, out of a Prussian sense of duty, inform Jack. But then, wasn't the risk part of it? Didn't it help add that—flavor?

"What would your husband do if he found out?" she asked June. "Cut you to bits? Jack would."

June said, "Mike has had several affairs of his own since we've been married. He'd be sore and possibly he'd give me a black eye and go off for a week or so with one of his girl friends, leaving me stuck with the kids, of course. But he'd get over it."

To herself, Silvia wondered if Jack had ever had an affair. It did not seem probable. She wondered how she would feel if he had and she found out—would it end the marriage? Yes, she thought. I'd get a lawyer right away. Or would I? There's no way to tell in advance. . . .

"How are you and your father-in-law getting along?" June asked.

"Oh, not badly. He and Jack and the Steiner boy are off somewhere today, taking a business trip. I don't see much of Leo, actually; he came mainly on busines —June, how many affairs have you had?"

"Six," June Henessy said.

"Gee," Silvia said. "And I haven't had any."

"Some women aren't built for it."

That sounded to Silvia like a rather personal, if not outright anatomical, insult. "What do you mean?"

"Aren't constituted psychologically," June explained glibly. "It takes a certain type of woman who can create and sustain a complex fiction, day after day. I enjoy it, what I make up to tell Mike. You're different. You have a simple, direct sort of mind; deception isn't your cup of tea. Anyhow, you have a nice husband." She emphasized the authority of her judgement by a lifting of her eyebrows.

"Jack used to be gone all week long," Silvia said. "I should have had one then. Now it would be so much harder." She wished, fervently, that she had something creative or useful or exciting to do that would fill up the long empty afternoons; she was bored to death with sitting in some other woman's

145

kitchen drinking coffee hour after hour. No wonder so many women had affairs. It was that or madness.

"If you're limited to your husband for emotional experience," June Henessy said, "you have no basis of judgment; you're more or less stuck with what he has to offer, but if you've gone to bed with other men you can tell better what your husband's deficiencies are, and it's much more possible for you to be objective about him. And what needs to be changed in him, you can insist that he change. And for your own part, you can see where you've been ineffective and with these other men you can learn how to improve yourself, so that you give your husband more satisfaction. I fail to see who loses by that."

Put that way, it certainly sounded like a good healthy idea for all concerned. Even the husband benefited.

While she sat sipping her coffee and meditating about that, Silvia looked out the window and saw to her surprise a 'copter landing. "Who's that?" she asked June.

"Heaven's sake, I don't know," June said, glancing out.

The 'copter rolled to a halt near the house; the door opened and a dark-haired, good-looking man wearing a bright nylon shirt and necktie, slacks, and stylish European loafers stepped out. Behind him came a Bleekman who lugged two heavy suitcases.

Inside her, Silvia Bohlen felt her heart quiver as she watched the dark-haired man stroll toward the house, the Bleekman following with the suitcases. This was the way she imagined June's Tony to look.

"Gosh," June said. "I wonder who he is. A salesman?" A rap sounded at the front door and she went to open it. Silvia set down her cup and followed along. At the door June halted. "I feel sort of—undressed." She put her hand nervously to her shorts. "You talk to him while I run into the bedroom and change. I wasn't expecting anybody strange to drop by; you know, we have to be careful, we're so isolated and our husbands are away—" She darted off to the bedroom, her hair flying.

Silvia opened the door.

"Good day," the good-looking man said, with a smile revealing perfect white Mediterranean teeth. He had a faint accent. "Are you the lady of the house?"

"I guess so," Silvia said, feeling timid and ill at ease; she glanced down at her own self, wondering if she were dressed modestly enough to be standing out here talking to this man.

146

"I wish to introduce a very fine line of health foods which you may be familiar with," the man said. He kept his eyes on her face, and yet Silvia had the distinct impression that somehow he managed at the same time to examine the rest of her detail by detail. Her self-consciousness grew, but she did not feel resentful; the man had a charming manner, simultaneously shy and yet oddly forthright.

"Health food," she murmured. "Well, I—"

The man gave a nod, and his Bleekman stepped up, laid down one of the suitcases, and opened it. Baskets, bottles, packages . . . she was very much interested.

"Unhomogenized peanut butter," the man declared. "Also dietetic sweets without calories, to keep your lovely slimness. Wheat germ. Yeast. Vitamin E; that is the vitamin of *vitality* . . . but of course for a young woman like yourself, not yet appropriate." His voice purred along as he indicated one item after another; she found herself bending down beside him, so close to him that their shoulders touched. Quickly she drew away, startled into apprehension.

At the door, June put in a momentary appearance, now wearing a skirt and a wool sweater; she hung about for a moment and then drew back inside and shut the door. The man failed to notice her.

"Also," he was saying, "there is much in the gourmet line that Miss might be interested in—these." He held up a jar. Her breath left her: it was caviar.

"Good grief," she said, magnetized. "Where did you get that?"

"Expensive, but well worth it." The man's dark eyes bored into hers. "Don't you agree? Reminder of days at Home, soft candlelight and dance music by an orchestra . . . days of romance in a whirl of places delightful to the ear and eye." He smiled long and openly at her.

Black market, she realized.

Her pulse hammered in her throat as she said, "Look, this isn't my house. I live about a mile down along the canal." She pointed. "I—am very much interested."

The man's smile seared her.

"You've never been by before, have you?" she said, now rattled and stammering. "I've never seen you. What's your name? Your firm name."

"I am Otto Zitte." He handed her a card, which she scarcely glanced at; she could not take her eyes from his face. "My business is long established but has just recently—due to an

147

unforeseen circumstance—been completely reorganized, so that now I am in a position to greet new customers direct. Such as yourself."

"You'll be by?"

"Yes, slightly later in the afternoon . . . and we can at leisure pore over a dazzling assortment of imported dainties of which I have exclusive distribution. Good afternoon." He rose cat-like to his feet.

June Henessy had reappeared. "Hello," she said in a low, cautious, interested voice.

"My card." Otto Zitte held the embossed white square out to her. Now both ladies had his card; each read hers intently.

Smiling his astute, insinuating, brilliant smile, Otto Zitte beckoned to his tame Bleekman to lay out and open the other suitcase.

As he sat in his office at Camp Ben-Gurion, Dr. Milton Glaub heard a woman's voice in the corridor, husky and full of authority but still unmistakably feminine. Listening, he heard the nurse defer to her, and he knew that it was Anne Esterhazy, come to visit her son Sam.

Opening the file he turned to *E*, and presently he had the folio *Esterhazy, Samuel* spread out before him on his desk.

It was interesting. The little boy had been born out of wedlock, a year or more after Mrs. Esterhazy had divorced Arnie Kott. And he had entered Camp B-G under her name, too. However it was undoubtedly Arnie Kott's progeny; the folio contained a great packet of information on Arnie, for the examining doctors had taken that blood relationship for granted throughout.

Evidently, even though their marriage had long been over, Arnie and Anne Esterhazy still saw one another, enough in fact to produce a child. Their relationship therefore was not merely a business one.

For a time Dr. Glaub ruminated as to the possible uses that this information could be put to. Did Arnie have enemies? None that he knew of; everybody liked Arnie—that is, everyone but Dr. Milton Glaub. Evidently Dr. Glaub was the sole person on Mars to have suffered at Arnie's hands, a realization that did not make Dr. Glaub feel any happier about it.

That man treated me in the most inhumane and cavalier fashion, he said to himself for the millionth time. But what could be done about it? He could still bill Arnie . . . hope to collect some trifle for his services. That, however, would not help. He wanted—was entitled to—much more. Again Dr. Glaub studied the folio. An odd sport, Samuel Esterhazy; he knew of no other case precisely like it. The boy seemed to be a throwback to some ancient line of near-man, or to some variant which had not survived: one which had lived partly in the water. It recalled to Glaub the theory being advanced by a number of anthropologists that man had descended from aquatic apes who had lived in the surf and shallows.

Sam's I.Q., he noted, was only 73. A shame.

—Especially so, he thought suddenly, in that Sam could beyond doubt be classified as mentally retarded rather than anomalous. Camp B-G had not been intended as an institution for the purely retarded, and its director, Susan Haynes, had sent back to their parents several pseudoautistic children who had turned out to be nothing more than standard imbeciles. The diagnostic problem had hampered their screening, of course. In the case of the Esterhazy boy, there was also the physical stigmata. . . .

No doubt of it, Dr. Glaub decided. I have the basis for it: I can send the Esterhazy child home. The Public School could teach him without trouble, could gear down to his level. It is only in the physical area that he could be called "anomalous," and it is not our task here to care for the physically disabled.

But what is my motive? he asked himself.

Possibly I am doing it to get back at Arnie Kott for treating me in a cruel manner.

No, he decided, that does not seem probable; I am not the psychological type who would seek revenge—that would be more the anal-expulsive or perhaps the oral-biting type. And long ago he had classified himself as the late genital type, devoted to the mature genital strivings.

On the other hand, his altercation with Arnie Kott had admittedly caused him to probe into the Esterhazy child's folio . . . so there was a small but finite causal connective.

Reading the folio through, he was struck once more by the bizarre relationship which it implied. Here they were, carrying on a sexual union years after their marriage had terminated. Why had they gotten divorced? Perhaps there had been a serious power-clash between them; Anne Esterhazy was clearly a domineering type of female with strong masculine components, what Jung called the "animus-ridden" woman. In successfully dealing with such a type, one had to play a definite role; one had to capture the position of authority right off

149

the bat and never relinquish it. One had to be the ancestral, or else be quickly defeated.

Dr. Glaub put the folio away and then sauntered down the corridor to the playroom. He located Mrs. Esterhazy; she was playing beanbag with her boy. Walking over, he stood observing them until she bacame aware of him and paused.

"Hello, Dr. Glaub," she said cheerfully.

"Good afternoon, Mrs. Esterhazy. Um, when you're finished visiting, may I see you in my office?"

It was rewarding to see the woman's competent, self-satisfied expression wilt with concern. "Of course, Dr. Glaub."

Twenty minutes later he sat facing her across his desk.

"Mrs. Esterhazy, when your boy first came to Camp B-G, there was a good deal of doubt as to the nature of his problem. It was believed for some time that it lay in the realm of mental disturbance, possibly a traumatic neurosis or—"

The woman broke in, firmly. "Doctor, you're going to tell me that since Sam has no problems except his defective learning ability, he is not to remain here; is that correct?"

"And the physical problem," Dr. Glaub said.

"But that is not your concern."

He made a gesture of resignation and agreement.

"When do I have to take him home?" She was white-faced and trembling; her hands gripped her purse, clutched at it.

"Oh, three or four days. A week."

Chewing her knuckle, Mrs. Esterhazy stared blindly down at the carpet of the office. Time passed. Then in a quavering voice she said, "Doctor, as you perhaps know, I have been active for some time in fighting a bill now before the UN which would close Camp B-G." Her voice gained strength. "If I am forced to remove Sam, I will withdraw my assistance in this matter, and you can be certain that the bill will be passed. And I will inform Susan Haynes as to the reason why I am withdrawing my assistance."

A slow cold wave of shock passed over Dr. Milton Glaub's mind. He could think of nothing to say.

"You understand, Doctor?" Mrs. Esterhazy said.

He managed to nod.

Rising to her feet, Mrs. Esterhazy said, "Doctor, I have been in politics a long time. Arnie Kott considers me a do-gooder, an amateur, but I am not. Believe me, in certain areas I am quite shrewd politically."

"Yes," Dr. Glaub said, "I see that you are." Automatically he too rose; he escorted her to the door of the office.

"Please don't ever bring up this issue about Sam again," the woman said, as she opened the door. "I find it too painful. It is much easier for me to regard him as anomalous." She faced him squarely. "It is not within my capacity to think of him as retarded." Turning, she walked swiftly off.

That did not work out too well, Dr. Glaub said to himself as he shakily closed his office door. The woman is obviously sadistic—strong hostility drives coupled with out-and-out aggression.

Seating himself at his desk he lit a cigarette and puffed at it despondently as he struggled to collect his aplomb.

When Jack Bohlen reached the bottom of the descent ramp he saw no sign of Manfred. Several children trotted by, no doubt on their way to their Teachers. He began to roam about, wondering where the boy had gone. And why so quickly? It was not good.

Ahead, a group of children had collected around a Teacher, a tall, white-haired, bushy-browed gentleman whom Jack recognized as Mark Twain. Manfred, however, was not among them.

As Jack started to walk past the Mark Twain it broke off its monolog to the children, puffed several times at its cigar, and called after Jack, "My friend, can I be of any assistance to you?"

Pausing, Jack said, "I'm looking for a little boy I brought here with me."

"I know all the young fellows," the Mark Twain Teaching Machine answered. "What is his name?"

"Manfred Steiner." He described the boy as the teaching machine listened alertly.

"Hmm," it said, when he had finished. It smoked for a moment and then once more lowered its cigar. "I believe you will find that young man over colloquizing with the Roman emperor Tiberius. Or at least so I am informed by the authorities in whose care this organization has been entrusted; I speak of the master circuit, sir."

Tiberius. He had not realized that such figures were represented here at the Public School: the base and deranged personages of history. Evidently from his expression the Mark Twain understood his thoughts.

"Here in the school," it informed him, "as examples not to be emulated but to be avoided with the most scrupulous zeal, you will find, sir, as you make your peregrinations about these halls, that many rascals, pirates, and scamps are on display, sermonizing in dolorous and lamentable tones their edifying histories for the enlightenment of the young." The Mark Twain, again puffing on its cigar, winked at him. Disconcerted, Jack hurried on.

At the Immanuel Kant he halted to ask directions. Several pupils, in their teens, stood aside for him.

"The Tiberius," it told him in heavily accented English, "can be found down that way." It pointed with absolute authority; it did not have any doubts, and Jack hurried at once down that particular hall.

A moment later he found himself approaching the slight, white-haired, fragile-looking figure of the Roman emperor. It seemed to be musing as he came up to it, but before he could speak it turned its head in his direction.

"The boy whom you are searching for has passed on. He was yours, was he? An exceeding attractive youth." Then it was silent, as if communing within itself. Actually, Jack knew, it was reconnecting itself with the master circuit of the school, which was now utilizing all the teaching machines in an attempt to locate Manfred for him. "He is talking to no one at this moment," the Tiberius said presently.

Jack went on, then. A sightless, middle-aged female figure smiled past him; he did not know who it was, and no children were conversing with it. But all at once it said, "The boy you want is with Philip Second of Spain." It pointed to the corridor to the right, and then it said in a peculiar voice, "Kindly hurry; we would appreciate it if you would remove him from the school as soon as possible. Thank you very much." It snapped off into silence. Jack hurried down the hall which it had pointed out.

Almost at once he turned a corridor and found himself before the bearded, ascetic figure of Philip the Second. Manfred was not there, but some intangible quality of his essence seemed still to hover in this area.

"He has only now departed, dear sir," the teaching machine said. Its voice held the same note of peculiar urgency as had the female figure's, a moment ago. "Kindly find him and remove him; it would be appreciated."

Without waiting any longer, Jack plunged down the corridor, a chill fear biting at him as he ran.

". . . Much appreciated," a seated, white-robed figure said, as he passed it. And then, as he passed a gray-haired man in a frock coat, it, too, took up the school's urgent litany. ". . . Soon as possible."

He turned the corner. And there was Manfred.

The boy was alone, seated on the floor, resting against the wall, his head down, apparently deep in thought.

Bending down, Jack said, "Why did you run off?"

The boy gave no response. Jack touched him, but still there was no reaction.

"Are you all right?" Jack asked him.

All at once the boy stirred, rose to his feet, and stood facing Jack.

"What is it?" Jack demanded.

There was no answer. But the boy's face was clouded with a blurred, distorted emotion that found no outlet; he gazed at Jack as if not seeing him. Totally absorbed in himself, unable to break out into the outside world.

"What happened?" Jack said. But he knew that he would never find out; no way existed for the creature before him to express itself. There was only silence, the total absence of communication between the two of them, the emptiness that could not be filled.

The boy looked away, then, and settled back down into a heap on the floor.

"You stay here," Jack said to him. "I'll have them go get David for me." Warily, he moved away from the boy, but Manfred did not stir. When he reached a teaching machine, Jack said to it, "I would like to have David Bohlen, please; I'm his father. I'll take him home."

It was the Thomas Edison Teaching Machine, an elderly man who glanced up, startled, and cupped his ear. Jack repeated what he had said.

Nodding, it said, "Gubble gubble."

Jack stared at it. And then he turned to look back at Manfred. The boy still sat slumped down, his back against the wall.

Again the Thomas Edison Teaching Machine opened its mouth and said to Jack, "Gubble gubble." There was nothing more; it became silent.

Is it me? Jack asked himself. Is this the final psychotic breakdown for me? Or—

He could not belive the alternative; it simply was not possible.

Down the hall, another teaching machine was addressing a

group of children; its voice came from a distance, echoing and metallic. Jack strained to listen.

"Gubble gubble," it was saying to the children.

He closed his eyes. He knew in a moment of perfect awareness that his own psyche, his own perceptions, had not misinformed him; it was happening, what he heard and saw.

Manfred Steiner's presence had invaded the structure of the Public School, penetrated its deepest being.

twelve

STILL AT HIS DESK in his office at Camp B-G, brooding over the behavior of Anne Esterhazy, Dr. Milton Glaub received an emergency call. It was from the master circuit of the UN's Public School.

"Doctor," its flat voice declared, "I am sorry to disturb you but we require assistance. There is a male citizen wandering about our premises in an evident state of mental confusion. We would like you to come and remove him."

"Certainly," Dr. Glaub murmured. "I'll come straight there."

Soon he was in the air, piloting his 'copter across the desert from New Israel toward the Public School.

When he arrived, the master circuit met him and escorted him at a brisk pace through the building until they reached a closed-off corridor. "We felt we should keep the children away from him," the master circuit explained as she caused the wall to roll back, exposing the corridor.

There, with a dazed expression on his face, stood a man familiar to Dr. Glaub. The doctor had an immediate reaction of satisfaction, in spite of himself. So Jack Bohlen's schizophrenia had caught up with him. Bohlen's eyes were without focus; obviously he was in a state of catatonic stupor, probably alternating with excitement—he looked exhausted. And with him was another person whom Dr. Glaub recognized. Manfred Steiner sat curled up on the floor, bent forward, likewise in an advanced state of withdrawal.

Your association did not cause either of you to prosper, Dr. Glaub observed to himself.

With the help of the master circuit he got both Bohlen and the Steiner boy into his 'copter, and presently he was flying back to New Israel and Camp B-G.

Hunched over, his hands clenched, Bohlen said, "Let me tell you what happened."

155

"Please do," Dr. Glaub said, feeling—at last—in control.

Jack Bohlen said in an uneven voice, "I went to the school to pick up my son. I took Manfred." He twisted in his seat to look at the Steiner boy, who had not come out of his catalepsy; the boy lay rolled up on the floor of the 'copter, as inert as a carving. "Manfred got away from me. And then—communication between me and the school broke down. All I could hear was—" He broke off.

"Folie á deux," Glaub murmured. Madness of two.

Bohlen said, "Instead of the school, I heard *him*. I heard his words coming from the Teachers." He was silent, then.

"Manfred has a powerful personality," Dr. Glaub said. "It is a drain on one's resources to be around him for long. I think it would be well for you, for your own health, to abandon this project. I think you risk too much."

"I have to see Arnie tonight," Bohlen said in a ragged, harsh whisper.

"What about yourself? What's going to become of you?" Bohlen said nothing.

"I can treat you," Dr. Glaub said, "at this stage of your difficulty. Later on—I'm not so sure."

"In there, in that damn school," Bohlen said, "I got completely confused; I didn't know what to do. I kept going on, looking for someone who I could still talk to. Who wasn't like —him." He gestured toward the boy.

"It is a massive problem for the schizophrenic to relate to the school," Glaub said. "The schizophrenic, such as yourself, very often deals with people through their unconscious. The teaching machines, of course, have no shadow personalities; what they are is all on the surface. Since the schizophrenic is accustomed constantly to ignore the surface and look beneath —he draws a blank. He is simply unable to understand them."

Bohlen said, "I couldn't understand anything they said; it was all just that—meaningless talk Manfred uses. That private language."

"You're fortunate you could come out of it," Dr. Glaub said.

"I know."

"So now what will it be for you, Bohlen? Rest and recovery? Or more of this dangerous contact with a child so unstable that—"

"I have no choice," Jack Bohlen said.

"That's right. You have no choice; you must withdraw."

Bohlen said, "But I learned something. I learned how great

the stakes are for me personally, in all this. Now I know what it would be like to be cut off from the world, isolated, the way Manfred is. I'd do anything to avoid that. I have no intention of giving up now." With shaking hands he got a cigarette from his pocket and lit up.

"The prognosis for you is not good," Dr. Glaub said.

Jack Bohlen nodded.

"There's been a remission of your difficulty, due no doubt to your being removed from the environment of the school. Shall I be blunt? There's no telling how long you'll be able to function; perhaps another ten minutes, another hour—possibly until tonight, and then you may well find yourself enduring a worse collapse. The nocturnal hours are especially bad, are they not?"

"Yes," Bohlen said.

"I can do two things for you. I can take Manfred back to Camp B-G and I can represent you at Arnie's tonight, be there as your official psychiatrist. I do that all the time; it's my business. Give me a retainer and I'll drop you off at your home."

"Maybe after tonight," Bohlen said. "Maybe you can represent me later on, if this gets worse. But tonight I'm taking Manfred with me to see Arnie Kott."

Dr. Glaub shrugged. Impervious to suggestion, he realized. A sign of autism. Jack Bohlen could not be persuaded; he was too cut off already to hear and understand. Language for him had become a hollow ritual, signifying nothing.

"My boy David," Bohlen said all at once. "I have to go back there to the school and pick him up. And my Yee Company 'copter; it's there, too." His eyes had become clearer, now, as if he were emerging from his state.

"Don't go back there," Dr. Glaub urged him.

"Take me back."

"Then don't go down into the school; stay up on the field. I'll have them send up your son—you can sit in your 'copter until he's up. That would be safe for you, perhaps. I'll deal with the master circuit for you." Dr. Glaub felt a rush of sympathy for this man, for his dogged instincts to go on in his own manner.

"Thanks," Bohlen said. "I'd appreciate that." He shot a smile at the doctor, and Glaub smiled back.

Arnie Kott said plaintively, "Where's Jack Bohlen?" It was six o'clock in the evening, and Arnie sat by himself in his living room, drinking a slightly too sweet Old Fashioned which Helio had fixed.

At this moment his tame Bleekman was in the kitchen preparing a dinner entirely of black-market goodies, all from Arnie's new stock. Reflecting that he now obtained his spread at wholesale prices, Arnie felt good. What an improvement on the old system, where Norbert Steiner made all the profit! Arnie sipped his drink and waited for his guests to arrive. In the corner, music emerged from the speakers, subtle and yet pervasive; it filled the room and lulled Goodmember Kott.

He was still in that trancelike mood when the noise of the telephone startled him awake.

"Arnie, this is Scott."

"Oh?" Arnie said, not pleased; he preferred to deal through his cunning code system. "Look, I've got a vital business meeting tonight here, and unless you've got something—"

"This is important, all right," Scott said. "There's somebody else hoeing away at our row."

Puzzled, Arnie said, "what?" And then he understood what Scott Temple meant.. "You mean the goodies?"

"Yes," Scott said. "And he's all set up. He's got his field, his incoming rockets, his route—he must have taken over Stein—"

"Don't talk any further," Arnie interrupted. "Come on over here right away."

"Will do." The phone clicked as Scott rang off.

How do you like that, Arnie said to himself. Just as I'm getting good and started, some bugger horns in. And I mean, I didn't even want to get into this black-market business in the first place—why didn't this guy tell me he wanted to take over where Steiner left off? But it's too late now; I'm in it, and nobody's going to force me out.

Half an hour later Scott appeared at the door, agitated; he paced about Arnie Kott's living room, eating hors d'oeuvres and talking away at a great rate. "He's a real pro, this guy; must have been in the business before sometime—he's already gone all over Mars, to practically everybody, including isolated houses way out in the goddam fringes, to those housewives out there who only buy maybe one jar of something; so he's leaving no stone unturned. There won't be any room for us, and we're just barely beginning to get our operation moving. This guy, let's face it, is running rings around us."

"I see," Arnie said, rubbing the bald part of his scalp.

"We've got to do something, Arnie."

"Do you know where his base of operations is?"

"No, but it's probably in the F.D.R. Mountains; that's where Norb Steiner had his field. We'll look there first." In his memo book, Scott made a note of that.

"Find his field," Arnie said, "and let me know. And I'll have a Lewistown police ship out there."

"Then he'll know who's against him."

"That's correct. I want him to know it's Arnie Kott he's got to contend with and not no ordinary opposition. I'll have the police ship drop a tactical A-bomb or some other minor demolition type of weapon and put an end to his field. So the bugger will see we're genuinely sore at him for his effrontery. And that's what it is, him coming in and competing against me, when I didn't even want to get into this business! It's bad enough without him making it harder."

In his memo book, Scott made notes of all that: *him making it even harder, etc.*

"You get me the location," Arnie concluded, "and I'll see that he's taken care of. I won't have the police get him, just his equipment; we don't want to find ourselves in trouble with the UN. I'm sure this'll blow over right away. Just one guy, do you think? It's not for instance a big outfit from Home?"

"The story I get is it's definitely one guy."

"Fine," Arnie said, and sent Scott off. The door shut after him and once more Arnie Kott was alone in his living room, while his tame Bleekman puttered in the kitchen.

"How's the bouillabaisse coming?" Arnie called into him.

"Fine, Mister," Heliogabalus said. "May I inquire who is to come this evening to eat all this?" At the stove he toiled surrounded by several kinds of fish, plus many herbs and spices.

Arnie said, "It'll be Jack Bohlen, Doreen Anderton and some autistic child Jack's working with that Dr. Glaub recommended . . . Norb Steiner's son."

"Low types all," Heliogabalus murmured.

Well, same to you, Arnie thought. "Just fix the food right," he said with irritation; he shut the kitchen door and returned to the living room. You black bastard, you got me into this, he thought to himself; it was you and your prognosticating stone that gave me the idea. And it better have worked out, because I got everything riding on it. And in addition—

The doorchimes sounded over the music from the speakers.

Opening the front door, Arnie found himself facing Doreen; she smiled warmly at him, as she entered the living room on high heels, a fur around her shoulders. "Hi. What smells so good?"

"Some darn fish thing." Arnie took her wrap; removed, it left her shoulders smooth, tanned and faintly freckled, bare. "No," he said at once, "this isn't that kind of evening; this is business. You go in and put on a decent blouse." he steered her to the bedroom. "Next time."

As he stood in the bedroom doorway watching her change he thought, What a terrific high-type looking woman I got, here. As she carefully laid her strapless gown out on the bed he thought, I gave her that. He recalled the model at the department store appearing wearing it. But Doreen looked a lot better; she had all that flaming red hair that plunged down the back of her neck like a drizzle of fire.

"Arnie," she said, turning to face him as she buttoned her blouse up, "you go easy on Jack Bohlen tonight."

"Aw hell," he protested, "whadya mean? All I want from good old Jack is results; I mean, he's had long enough—time's run out!"

Doreen repeated, "Go easy, Arnie. Or I'll never forgive you."

Grumbling, he walked away, to the sideboard in the living room, and began fixing her a drink. "What'll you have? I got a bottle of this ten-year-old Irish whisky; it's O.K."

"I'll have that, then," Doreen said, emerging from the bedroom. She seated herself on the couch and smoothed her skirt over her crossed knees.

"You look good in anything," Arnie said.

"Thank you."

"Listen, what you're doing with Bohlen has my sanction, of course, as you know. But it's all on the surface, what you're doing; right? Deep inside you're saving yourself for me."

Quizzically, Doreen said, "What do you refer to by 'deep inside'?" She eyed him until he laughed. "Watch it," she said. "Yes, of course I'm yours, Arnie. Everything here in Lewistown is yours, even the bricks and straw. Every time I pour a little water down the kitchen drain I think of you."

"Why me?"

"Because you're the totem god of wasted water." She smiled at him. "It's a little joke, that's all; I was thinking about your steam bath with all its run-off."

"Yeah," Arnie said. "Remember that time you and I went there late at night, and I unlocked it with my key, and we went in, like a couple of bad kids . . . sneaked in, turned on the hot water showers until the whole place was nothing but steam. And then we took off our clothes—we really must have been drinking—and we ran all around naked in the steam, hiding from each other. . . ." He grinned. "And I caught you, too, right there where that bench is where the masseuse pounds on you to flatten your ass out. And we sure had fun there on that bench."

"Very primordial," Doreen said, recalling.

"I felt like I was nineteen again that night," Arnie said. "I really am young, for an old guy—I mean, I got a lot left to me, if you know what I mean." He paced about the room. "When is that Bohlen going to get here, for chrissakes?"

The telephone rang.

"Mister," Heliogabalus called from the kitchen. "I am unable to attend to that; I must ask you to get it."

To Doreen, Arnie said, "If it's Bohlen calling to say he can't make it—" He made a dour, throat-cutting motion and picked up the receiver.

"Arnie," a man's voice came. "Sorry to bother you; this is Dr. Glaub."

Relieved, Arnie said, "Hi, Doc Glaub." To Doreen he said, "It's not Bohlen."

Dr. Glaub said, "Arnie, I know you're expecting Jack Bohlen tonight—he's not there yet, is he?"

"Naw."

Hesitating, Glaub said, "Arnie, I happen to have spent some time with Jack today, and although—"

"What's the matter, has he had a schizophrenic seizure?" With acute intuition, Arnie knew it was so; that was the point of the doctor's call. "O.K." Arnie said, "he's under a strain, under the pressure of time; granted. But so are we all. I gotta disappoint you if you want me to excuse him like some kid who's too sick to go to school. I can't do that. Bohlen knew what he was getting into. If he doesn't have any results to show me tonight, I'll fix him so he never repairs another toaster on Mars the rest of his life."

Dr. Glaub was silent and then he said, "It's people like you with your harsh driving demands that create schizophrenics."

"So what? I've got standards; he's got to meet them; that's all. Very high standards, I know that."

"So does he have high standards."

Arnie said, "Not as high as mine. Well, you got anything else to say, Doc Glaub?"

"No," Glaub said. "Except that—" His voice shook. "Nothing else. Thanks for your time."

"Thanks for calling." Arnie hung up. "That gutless wonder; he's too cowardly to say what he was thinking." Disgustedly, he walked away from the phone. "Afraid to stick up for what he believes in; I got nothing but contempt for him. Why'd he call if he's got no guts?"

Doreen said, "I'm amazed he called. Sticking his neck out. What did he say about Jack?" Her eyes were darkened by concern; she rose and approached Arnie, putting her hand on his arm to stop his pacing. "Tell me."

"Aw, he just said he was with Bohlen today for a while; I suppose Bohlen had some sort of fit, his ailment, you know."

"Is he coming?"

"Christ, I don't know. Why does everything have to be so complicated? Doctors calling, you pawing at me like a whipped dog or something." With resentment and aversion he loosened her fingers from his arm and pushed her aside. "And that nutty nigger in the kitchen; Christ! Is he baking some witch-doctor brew in there? He's been going for hours!"

In a faint but controlled voice Doreen said, "Arnie, listen. If you push Jack too far and injure him, I'll never go to bed with you again. I promise."

"Everybody's protecting him, no wonder he's sick."

"He's a good person."

"He better be a good technician, too; he better have that kid's mind spread out like a road map for me to read."

They faced each other.

Shaking her head, Doreen turned away, picking up her drink, and moved off, her back to Arnie. "O.K. I can't tell you what to do. You can pick up a dozen women as good in bed as me; what am I to big Arnie Kott?" Her voice was bleak and envenomed.

He followed after her awkwardly. "Hell, Dor, you're unique, I swear, you're incredible, like what a swell smooth back you got, that dress you wore here, it showed it." He stroked her neck. "A knockout, even by Home standards."

The door chimes sounded.

"That's him," Arnie said, moving at once toward the door.

He opened the door, and there stood Jack Bohlen, looking tired. With him was a boy who danced unceasingly about on tiptoe, from one side of Jack to the other, his eyes shining, taking in everything and yet not focusing on any one thing.

The boy at once slithered past Arnie and into the living room, where Arnie lost sight of him.

Disconcerted, Arnie said to Jack Bohlen, "Enter."

"Thanks, Arnie," Jack said, coming in. Arnie shut the door, and the two of them looked around for Manfred.

"He went in the kitchen," Doreen said.

Sure enough, when Arnie opened the kitchen door, there stood the boy, raptly observing Heliogabalus. "What's the matter?" Arnie said to the boy. "You never saw a Bleekman before?"

The boy said nothing.

"What's that dessert you're making, Helio?" Arnie said.

"Flan," Heliogabalus said. "A filipino dish, a custard with a caramel sauce. From Mrs. Rombauer's cookbook."

"Manfred," Arnie said, "this here is Heliogabalus."

Standing at the kitchen doorway, Doreen and Jack watched, too. The boy seemed deeply affected by the Bleekman, Arnie noticed. As if under a spell, he followed with his eyes every move Helio made. With painstaking care, Helio was pouring the flan into molds which he carried to the freezing compartment of the refrigerator.

Almost shyly, Manfred said, "Hello."

"Hey," Arnie said. "He said an actual word."

Helio said in a cross voice, "I must ask all of you to leave the kitchen. Your presence makes me self-conscious so that I cannot work." He glared at them until, one by one, they left the kitchen. The door, shut from within, swung closed after them, cutting off the sight of Helio at his job.

"He's sort of odd," Arnie apologized. "But he sure can cook."

Jack said to Doreen, "That's the first time I've heard Manfred do that." He seemed impressed, and he walked off by himself, ignoring the rest of them, to stand at the window.

Joining him, Arnie said, "What do you want to drink?"

"Bourbon and water."

"I'll fix it," Arnie said. "I can't bother Helio with trivia like this." He laughed, but Jack did not.

The three of them sat with their drinks, for a time. Manfred, given some old magazines to read, stretched out on the carpet, once more oblivious to their presence.

"Wait'll you taste this meal," Arnie said.

"Smells wonderful," Doreen said.

"All black market," Arnie said.

Both Doreen and Jack, together on the couch, nodded.

"This is a big night," Arnie said.

Again they nodded.

Raising his drink, Arnie said, "Here's to communication. Without which there wouldn't be a goddamn nothin'."

Somberly, Jack said, "I'll drink to that, Arnie." However, he had already finished his drink; he gazed at the empty glass, evidently at a loss.

"I'll get you another," Arnie said, taking it from him.

At the sideboard, as he fixed a fresh drink for Jack, he saw that Manfred had grown bored with the magazines; once more the boy was on his feet, roaming around the room. Maybe he'd like to cut out and paste, Arnie decided. He gave Jack his fresh drink and then went into the kitchen.

"Helio, get some glue and scissors for the kid, and some paper for him to paste things on."

Helio had finished with the flan; his work evidently was done, and he had seated himself with a copy of *Life*. With reluctance he got up and went in search of glue, scissors, and paper.

"Funny kid, isn't he?" Arnie said to Helio, when the Bleekman returned. "What's your opinion about him, is it the same as mine?"

"Children are all alike," Helio said, and went out of the kitchen, leaving Arnie alone.

Arnie followed. "We'll eat pretty soon," he announced. "Everybody had some of these Danish blue cheese hors d'oeuvres? Anybody need anything at all?"

The phone rang. Doreen, who was closest, answered it. She handed it to Arnie. "For you. A man."

It was Dr. Glaub again. "Mr. Kott," Dr. Glaub said in a thin, unnatural voice, "it is essential to my integrity to protect my patients. Two can play at this bullying game. As you know, your out-of-wedlock child Sam Esterhazy is at Camp B-G, where I am in attendance."

Arnie groaned.

"If you do not treat Jack Bohlen fairly," Glaub continued, "if you apply your inhumane, cruel, aggressive, domineering tactics on him, I will retaliate by discharging Sam Esterhazy from Camp B-G on the grounds that he is mentally retarded, Is that comprehended?"

"Oh, Christ, anything you say," Arnie groaned. "I'll talk to you about it tomorrow. Go to bed or something. Take a pill Just get off me." He slammed down the phone.

The tape on the tape transport had reached its end; the music had ceased a long time ago, Arnie stalked over to his tape library and snatched up a box at random. That doctor, he said to himself. I'll get him, but not now. No time now. There must be something the matter with him; he must have some wild hair up his bung.

Examining the box he read:

W.A. Mozart, Symphony 40 in G mol., K. 550

"I love Mozart," he said to Doreen, Jack Bohlen, and the Steiner boy. "I'll put this on." He removed the reel of tape from the box and put it on the transport; he fiddled with the knobs of the amplifier until he could hear the hiss of the tape as it passed through the head. "Bruno Walter conducting," he told his guests, "A great rarity from the golden age of recordings."

A hideous racket of screeches and shrieks issued from the speakers. Noises like the convulsions of the dead, Arnie thought in horror. He ran to shut off the tape transport.

Seated on the carpet, snipping pictures from the magazines with his scissors and pasting them into new configurations, Manfred Steiner heard the noise and glanced up. He saw Mr. Kott hurry to the tape machine to shut it off. How blurred Mr. Kott became, Manfred noticed. It was hard to see him when he moved so swiftly; it was as if in some way he had managed to disappear from the room and then reappear in another spot. The boy felt frightened.

The noise, too, frightened him. He looked to the couch where Mr. Bohlen sat, to see if he were upset. But Mr. Bohlen remained where he was with Doreen Anderton, interlinked with her in a fashion that made the boy cringe with concern. How could two people stand being so close? It was, to Manfred, as if their separate identities had flowed together, and the idea that such a muddling could be terrified him. He pretended not to see; he saw past them, at the safe, unblended wall.

The voice of Mr. Kott broke over the boy, harsh and jagged tones that he did not understand. Then Doreen Anderton spoke, and then Jack Bohlen; they were all chattering in a chaos, now, and the boy clapped his hands to his ears. All at once, without warning of any kind, Mr. Kott shot across the room and vanished entirely.

Where had he gone? No matter where he looked the boy could not find him. He began to tremble, wondering what was going to happen. And then he saw, to his bewilderment, that Mr. Kott had reappeared in the room where the food was; he was chattering to the dark figure there.

The dark figure, with rhythmic grace, ebbed from his spot on top of the high stool, flowed step by step across the room and got a glass from the cabinet. Awed by the movement of the man, Manfred looked directly at him, and at that moment the dark man looked back, meeting his gaze.

"You must die," the dark man said to him in a far-off voice. "Then you will be reborn. Do you see, child? There is nothing for you as you are now, because something went wrong and you cannot see or hear or feel. No one can help you. Do you see, child?"

"Yes," Manfred said.

The dark figure glided to the sink, put some powder and water into the glass, presented it to Mr. Kott, who drank down the contents, chattering all the while. How beautiful the dark figure was. Why can't I be like that? Manfred thought. No one else looked like that.

His glimpse, his contact with the shadow-like man, was cut off. Doreen Anderton had passed between them as she ran into the kitchen and began talking in high-pitched tones. Once more Manfred put his hands to his ears, but he could not shut out the noise.

He looked ahead, to escape. He got away from the sound and the harsh, blurred comings and goings.

Ahead of him a mountain path stretched out. The sky overhead was heavy and red, and then he saw dots: hundreds of gigantic specks that grew and came closer. Things rained down from them, men with unnatural thoughts. The men struck the ground and dashed about in circles. They drew lines, and then great things like slugs landed, one after another, without thoughts of any sort, and began digging.

He saw a hole as large as a world; the earth disappeared and became black, empty, and nothing. . . . Into the hole the men jumped one by one, until none of them were left. He was alone, with the silent world-hole.

At the rim of the hole he peeped down. At the bottom, in the nothing, a twisted creature unwound as if released. It snaked up, became wide, contained square space, and grew color.

I am in you, Manfred thought. Once again.

A voice said, "He has been here at AM-WEB longer than

166

anyone else. He was here when the rest of us came. He is extremely old."

"Does he like it?"

"Who knows? He can't walk or feed himself. The records were lost in that fire. Possibly he's two hundred years old. They amputated his limbs and of course most of his internal organs were taken out on entry. Mostly he complains about hayfever."

No, Manfred thought. I can't stand it; my nose burns. I can't breathe. Is this the start of life, what the dark shadow-figure promised? A new begininng where I will be different and someone can help me?

Please help me, he said. I need someone, anyone. I can't wait here forever; it must be done soon or not at all. If it is not done I will grow and become the world-hole, and the hole will eat up everything.

The hole, beneath AM-WEB, waited to be all those who walked above, or had ever walked above; it waited to be everyone and everything. And only Manfred Steiner held it back.

Setting down his empty glass, Jack Bohlen felt the coming apart of every piece of his body. "We're out of booze," he managed to say to the girl beside him.

To him, Doreen said in a rapid whisper, "Jack, you must remember, you've got friends. I'm your friend, Dr. Glaub called—he's your friend." She looked into his face anxiously. "Will you be O.K.?"

"God sake," Arnie yelled. "I got to hear how you've done, Jack. Can't you give me anything?" With envy he faced the two of them; Doreen drew away from Jack imperceptibly. "Are you two just going to sit there necking and whispering? I don't feel good." He left them, then, going into the kitchen.

Leaning toward Jack until her lips almost touched his, Doreen whispered, "I love you."

He tried to smile at her. But his face had become stiff; it would not yield. "Thanks," he said, wanting her to know how much it meant to him. He kissed her on the mouth. Her lips were warm, soft with love; they gave what they had to him, holding nothing back.

Her eyes full of tears, she said, "I feel you sliding away farther and farther into yourself again."

"No," he said. "I'm O.K." But it was not so; he knew it.

"Gubble gubble," the girl said.

Jack closed his eyes. I can't get away, he thought. It has closed over me completely.

When he opened his eyes he found that Doreen had gotten up from the couch and was going into the kitchen. Voices, hers and Arnie's, drifted to him where he sat.

"Gubble gubble gubble."

"Gubble."

Turning toward the boy who sat snipping at his magazines on the rug, Jack said to him, "Can you hear me? Can you understand me?"

Manfred glanced up and smiled.

"Talk to me," Jack said. "Help me."

There was no response.

Getting to his feet, Jack made his way to the tape recorder; he began inspecting it, his back to the room. Would I be alive now, he asked himself, if I had listened to Dr. Glaub? If I hadn't come here, had let him represent me? Probably not. Like the earlier attack: it would have happened anyhow. It is a process which must unfold; it must work itself out to its conclusion.

The next he knew he was standing on a black, empty sidewalk. The room, the people around him, were gone; he was alone.

Buildings, gray, upright surfaces on both sides. Was this AM-WEB? He looked about frantically. Lights, here and there; he was in a town, and now he recognized it as Lewistown. He began to walk.

"Wait," a voice, a woman's voice, called.

From the entrance of a building a woman in a fur wrap hurried, her high heels striking the pavement and setting up echoes. Jack stopped.

"It didn't go so bad after all," she said, catching up with him, out of breath. "Thank God it's over; you were so tense— I felt it all evening. Arnie is dreadfully upset by the news about the co-op; they're so rich and powerful, they make him feel so little."

Together, they walked in no particular direction, the girl holding on to his arm.

"And he did say," she said, "that he's going to keep you on as his repairman; I'm positive he means it. He's sore, though, Jack. All the way through him. I know; I can tell."

He tried to remember, but he could not.

"Say something," Doreen begged.

After a bit he said, "He—would make a bad enemy."

168

"I'm afraid that's so." She glanced up into his face. "Shall we go to my place? Or do you want to stop somewhere and get a drink?"

"Let's just walk," Jack Bohlen said.

"Do you still love me?"

"Of course," he said.

"Are you afraid of Arnie? He may try to get revenge on you, for—he doesn't understand about your father; he thinks that on some level you must have—" She shook her head. "Jack, he will try to get back at you; he does blame you. He's so goddamn primitive."

"Yes," Jack said.

"*Say* something," Doreen said. "You're just like wood, like you're not alive. Was it so terrible? It wasn't, was it? You seemed to pull yourself together."

With effort he said, "I'm—not afraid of what he'll do."

"Would you leave your wife for me. Jack? You said you loved me. Maybe we could emigrate back to Earth, or something."

Together, they wandered on.

thirteen

For OTTO ZITTE it was as if life had once more opened up; since Norb Steiner's death he moved about Mars as in the old days, making his deliveries, selling, meeting people face to face and gabbing with them.

And, most particularly, he had already encountered several good-looking women, lonely housewives stranded out in the desert in their homes day after day, yearning for companionship . . . so to speak.

So far he had not been able to call at Mrs. Silvia Bohlen's house. But he knew exactly where it was; he had marked it on his map.

Today he intended to go there.

For the occasion he put on his best suit: a single-breasted gray English sharkskin suit he had not worn for years. The shoes, regrettably, were local, and so was the shirt. But the tie: ah. It had just arrived from New York, the latest in bright, cheerful colors; it divided at the bottom into a wild fork shape. Holding it up before him he admired it. Then he put it on and admired it there, too.

His long dark hair shone. He felt happy and confident. This day begins it all afresh for me, with a woman like Silvia, he said to himself as he put on his wool topcoat, picked up his suitcases, and marched from the storage shed—now made over into truly comfortable living quarters—to the 'copter.

In a great soaring arc he lifted the 'copter into the sky and turned it east. The bleak F.D.R. Mountains fell away behind him; he passed over the desert, saw at last the George Washington Canal by which he oriented himself. Following it, he approached the smaller canal system which branched from it, and soon he was above the junction of the William Butler Yeats and the Herodotus, near which the Bohlens lived.

Both those women, he ruminated, are attractive, that June

170

Henessy and Silvia Bohlen, but of the two of them, Silvia's more to my liking; she has that sleepy, sultry quality that a deeply emotional woman always has. June is too pert and frisky; that kind talks on and on, sort of wiseguy-like. I want a woman who's a good listener.

He recalled the trouble he had gotten into before. Wonder what her husband's like, he wondered. Must inquire. A lot of these men take the pioneer life seriously, especially the ones living far out from town; keep guns in their houses and so forth.

However, that was the risk one ran, and it was worth it.

Just in case trouble did occur, Otto Zitte had a gun of his own, a small pistol, .22 caliber, which he kept in a hidden side-pocket of one of his suitcases. It was there now, and fully loaded.

Nobody messes around with me, he said to himself. If they want trouble—they'll soon find it.

Cheered by that thought, he dipped his 'copter, scouted out the land below—there was no 'copter parked at the Bohlen house—and prepared to land.

It was innate caution which caused him to park the 'copter over a mile from the Bohlen house, at the entrance of a service canal. From there he hiked on foot, willing to enduro tho weight of the suitcase; there was no alternative. A number of houses stood between him and the Bohlen place, but he did not pause to knock at any door; he went directly along the canal without halting.

When he neared the Bohlen place he slowed, regaining his wind. He eyed the nearby houses carefully . . . from the one right next door there came the racket of small children. People home, there. So he approched the Bohlen place from the opposite side, walking silently and in a line which kept him entirely hidden from the house where he heard the children's voices.

He arrived, stepped up on the porch, rang the bell.

Someone peeped out at him from behind the red drapes of the living-room window. Otto maintained a formal, correct smile on his face, one that would do in any eventuality.

The front door opened; there stood Silvia Bohlen, with her hair expertly done, lipstick, wearing a jersey sweater and tight pink capri pants, sandals on her feet. Her toenails were painted a bright scarlet; he noticed that from the corner of his eye. Obviously, she had fixed herself up in expectation of his visit. However, she of course assumed a bland, detached pose; she regarded him in aloof silence, holding on to the door knob.

"Mrs. Bohlen," he said in his most intimate tone of voice. Bowing, he said, "Passage across barren miles of desert wastelands finds its just reward in seeing you once more at last. Would you be interested in seeing our special in kangaroo-tail soup? It is incredible and delightful, a food never before available on Mars at any price. I have come straight here to you with it, seeing that you are qualified in judging fine foods and can discriminate the worthy without consulting the expense." And all this time, as he reeled off his set speech, he edged himself and his wares toward the open door.

A trifle stiffly and hesitantly, Silvia said, "Uh, come in." She let the door swing freely open, and he at once passed on inside and laid his suitcases on the floor by the low table in the living room.

A boy's bow and quiver of arrows caught his eye. "Is your young son about?" he inquired.

"No," Silvia said, moving edgily about the room with her arms folded before her. "He's at the school today." She tried to smile. "And my father-in-law went into town; he won't be home until very late."

Well, Otto thought; I see.

"Please be seated," he urged her. "So that I may display to you properly, don't you agree?" In one motion, he moved a chair, and Silvia perched on the edge of it, her arms still hugged about her, lips pressed together. How tense she is, he observed. It was a good sign because it meant that she was fully aware of the meaning of all that went on, his visit here, the absence of her son, the fact that she had carefully closed the front door; the living-room drapes still shut, he noticed.

Silvia blusted out, "Would you like coffee?" She bolted from her chair and dived into the kitchen. A moment later she reappeared with a tray on which was a pot of coffee, sugar, cream, two china cups.

"Thank you," he purred. During her absence he had drawn another chair up beside hers.

They drank coffee.

"Are you not frightened to live out here alone so much of the time?" he asked. "In this desolate region?"

She glanced at him sideways. "Golly, I guess I'm used to it."

"What part of Earth are you from originally?"

"St. Louis."

"It is much different here. A new, freer life. Where one can cast off the shackles and be oneself; do you agree? The old mores and customs, an antiquated Old World, best forgotten in its own dust. Here—" He glanced about the living room, with its commonplace furnishings; he had seen such chairs, carpeting, bric-a-brac hundreds of times, in similar homes. "Here we see the clash of the extraordinary, the pulse, Mrs. Bohlen, of opportunity which strikes the brave person only once—once—in his lifetime."

"What else do you have beside kangaroo-tail soup?"

"Well," he said, frowning inwardly, "quail eggs; very good. Real cow butter. Sour cream. Smoked oysters. Here—you please bring forth ordinary soda crackers and I will supply the butter and caviar, as a treat." He smiled at her, and was rewarded by a spontaneous, beaming smile in return; her eyes sparkled with anticipation and she hopped impulsively to her feet to go scampering, like a little child, to the kitchen.

Presently they sat together, huddled over the table, scraping the black, oily fish eggs from the tiny jar onto crackers.

"There's nothing like genuine caviar," Silvia said, sighing. "I only had it once before in my life, at a restaurant in San Francisco."

"Observe what else I have." From his suitcase he produced a bottle. "Green Hungarian, from the Buena Vista winery in California; the oldest winery in that state!"

They sipped wine from long-stemmed glasses. (He had brought the glasses, too.) Silvia lay back against the couch, her eyes half-closed. "Oh, dear. This is like a fantasy. It can't really be happening."

"But it is." Otto set his glass down and leaned over her. She breathed slowly, regularly, as if asleep; but she was watching him fixedly. She knew exactly what was going on. And as he bent nearer and nearer she did not stir; she did not try to slide away.

The food and wine, he reckoned as he took hold of her, had set him back—in retail value—almost a hundred UN dollars. It was well worth it, to him, at least.

His old story, repeating itself. Again, it was not union scale. It was much more, Otto thought a little later on, when they had moved from the living room to the bedroom with its window shades pulled down, the room in unstirring gloom, silent and receptive to them, made, as he well knew, for just such happenings as this.

"Nothing like this," Silvia murmured, "has ever happened

before in my entire life." Her voice was full of contentment and acquiescence, as if emerging from far away. "Am I drunk, is that it? Oh, my Lord."

For a long time, then, she was silent.

"Am I out of my mind?" she murmured, later on. "I must be insane. I just can't believe it, I know it isn't real. So how can it matter, how can what you do in a dream be wrong?"

After that, she said nothing at all.

She was exactly the kind he liked: the kind that didn't talk a lot.

What is insanity? Jack Bohlen thought. It was, for him, the fact that somewhere he had lost Manfred Steiner and did not remember how or when. He remembered almost nothing of the night before, at Arnie Kott's place; piece by piece, from what Doreen told him, he had managed to patch together an image of what had taken place. Insanity—to have to construct a picture of one's life, by making inquiries of others.

But the lapse in memory was a symptom of a deeper disturbance. It indicated that his psyche had taken an abrupt leap ahead in time. And this had taken place after a period in which he had lived through, several times, on some unconscious level, that very section which was now missing.

He had sat, he realized, in Arnie Kott's living room again and again, experiencing that evening before it arrived; and then, when at last it had taken place in actuality, he had bypassed it. The fundamental disturbance in time-sense, which Dr. Glaub believed was the basis of schizophrenia, was now harassing him.

That evening at Arnie's had taken place, and had existed for him . . . but out of sequence.

In any case, there was no way that it could be restored. For it now lay in the past. And a disturbance of the sense of past time was not symptomatic of schizophrenia but of compulsive-obsessive neurosis. His problem—as a schizophrenic—lay entirely with the future.

And his future, as he now saw it, consisted mostly of Arnie Kott and Arnie's instinctive drive for revenge.

What chance do we have against Arnie? he asked himself. Almost none.

Turning from the window of Doreen's living room, he walked slowly into the bedroom and gazed down at her as she lay, still asleep, in the big, rumpled double bed.

While he stood there looking at her, she woke, saw him, smiled up at him. "I was having the strangest dream," she said. "In the dream I was conducting the Bach B minor Mass, the Kyrie part. It was in four-four time. But when I was right in the middle, someone came along and took away my baton and said it wasn't in four-four time." She frowned. "But it really is. Why would I be conducting that? I don't even like the Bach B minor Mass. Arnie has a tape of it; he plays it all the time, very late in the evening."

He thought of the dreams he had been having of late, vague forms that shifted, flitted away; something to do with a tall building of many rooms, hawks or vultures circling endlessly overhead. And some dreadful thing in a cupboard . . . he had not seen it, had only felt its presence there.

"Dreams usually relate to the future," Doreen said. "They have to do with the potential in a person. Arnie wants to start a symphony orchestra at Lewistown; he's been talking to Bosley Touvim at New Israel. Maybe I'll be the conductor; maybe that's what my dream means." She slid from the bed and stood up, naked and slim and smooth.

"Doreen," he said steadily, "I don't remember last night. What became of Manfred?"

"He stayed with Arnie. Because he has to go back to Camp B-G, now, and Arnie said he'd take him. He goes to New Israel all the time to visit his own boy there, Sam Esterhazy. He's going there today, he told you." After a pause she said, "Jack . . . have you ever had amnesia before?"

"No," he said.

"It's probably due to the shock of quarreling with Arnie; it's awfully hard on a person to tangle with Arnie, I've noticed."

"Maybe that's it," he said.

"What about breakfast?" Now she began getting fresh clothes from her dresser drawers, a blouse, underwear. "I'll cook bacon and eggs—delicious canned Danish bacon." She hesitated and then she said, "More of Arnie's black-market goodies. But they really are good."

"It's fine with me," he said.

"After we went to bed last night I lay awake for hours wondering what Arnie will do. To us, I mean. I think it'll be your job, Jack; I think he'll put pressure on Mr. Yee to let you go. You must be prepared for that. We both must be. And of course, he'll just dump me; that's obvious. But I don't mind—I have you."

"Yes that's so, you do have me," he said, as by reflex.

"The vengeance of Arnie Kott," Doreen said, as she washed her face in the bathroom. "But he's so human; it's not so scary. I prefer him to that Manfred; I really couldn't stand that child. Last night was a nightmare—I kept feeling awful cold squishy tendrils drifting around the room and in my mind . . . intimations of filth and evil that didn't seem to be either in me or outside of me—just nearby. I know where they came from." After a moment she finished, "It was that child. It was his thoughts."

Presently she was frying the bacon and heating coffee; he set the table, and then they sat down to eat. The food smelled good, and he felt much better, tasting it and seeing it and smelling it, and being aware of the girl across from him, with her red hair, long and heavy and sleek, tied back with a gay ribbon.

"Is your son at all like Manfred?" she asked.

"Oh, hell, no."

"Does he take after you or—"

"Silvia," he said. "He takes after his mother."

"She's pretty, isn't she?"

"I would say so."

"You know, Jack, last night when I was lying there awake and thinking . . . I thought, Maybe Arnie won't turn Manfred over to Camp B-G. What would he do with him, with a creature like that? Arnie's very imaginative. Now this scheme to buy into the F·D·R. land is over . . . maybe he'll find an an entirely new use for Manfred's precognition. It occurred to me—you'll laugh. Maybe he'll be able to contact Manfred through Heliogabalus, that tame Bleekman of his." She was quiet, then, eating breakfast and staring down at the plate.

Jack said, "You could be right." He felt bad, just to hear her say it. It rang so true; it was so plausible.

"You never talked to Helio," Doreen said. "He's the most cynical, bitter person I ever met. He's even sardonic with Arnie; he hates everybody. I mean, he's really twisted inside."

"Did I ask Arnie to take the boy? Or was it his idea?"

"Arnie suggested it. At first you wouldn't agree. But you had become so—inert and withdrawn. It was late and we all had drunk a lot—do you remember that?"

He nodded.

"Arnie serves that Black Label Jack Daniels. I must have drunk a whole fifth of it alone." She shook her head mournfully. "Nobody else on Mars has the liquor Arnie has; I'll miss it."

"There isn't much I can do along that line," Jack said.

"I know. That's O.K. I don't expect you to; I don't expect anything, in fact. It all happened so fast last night; one minute we were all working together, you and I and Arnie—then, it seemed like all of a sudden, it was obvious that we were on opposite sides, that we'd never be together again, not as friends, anyhow. It's sad." She put up the side of her hand and rubbed at her eye. A tear slid down her cheek. "Jesus. I'm crying," she said with anger.

"If we could go back and relive last night—"

"I wouldn't change it," she said. "I don't regret anything. And you shouldn't either."

"Thanks," he said. He took hold of her hand. "I'll do the best I can by you. As the guy said, I'm not much but I'm all I have."

She smiled, and, after a moment, resumed eating her breakfast.

At the front counter of her shop, Anne Esterhazy wrapped a package for mailing. As she began addressing the label, a man strode into the store; she glanced up, saw him, a tall, thin man wearing glasses much too large for him. Memory brought distaste as she recognized Dr. Glaub.

"Mrs. Esterhazy," Dr. Glaub said, "I want to talk to you, if I may. I regret our altercation; I behaved in a regressive, oral-sucking fashion, and I'd like to apologize."

She said coolly, "What do you want, Doctor? I'm busy."

Lowering his voice, he said in a rapid monotone, "Mrs. Esterhazy, this has to do with Arnie Kott and a project he has with an anomalous boy whom he took from the camp. I want you to use your influence over Mr. Kott and your great zeal for humanitarian causes to see that a severe cruelty is not done to an innocent, introverted schizoid individual who was drawn into Mr. Kott's scheme due to his line of work. This man—"

"Wait," she interrupted. "I can't follow." She beckoned him to accompany her to the rear of the store, where no one entering would overhear.

"This man, Jack Bohlen," Dr. Glaub said, even more rapidly than before, "could become permanently psychotic as a result of Kott's desire for revenge, and I ask you, Mrs. Esterhazy—" He pleaded on and on.

Oh, good grief, she thought. Another cause that somebody wants to enlist me in—don't I have enough already?

But she listened; she had no choice. And it was her nature.

On and on mumbled Dr. Glaub, and gradually she began to build up an idea of the situation which he was trying to describe. It was clear that he held a grudge against Arnie. And yet—there was more. Dr. Glaub was a curious mixture of the idealistic and the childishly envious, a queer sort of person, Anne Esterhazy thought as she listened.

"Yes," she said at one point, "that does sound like Arnie."

"I thought of going to the police." Dr. Glaub rambled on. "Or to the UN authorities, and then I thought of you, so I came here." He peered at her, disingenuously but with determination.

At ten o'clock that morning Arnie Kott entered the front office of the Yee Company at Bunchewood Park. An elongated, intelligent-looking Chinese in his late thirties approached him and asked what he wished.

"I am Mr. Yee." They shook hands.

"This guy Bohlen that I'm leasing from you."

"Oh, yes. Isn't he a top-drawer repairman? Naturally, he is." Mr. Yee regarded him with shrewd caution.

Arnie said, "I like him so much I want to buy his contract from you." He got out his checkbook. "Give me the price."

"Oh, we must keep Mr. Bohlen," Mr. Yee protested, throwing up his hands. "No, sir, we can only lease him, not ever part with him."

"Name me the price." You skinny, smart cookie, Arnie thought.

"To part with Mr. Bohlen—we couldn't replace him!"

Arnie waited.

Considering, Mr. Yee said, "I suppose I could go over our records. But it would take hours to determine Mr. Bohlen's even approximate value."

Arnie waited, checkbook in hand.

After he had purchased Jack Bohlen's work contract from the Yee Company, Arnie Kott flew back home to Lewistown. He found Helio with Manfred, in the living room together; Helio was reading aloud to the boy from a book. "What's all this mumbo-jumbo?" Arnie demanded.

Helio, lowering his book, said, "This child has a speech impediment which I am overcoming."

"Bull," Arnie said, "you'll never overcome it." He took off his coat and held it out to Helio. After a pause the Bleekman reluctantly laid down the book and accepted the coat; he moved off to hang it in the hall closet·

From the corner of his eye Manfred seemed to be looking at Arnie.

"How you doin', kid," Arnie said in a friendly voice. He whacked the boy on the back. "Listen, you want to go back to that nuthouse, that no-good Camp B-G? Or do you want to stay with me? I'll give you ten minutes to decide."

To himself, Arnie thought, You're staying with me, no matter what you decide. You crazy fruity dumb kid, you and your dancing around on your toes and not talking and not noticing anybody. And your future-reading talent, which I know you got down there in that fruity brain of yours, which last night proved there's no doubt of.

Returning, Helio said, "He wants to stay with you, Mister."

"Sure he does," Arnie said, pleased.

"His thoughts," Helio said, "are as clear as plastic to me, and mine likewise to him. We are both prisoners, Mister, in a hostile land."

At that Arnie laughed loud and long.

"Truth always amuses the ignorant," Helio said.

"O.K.," Arnie said, "so I'm ignorant. I just get a kick out of you liking this warped kid, that's all. No offense. So you got something in common, you two? I'm not surprised." He swept up the book which Helio had been reading. "Pascal," he read. "*Provincial Letters*. Christ on the cross, what's the point of this? Is there a point?"

"The rhythms," Helio said, with patience. "Great prose establishes a cadence which attracts and holds the boy's wandering attention."

"Why does it wander?"

"From dread."

"Dread of what?"

"Of death," Helio said.

Sobered, Arnie said, "Oh. Well. His death? Or just death in general?"

"This boy experiences his own old age, his lying in a dilapidated state, decades from now, in an old persons' home which is yet to be built here on Mars, a place of decay which he loathes beyond expression. In this future place he passes empty, weary years, bedridden—an object, not a person, kept alive through stupid legalities. When he tries to fix his eyes

179

on the present, he almost at once is smitten by that dread vision of himself once again."

"Tell me about this old persons' home," Arnie said.

"It is to be built soon," Helio said. "Not for that purpose, but as a vast dormitory for immigrants to Mars."

"Yeah," Arnie said, recognizing it. "In the F.D.R. range."

"The people arrive," Helio said, "and settle, and live, and drive the wild Bleekmen from their last refuge. In turn, the Bleekmen put a curse on the land, sterile as it is. The Earth settlers fail; their buildings deteriorate year after year. Settlers return to Earth faster than they come here. At last this other use is made of the building: it becomes a home for the aged, for the poor, the senile and infirm."

"Why doesn't he talk? Explain that."

"To escape from his dread vision he retreats back to happier days, days inside his mother's body where there is no one else, no change, no time, no suffering. The womb life. He directs himself there, to the only happiness he has ever known. Mister, he refuses to leave that dear spot."

"I see," Arnie said, only half-believing the Bleekman.

"His suffering is like our own, like all other persons'. But in him it is worse, for he has his preknowledge, which we lack. It is a terrible knowledge to have. No wonder he has become—dark within."

"Yeah, he's as dark as you are," Arnie said, "and not outside, either, but like you said—inside. How can you stand him?"

"I stand everything," the Bleekman said.

"You know what I think?" Arnie said. "I think he does more than just see into time. I think he controls time."

The Bleekman's eyes became opaque. He shrugged.

"Doesn't he?" Arnie persisted. "Listen, Heliogabalus, you black bastard; this kid fooled around with last night. I know it. He saw it in advance and he tried to tamper with it. Was he trying to make it not happen? He was trying to halt time."

"Perhaps," Helio said.

"That's quite a talent," Arnie said. "Maybe he could go back into the past, like he wants to, and maybe alter the present. You keep working with him, keep after this. Listen, has that Doreen Anderton called or stopped by this morning? I want to talk to her."

"No."

"You think I'm nuts? As to what I imagine about this kid and his possible abilities?"

"You are driven by rage, Mister," the Bleekman said. "A man driven by rage may stumble, in his passion, onto truth."

"What crap," Arnie said, disgusted. "Can't you just say yes or no? Do you have to babble like you do?"

Helio said, "Mister, I will tell you something about Mr. Bohlen, whom you wish to injure. He is very venerable—"

"Vulnerable," Arnie corrected.

"Thank you. He is frail, easily hurt. It should be easy for you to put an end to him. However, he has with him a charm, given to him by someone who loves him or perhaps by several who love him. A Bleekman water witch charm. It may guarantee him in safety."

After an interval, Arnie said, "We'll see."

"Yes," Helio said in a voice which Arnie had never heard him use before. "We will have to wait and see what strength still lives in such ancient items."

"The living proof that such junk is just so much worthless crap is you yourself. That you'd rather be here, taking orders from me, serving me my food and sweeping the floor and hanging up my coat, than roaming around out on that Martian desert like you were when I found you. Out there like a dying beast, begging for water."

"Hmm," the Bleekman murmured. "Possibly so."

"And keep that in mind," Arnie said. Or you might find yourself back out there again, with your paka eggs and your arrows, stumbling along going nowhere, nowhere at all, he thought to himself. I'm doing you a big favor, letting you live here like a human.

In the early afternoon Arnie Kott received a message from Scott Temple. He placed it on the spindle of his decoding equipment, and soon he was listening to the message.

"We located this character's field, Arnie, out in the F.D.R. range, all right. He wasn't there, but a slave rocket had just landed; in fact, that's how we found it right off—we followed the trail of the rocket in. Anyhow, the guy had a large storage shed full of goodies; we took all the goodies, and they're in our warehouse now. Then we planted a seed-type A-weapon and blew up the field and the shed and all the equipment lying around."

Good deal, Arnie thought.

"And, like you said, so he'd realize who he's up against, we left a message. We stuck a note up on the remains of the landing field guidance tower that said, *Arnie Kott doesn't like what you stand for.* How does that strike you. Arnie?"

"That strikes me fine," Arnie said aloud, although it did seem a little—what was the word? Corny.

The message continued, "And he'll discover it when he gets back. And I thought—this is my idea, subject to your correction—that we'd take a trip out there later in the week, just to be sure he's not rebuilding. Some of these independent operators are sort of screwy, like those guys last year that tried to set up their own telephone system. Anyhow, I believe that takes care of it. And by the way—he was using Norb Steiner's old gear; we found records around with Steiner's name on them. So you were right. It's a good thing we moved right onto this guy, because he could have been trouble."

The message ended. Arnie put the reel on his encoder, seated himself at the mike, and answered.

"Scott, you did good. Thanks. I trust we've heard the last from that guy, and I approve your confiscating his stock; we can use it all. Drop by some evening and have a drink." He stopped the mechanism, then, and rewound the reel.

From the kitchen came the insistent, muffled sound of Heliogabalus reading aloud to Manfred Steiner. Hearing it, Arnie felt irritation, and then his resentment toward the Bleekman surged up. Why'd you let me get mixed up with Jack Bohlen when you could read the kid's mind? he demanded. Why didn't you speak up?

He felt outright hatred for Heliogabalus. You betrayed me, too, he said to himself. Like the rest of them, Anne and Jack and Doreen; all of them.

Going to the kitchen door he yelled in, "You getting results, or aren't you?"

Heliogabalus lowered his book and said, "Mister, this requires time and effort."

"Time!" Arnie said. "Hell, that's the whole problem. Send him back into the past, say two years ago, and have him buy the Henry Wallace in my name—can you do that?"

There was no answer. The question, to Heliogabalus, was too absurd even to consider. Flushing, Arnie slammed the kitchen door shut and stalked back into the living room.

Then have him send me back into the past, Arnie said to himself. This time-travel ability must be worth something; why can't I get the kind of results I want? What's the matter with everyone?

They're making me wait just to annoy me, he said to himself.

And, he decided, I'm not going to wait much longer.

By one o'clock in the afternoon still no service calls had come in from the Yee Company. Jack Bohlen, waiting by the phone in Doreen Anderton's apartment, knew that something was wrong.

At one-thirty he phoned Mr. Yee.

"I assumed that Mr. Kott would inform you, Jack," Mr. Yee said in his prosaic manner. "You are no longer my employee, Jack; you are his. Thank you for your fine service record."

Demoralized by the news, Jack said, "Kott bought my contract?"

"That is the case, Jack."

Jack hung up the phone.

"What did he say?" Doreen asked, watching him wide-eyed.

"I'm Arnie's."

"What's he going to do?"

"I don't know," he said. "I guess I better call him and find out. It doesn't look as if he's going to call me." Playing with me, he thought. Sadistic games . . . enjoying himself, perhaps.

"There's no use telephoning him," Doreen said. "He never says anything on the phone. We'll have to go over to his place. I want to go along; please let me."

"O.K.," he said, going to the closet to get his coat. "Let's go," he said to her.

fourteen

AT TWO O'CLOCK in the afternoon Otto Zitte poked his head out the side door of the Bohlen house and ascertained that no one was watching. He could leave safely, Silvia Bohlen realized, as she saw what he was doing.

What have I done? she asked herself as she stood in the middle of the bedroom clumsily buttoning her blouse. How can I expect to keep it secret? Even if Mrs. Steiner doesn't see him, he'll surely tell that June Henessy, and she'll blab it to everybody along the William Butler Yeats; she loves gossip. I know Jack will find out. And Leo might have come home early—

But it was too late now. Over and done with. Otto was gathering up his suitcases, preparing to depart.

I wish I was dead, she said to herself.

"Goodbye, Silvia," Otto said hurriedly as he started toward the front door, "I will call you."

She did not answer; she concentrated on putting on her shoes.

"Aren't you going to say goodbye?" he asked, pausing at the bedroom door.

Shooting a glance at him she said, "No. And get out of here. Don't ever come back—I hate you, I really do."

He shrugged. "Why?"

"Because," she said, with perfect logic, "you're a horrible person. I never had anything to do with a person like you before. I must be out of my mind, it must be the loneliness."

He seemed genuinely hurt. Flushed red, he hung around at the doorway of the bedroom. "It was as much your idea as mine," he mumbled finally, glaring at her.

"Go away," she said, turning her back to him.

At last the front door opened and shut. He had gone.

Never, never again, Silvia said to herself. She went to the

184

medicine cabinet in the bathroom and got down her bottle of phenobarbital; hastily pouring herself a glass of water, she took 150 milligrams, gulping them down and gasping.

I shouldn't have been so mean to him, she realized in a flash of conscience. It wasn't fair; it wasn't really his fault, it was mine. If I'm no good, why blame him? If it hadn't been him it would have been someone else, sooner or later.

She thought, *Will he ever come back?* Or have I driven him off forever? Already she felt lonely, unhappy and completely at a loss once more, as if she were doomed to drift in a hopeless vacuum for ever and ever.

He was actually very nice, she decide. Gentle and considerate. I could have done a lot worse.

Going into the kitchen, she seated herself at the table, picked up the telephone, and dialed June Henessy's number.

Presently June's voice sounded in her ear. "Hello?"

Silvia said, "Guess what."

"Tell me."

"Wait'll I light a cigarette." Silvia Bohlen lit a cigarette, got an ashtray, moved her chair so that she was comfortable, and then, with an infinitude of detail, plus a little essential invention at critical points, she told her.

To her surprise she found the telling to be as enjoyable as the experience itself·

Perhaps even a bit more so.

Flying back across the desert to his base in the F.D.R. Mountains, Otto Zitte ruminated on his assignation with Mrs. Bohlen and congratulated himself; he was in a good mood, despite Silvia's not unnatural fit of remorse and accusation just as he was leaving.

You have to expect that, he advised himself.

It had happened before; true, it always upset him, but that was one of the odd little tricks typical of a woman's mind: there always came a point when they had to sidestep reality and start casting blame in all directions, toward anyone and anything handy.

He did not much care; nothing could rob him of the memory of the happy time which the two of them had engaged in.

So now what? Back to the field to have lunch, rest up, shave, shower and change his clothes. . . . There would still be time enough to start out once more on an authentic selling trip with nothing else in mind this time but pure business itself.

Already, he could see the ragged peaks of the mountains ahead; he would soon be there.

It seemed to him that he saw a plume of ugly gray smoke drifting up from the mountains directly ahead.

Frightened, he stepped up the velocity of the 'copter. No doubt of it; the smoke rose at or near his field. They found me! he said to himself with a sob. The UN—they wiped me out and they're waiting for me. But he went on anyhow; he had to know for sure.

Below lay the remains of his field. A smoking, rubble-strewn ruin. He circled aimlessly, crying openly, tears spilling down his cheeks. There was no sign of the UN, however, no military vehicles or soldiers.

Could an incoming rocket have exploded?

Quickly, Otto landed the 'copter; on foot he ran across the hot ground, toward the debris that had been his storage shed.

As he reached the signal tower of the field he saw, pinned to it, a square of cardboard.

ARNIE KOTT DOESN'T LIKE WHAT YOU STAND FOR

Again and again he read it, trying to understand it. Arnie Kott—he was just getting ready to call on him—Arnie had been Norb's best customer. What did this mean? Had he already provided poor service to Arnie, or how else had he made Arnie mad? It didn't make sense—what had he done to Arnie Kott to deserve this?

Why? Otto asked. What did I do to you? Why have you destroyed me?

Presently he made his way over to the shed, hoping beyond hope that some of the stocks could be salvaged, hoping to find something among the remains. . . .

There were no remains. The stock had been taken; he saw no single can, glass jar, package, or bag. The litter of the building itself, yes, but only that. Then they—those who had dropped the bomb—had come in first and pilfered the stock.

You bombed me, Arnie Kott, and you stole my goods, Otto said, as he wandered in a circle, clenching and unclenching his fists and darting glances of rage and frenzy up at the sky.

And still he did not understand why.

There has to be a reason, he said to himself. And I will find it out; I will not rest, goddamn you, Arnie Kott, until I know. And when I find out I will get you. I will pay you back for what you did.

He blew his nose, snuffled, dragged himself back to his 'copter with slow steps, seated himself inside, and stared ahead for a long, long time.

At last he opened one of the suitcases. From it he took the .22-caliber pistol; he sat holding it on his lap, thinking about Arnie Kott.

To Arnie Kott, Heliogabalus said, "Mister, excuse me for disturbing you. But if you are ready I will explain to you what you must do."

Delighted, Arnie stopped at his desk. "Fire away."

With a sad and haughty expression on his face, Helio said, "You must take Manfred out into the desert and cross, on foot, to the Franklin Delano Roosevelt Mountains. There your pilgrimage must end when you bring the boy to Dirty Knobby, the Rock which is sacred to the Bleekmen. Your answer lies there, when you have introduced the boy to Dirty Knobby."

Wagging his finger at the tame Bleekman, Arnie said slyly, "And you told me it was a fraud." He had felt all the time that there was something to the Bleekman religion. Helio had tried to deceive him.

"At the sanctuary of the rock you must commune. The spirit which animates Dirty Knobby will receive your collective psyches and perhaps if it is merciful, it will grant what you request." Helio added, "It is in actuality the capacity within the boy which you must depend on. The rock alone is powerless. However, it is as follows: time is weakest at that spot where Dirty Knobby lies. Upon that fact the Bleekman has prevailed for centuries."

"I see," Arnie said. "A sort of puncture in time. And you guys get at the future through it. Well, it's the past I'm interested in, now, and frankly this all sounds fishy to me. But I'll try it. You've told me so many different yarns about that rock—"

Helio said, "What I said before is true. Alone, Dirty Knobby could have done nothing for you." He did not cringe; he met Arnie's gaze.

"You think Manfred will cooperate?"

"I have told him of the rock and he is excited at the idea of seeing it. I said that, in that place, one might escape backward into the past. That idea enthralls him. However—" Helio paused. "You must repay the boy for his effort."

"You can offer him something of priceless value.... Mister, you can banish the specter of AM-WEB from his life forever. Promise him that you will send him back to Earth. Then no matter what becomes of him, he will never see the interior of that abominable building. If you do that for him, he will turn all his mental powers in your behalf."

"It sounds fine to me," Arnie said.

"And you will not fail the boy."

"Oh, heck, no," Arnie promised. "I'll make all the arrangements with the UN right away—it's complicated, but I got lawyers who can handle stuff like that without even half trying."

"Good," Helio said, nodding. "It would be foul to let the boy down. If you could for a moment experience his terrible anxiety about his future life in that place—"

"Yeah, it sounds awful," Arnie agreed.

"What a shame it would be," Helio said, eying him, "if you yourself did ever have to endure that."

"Where is Manfred right now?"

"He is walking about the streets of Lewistown," Helio said. "Taking in the sights."

"Cripes, is it safe?"

"I think so," Helio said. "He is much excited by the people and stores and activity; it is all new to him."

"You sure have helped that kid," Arnie said.

The door chimes sounded, and Helio went to answer. When Arnie looked up, there stood Jack Bohlen and Doreen Anderton, both of them with fixed, high-strung expressions.

"Oh, hi," Arnie said, preoccupied. "Come on in; I was about to call you, Jack. Listen, I got a job for you."

Jack Bohlen said, "Why did you buy my contract from Mr. Yee?"

"Because I need you," Arnie said. "I'll tell you why right now. I'm going on a pilgrimage with Manfred and I want somebody to circle around overhead so we don't get lost and die of thirst. We got to walk across the desert to the F.D.R. Mountains; isn't that right, Helio?"

"Yes, Mister," Helio said.

"I want to get started right away," Arnie explained. "I figure it's about a five-day hike. We'll take a portable communications rig with us so we can notify you when we need something like food or water. At night you can land the

188

'copter and pitch a tent for us to sleep in. Make sure you get medical supplies on board in case either Manfred or I get bit by a desert animal; I hear there's Martian snakes and rats running around wild out there." He examined his watch. "It's three now; I'd like to get started by four and get in maybe five hours tonight."

"What's the purpose of this—pilgrimage?" Doreen asked presently.

"I got business out there to attend to," Arnie said. "Out among those desert Bleekman. Private business. Are you coming along in the 'copter? If so you better put on something different, maybe boots and heavy pants, because it's always possible you fellas might get forced down. That's a long time, five days, to keep circling. Make sure in particular about the water."

Doreen and Jack looked at each other.

"I'm serious," Arnie said. "So let's not stop to mess around. O.K?"

"As far as I can tell," Jack said to Doreen, "I have no choice. I have to do what he tells me."

"That's the truth, buddy," Arnie agreed. "So start rounding up the equipment we'll need. Portable stove to cook on, portable light, portable bathroom, food and soap and towels, a gun of some sort. You know what we'll need; you've been living on the edge of the desert."

Jack nodded slowly.

"What is this business?" Doreen said. "And why do you have to walk? If you have to go there, why can't you fly as you usually do?"

"I just have to walk," Arnie said with irritation. "That's the way it is; it wasn't my idea." To Helio he said, "I can fly back, can't I?"

"Yes, Mister," Helio said. "You may return any way you prefer."

"It's a good thing I'm in top-notch physical shape," Arnie said, "or this would be out of the question. I hope Manfred can make it."

"He is quite strong, Mister," Helio said.

"You're taking the boy," Jack murmured.

"That's right," Arnie said. "Any objections?"

Jack Bohlen did not answer, but he looked more grim than ever. Suddenly he burst out, "You can't make the boy walk for five days across the desert—it'll kill him."

"Why can't you go in some surface vehicle?" Doreen asked.

"One of those little tractor-jitneys that the UN post office people use to deliver the mail. It would still take a long time; it would still be a pilgrimage."

"What about that?" Arnie said to Helio.

After some reflection, the Bleekman said, "I suppose that little cart of which you speak would do."

"Fine," Arnie said, deciding then and there. "I'll phone a couple of guys I know and pick up one of those PO jitneys. That's a good idea you gave me, Doreen; I appreciate it. Of course, you two still have to be there overhead to make sure we don't break down."

Both Jack and Doreen nodded.

"Maybe when I get there, where I'm going," Arnie said, "you'll maybe find out what I'm up to." In fact you darn well are going to, he said to himself; there's no doubt about that.

"This is all very strange," Doreen said; she stood close to Jack Bohlen, holding on to his arm.

"Don't blame me," Arnie said. "Blame Helio." He grinned.

"That is true," Helio said. "It was my idea."

But their expressions remained.

"Talked to your dad yet today?" Arnie asked Jack.

"Yes. Briefly, on the phone."

"His claim filed now, all recorded? No hitches?"

Jack said, "He says it was processed properly. He's preparing to return to Earth."

"Efficient operation," Arnie said. "I admire that. Shows up here on Mars, stakes out his claim, goes to the abstract office and records it, then flies back. Not bad."

"What are you up to, Arnie?" Jack said in a quiet voice.

Arnie shrugged. "I got this holy pilgrimage to make, along with Manfred. That's all." He was, however, still grinning; he could not help it. He could not stop, and he did not bother to try.

Use of the UN post office jitney cut the proposed pilgrimage from Lewistown to Dirty Knobby from five days to a mere eight hours; or so Arnie calculated. Nothing to do now but go, he said to himself as he paced about his living room.

Outside the building, at the curb, Helio sat in the parked jitney with Manfred. Through the window Arnie could see them, far below. He got his gun from his desk drawer, strapped it on inside his coat, locked up the desk, and hurried out into the hall.

A moment later he emereged on the sidewalk and made for the jitney.

"Here we go," he said to Manfred. Helio stepped from the jitney, and Arnie seated himself behind the tiller. He revved up the tiny turbine engine; it made a noise like a bumblebee in a bottle. "Sounds good," he said heartily. "So long, Helio. If this goes off O.K., there's a reward for you—remember that."

"I expect no reward," Helio said. "I am only doing my duty by you, Mister; I would do it for anyone."

Releasing the parking brake, Arnie pulled out into downtown Lewistown late-afternoon traffic. They were on their way. Overhead, Jack Bohlen and Doreen were no doubt cruising in the 'copter; Arnie did not bother to search for sign of them, taking it for granted that they were there. He waved goodbye to Helio, and then a huge tractor-bus filled in all the space behind the jitney; Helio was cut off from view.

"How about this, Manfred?" Arnie said, as he guided the jitney toward the perimeter of Lewistown and the desert beyond. "Isn't this something? It makes almost fifty miles an hour, and that isn't hay."

The boy did not respond, but his body trembled with excitement.

"This is the nuts," Arnie declared, in answer to his own query.

They had almost left Lewistown when Arnie became aware of a car which had pulled up beside them and was proceeding at the same speed as theirs. He saw, within the car, two figures, a man and a woman; at first he thought it was Jack and Doreen, and then he discovered that the woman was his ex-wife Anne Esterhazy and the man was Dr. Milton Glaub.

What the hell do they want? Arnie wondered. Can't they see I'm busy, I can't be bothered, whatever it is?

"Kott," Dr. Glaub yelled, "pull over to the curb so we can talk to you! This is vital!"

"The hell," Arnie said, increasing the speed of the jitney. He felt with his left hand for his gun. "I got nothing to say, and what are you two doing in cahoots?" He didn't like the look of it one bit. Just like them to gang up, he said to himself. I should have expected it. Snapping on the portable communications rig, he put in a call to his steward, Eddy Goggins at Union Hall. "This is Arnie. My gyrocompass point is 8.

45702, right at the edge of town. Get over here quick—I got a party that has to be took care of. Make it fast, they're gaining on me." They had, in fact, never fallen behind; it was easy for them to match the speed of the little jitney, and even to exceed it.

"Will do, Arnie," Eddy Goggins said. I'll send some of the boys on the double; don't worry."

Now the car edged ahead and drew toward the curb. Arnie reluctantly slowed the jitney to a stop. The car placed itself in a position to block escape, and then Glaub jumped from it and scuttled up crablike to the jitney, waving his arms.

"This ends your career of bullying and domineering," he shouted at Arnie.

Kee-rist, Arnie thought. At a time like this. "What do you want?" he said. "Make it snappy; I got business."

"Leave Jack Bohlen alone," Dr. Glaub panted. "I represent him, and he needs rest and quiet. You'll have to deal with me."

From the car Anne Esterhazy emerged; she approached the jitney and confronted Arnie. "As I understand the situation—" she began.

"You understand nothin'," Arnie said, with venom. "Let me by, or I'll take care of both of you."

Overhead, a 'copter with the Water Workers' Union marking on it appeared and began to descend; it was Jack and Doreen, Arnie guessed. And behind it came a second 'copter at tremendous speed; that no doubt was Eddy and the Goodmembers. Both 'copters prepared to land close by.

Anne Esterhazy said, "Arnie, I know that something bad is going to happen to you if you don't stop what you're doing."

"To me? he said, amused and incredulous.

"I feel it. Please, Arnie. Whatever it is you're up to—think twice. There's so much good in the world; must you have your revenge?"

"Go back to New Israel and tend your goddamn store." He fast-idled the motor of the jitney.

"That boy," Anne said. "That's Manfred Steiner, isn't it? Let Milton take him back to Camp B-G; it's better for everyone, better for him and for you."

One of the 'copters had landed. From it hopped three or four WWU men; they came running up the street, and Dr. Glaub, seeing them, plucked dolefully at Anne's sleeve.

"I see them." She remained unruffled. "Please, Arnie. You and I have worked together so often, on so many worthwhile things . . . for my sake, for Sam's sake—if you go ahead with this, I know you and I will never be together again in any way whatever. Can't you feel that? Is this so important as all that, to lose so much?"

Arnie said nothing.

Puffing, Eddy Goggins appeared beside the jitney. The union men fanned out toward Anne Esterhazy and Dr. Glaub. Now the other 'copter had landed, and from it stepped Jack Bohlen.

"Ask him," Arnie said. "He's coming of his own free will; he's a grown man, he knows what he's doing. Ask him if he isn't voluntarily coming along on this pilgrimage."

As Glaub and Anne Esterhazy turned toward Jack, Arnie Kott backed up the jitney; he shifted into forward and shot around the side of the parked car. A scuffle broke out, as Glaub tried to get back into the car; two Goodmembers grabbed him and they wrestled. Arnie steered the jitney straight ahead, and the car and the people fell behind.

"Here we go," he said to Manfred.

Ahead, the street became a vague level strip passing from the city out onto the desert, in the direction of the hills far beyond. The jitney bumped along at near top speed, and Arnie smiled. Beside him the boy's face shone with excitement.

Nobody can stop me, Arnie said to himself.

The sounds of the squabble faded from his ears; he heard now only the buzz of the tiny turbine of the jitney. He settled back.

Dirty Knobby, get ready, he said to himself. And then he thought of Jack Bohlen's magic charm, the water witch which Helio said the man had on him, and Arnie frowned. But the frown was momentary. He did not slow down.

Beside him Manfred crowed excitedly, "Gubble gubble!"

"What's that mean, gubble gubble?" Arnie asked.

There was no answer, as the two of them bounced along in the UN post office jitney toward the F.D.R. Mountains directly ahead.

Maybe I'll find out what it means when we get there, Arnie said to himself. I'd like to know. For some reason the sounds which the boy made, the unintelligible words, made him nervous, more so than anything else. He wished suddenly that Helio was along.

"Gubble gubble!" Manfred cried as they sped along.

fifteen

THE BLACK, LOPSIDED projection of sandstone and volcanic glass which was Dirty Knobby poked up huge and gaunt ahead of them in the glow of early morning. They had spent the night on the desert, in a tent, the 'copter parked close by. Jack Bohlen and Doreen Anderton had exchanged no words with them; at dawn the 'copter had taken off to circle overhead. Arnie and the boy Manfred Steiner had eaten a good breakfast and then packed up and resumed their trip.

Now the trip, the pilgrimage to the sacred rock of the Bleekmen, was over.

Seeing Dirty Knobby close up like this, Arnie thought, There's the place that'll cure us all of whatever ails us. Letting Manfred take the tiller of the jitney, he consulted the map which Heliogabalus had drawn. It showed the path up into the range to the rock. There was, Helio had told him, a hollowed-out chamber on the north side of the rock, where a Bleekman priest could generally be found. Unless, Arnie said to himself, he's off somewhere sleeping off a binge. He knew the Bleekmen priests; they were old winos, for the most part. Even the Bleekmen had contempt for them.

At the base of the first hill, in the shadows, he parked the jitney and shut off its engine. "From here we climb on foot," he said to Manfred. "We'll carry as much gear as we can, food and water naturally, and the communications rig, and I guess if we need to cook we can come back for the stove. It's only supposed to be a few more miles."

The boy hopped from the jitney. He and Arnie unloaded the gear, and soon they were trudging up a rocky trail, into the F.D.R. range.

Glancing about with apprehension, Manfred huddled and shivered. Perhaps the boy was experiencing AM-WEB once more. Arnie conjectured. The Henry Wallace was only a hundred miles from here. The boy might well have picked up the emanations of the structure to come, close as they were, now. In fact he could almost feel them himself.

Or was it the rock of the Bleekmen which he felt?

He did not like the sight of it. Why make a shrine out of this? he asked himself. Perverse—this arid place. But maybe a long time ago this region had been fertile. Evidence of one-time Bleekmen camps could be made out along the path. Maybe the Martians had originated here; the land certainly had an old, used appearance. As if, he thought, a million gray-black creatures had handled all this throughout the ages. And now what was it? A last remains for a dying race. A relic for those who were not going to be around much longer.

Wheezing from the exertion of climbing with a heavy load, Arnie halted. Manfred toiled up the steep acclivity after him, still casting anxiety-stricken looks around.

"Don't worry," Arnie said encouragingly. "There's nothing here to be scared of." Was the boy's talent already blending with that of the rock? And, he wondered, had the rock itself become apprehensive, too? Was it capable of that?

The trail leveled out and became wider. And all was in shadow; cold and damp hung over everything, as if they were treading within a great tomb. The vegetation that grew thin and noxious along the surface of rocks had a dead quality to it, as if something had poisoned it in its act of growing. Ahead lay a dead bird on the path, a rotten corpse that might have been there for weeks; he could not tell. It had a mummified appearance.

I sure don't enjoy this place, Arnie said to himself.

Halting at the bird, Manfred bent down and said, "Gubbish."

"Yeah," Arnie murmured. "Come on, let's go."

They arrived all at once at the base of the rock.

Wind rustled the leaves of vegetation, the shrubs which looked as if they had been skinned down to their elements: bare and picked over, like bones stuck upright in the soil. The wind emerged from a crack in Dirty Knobby and it smelled, he thought, as if some sort of animal lived there. Maybe the priest himself; he saw with no real surprise an empty wine bottle lying off to one side, with other bits of debris caught on the sharp foliage nearby.

"Anybody around?" Arnie called.

After a long time an old man, a Bleekman, gray as if

195

wrapped in webs, edged out of the chamber within the rock. The wind seemed to blow him along, so that he crept sideways, pausing against the side of the cavity and then stirring forward once more. His eyes were red-rimmed.

"You old drunk," Arnie said in a low voice. And then from a piece of paper Helio had given him he greeted the old man in Bleeky.

The priest mumbled a toothless, mechanical response.

"Here." Arnie held out a carton of cigarettes. The priest, mumbling, sidled forward and took the carton in his claws; he tucked the carton beneath his gray-webbed robes. "You like that, huh?" Arnie said. "I thought you would."

From the piece of paper he read, in Bleeky, the purpose of his visit and what he wanted the priest to do. He wanted the priest to leave him and Manfred in peace for an hour or so, at the chamber, so that they could summon the spirit of the rock.

Still mumbling, the priest backed away, fussed with the hem of his robes, then turned and shambled off. He disappeared down a side trail without a backward look at Arnie and Manfred.

Arnie turned the paper over and read the instructions that Helio had written out.

(1) Enter chamber.

Taking Manfred by the arm, he led him step by step into the dark cleft of the rock; flashing on his light, he led the boy along until the chamber became large. It still smelled bad, he thought, as if it had been kept closed up for centuries. Like an old box full of decayed rags, a vegetable rather than animal scent.

Now what? Again he consulted Helio's paper.

(2) Light fire.

An uneven ring of boulders surrounded a blackened pit in which lay fragments of wood and what appeared to be bones. . . . It looked as if the old wino fixed his meals here.

In his pack Arnie had kindling; he got it out now, laying the pack on the floor of the cavern and fumbling stiff-fingered with the straps. "Don't get lost, kid," he said to Manfred. I wonder if we're ever coming out of here again? he asked himself.

Both of them felt better, however, when the fire had been lit. The cavern became warmer, but not dry; the smell of mold persisted and even seemed to become stronger, as if the fire were attracting it, whatever it was.

The next instruction bewildered him; it did not seem to fit in, but nonetheless he complied.

(3) Turn on portable radio to 574 kc.

Arnie got out the little Japanese-made transistor portable and turned it on. At 574 kc. nothing but static issued forth. It seemed, though, to obtain a response from the rock around them; the rock seemed to change and become more alert, as if the noise from the radio had awakened it to their presence. The next instruction was equally annoying.

(4) Take Nembutal (boy not take).

Using the canteen, Arnie swallowed the Nembutal down, wondering if its purpose was to blur his senses and make him credulous. Or was it to stifle his anxiety?

Only one instruction remained.

(5) Throw enclosed packet on fire.

Helio had put into Arnie's pack a small paper, a wadded-up page from the New York Times, with some kind of grass within it. Kneeling by the fire, Arnie carefully unwrapped the packet and dumped the dark, dry strands into the flames. A nauseating smell arose and the flames died down. Smoke billowed out, filling the chamber; he heard Manfred cough. Goddamn, Arnie thought, it'll kill us yet if we keep on.

The smoke disappeared almost at once. The cavern seemed now dark and empty and much larger than before, as if the rock around them had receded. He felt, all at once, as if he were going to fall; he seemed no longer to be standing precisely upright. Sense of balance gone, he realized. Nothing to use as bearing.

"Manfred," he said, "now listen. On account of me you don't have to worry about that AM-WEB any more, like Helio explained. You got that? O.K. Now regress back around three weeks. Can you do that? Really put your back into it, try hard as you can."

In the gloom the boy peeped at him, eyes wide with fear.

"Back to before I knew Jack Bohlen," Arnie said. "Before I met him out on the desert that day those Bleekmen were dying of thirst. You get it?" He walked toward the boy—

He fell flat on his face.

The Nembutal, he thought. Better get back up before I pass out entirely. He struggled up, groping for something to catch on to. Light flared, searing him; he put his hands . . . and then he was in water. Warm water poured over him, over his face; he spluttered, choked, saw around him billowing steam, felt beneath his feet familiar tile.

He was in his steam bath.

Voices of men conversing. Eddy's voice, saying, "Right, Arnie." Then the outline of shapes around him, other men taking showers.

Down inside him, near his groin, his duodenal ulcer began to burn and he realized that he was terribly hungry. He stepped from the shower and with weak, unwilling legs padded across the warm, wet tiles, searching for the attendant so that he could get his great terrycloth bathtowel.

I been here before, he thought. I've done all this, said what I'm going to say; it's uncanny. What do they call it? French word . . .

Better get some breakfast. His stomach rumbled and the ulcer pain increased.

"Hey, Tom," he called to the attendant. "Dry me off and get me dressed so I can go eat; my ulcer's killing me." He had never felt such pain from it before.

"Right, Arnie," the attendant said, stepping toward him, holding out the huge soft white towel.

When he had been dressed by the attendant, in his gray flannel trousers and T-shirt, soft leather boots, and nautical cap, Goodmember Arnie Kott left the steam bath and crossed the corridor of the Union Hall to his dining room, where Heliogabalus had his breakfast waiting.

At last he sat before a stack of hotcakes and bacon, genuine Home coffee, a glass of orange juice from New Israel oranges, and the previous week's New York Times, the Sunday edition.

He trembled with consternation as he reached to pick up the glass of chilled, strained, sweet orange juice; the glass was slippery and smooth to the touch and almost eluded him in mid-trip. . . . He thought, I have to be careful, slow down and take it easy. *It's really so; I'm back here where I was, several weeks ago. Manfred and the rock of the Bleekmen*

198

did it together. Wow, he thought, his mind a hubbub of anticipation. This is something! He sipped at the orange juice, enjoying each swallow of it until the glass had been emptied.

I got what I wanted, he said to himself.

Now, I have to be careful, he told himself; there are some things I sure don't want to change. I want to be sure I don't foul up my black-market business by doing the natural thing and interfering so that old Norb Steiner doesn't take his own life. I mean, it's sad about him, but I don't intend to get out of the business; so that stays as it is. As it's going to be, he corrected himself.

Mainly I got two things to do. First, I see that I get a legal deed to land in the F.D.R. range all around the Henry Wallace area, and that deed'll predate old man Bohlen's deed by several weeks. So the hell with the old speculator, flying out here from Earth. When he does come, weeks from now, he'll discover the land's been bought. Trip all the way here and back for nothing. Maybe he'll have a heart attack. Arnie chuckled, thinking about that. Too bad.

And then the other thing. Jack Bohlen himself.

I'm going to fix him, he said to himself, a guy I haven't met yet, that doesn't know me, although I know him.

What I am to Jack Bohlen now is fate.

"Good morning, Mr. Kott."

Annoyed at having his meditation interrupted, he glanced up and saw that a girl had entered the room and was standing by his desk expectantly. He did not recognize her. A girl from the secretary pool, he realized, come to take the morning's dictation.

"Call me Arnie," he muttered. "Everybody's supposed to call me that. How come you didn't know, you new around here?"

The girl, he thought, was not too good-looking, and he returned to his newspaper. But on the other hand, she had a heavy, full figure. The black silk dress she wore: there isn't much on under that, he said to himself as he observed her around the side of the newspaper. Not married; he saw no wedding ring on her finger.

"Come over here," he said. "You scared of me because I'm the famous great Arnie Kott, in charge of this whole place?"

The girl approached in a luxuriant sidling motion that surprised him; she seemed to creep sideways over to the desk. And in an insinuating, hoarse voice, she said, "No, Arnie, I'm not scared of you." Her blunt stare did not seem to be one of innocence; on the contrary, its implied knowledge jolted him. It seemed to him as if she were conscious of every whim and urge in him, especially those that applied to her.

"You been working here long?" he asked.

"No, Arnie." She moved closer, now, and rested against the edge of the desk so that one leg—he could hardly believe it—gradually came in to contact with his own.

Methodically, her leg undulated against his own in a simple, reflexive, rhythmic way that made him recoil and say weakly, "Hey."

"What's the matter, Arnie?" the girl said, and smiled. It was a smile like nothing he had ever seen in his life before, cold and yet full of intimation; utterly without warmth, as if a machine had stamped it there, constructed it by pattern out of lips, teeth, tongue . . . and yet it swamped him with its sensuality. It poured forth a saturated, sopping heat that made him sit rigid in his chair, unable to look away. Mostly it was the tongue, he thought. It vibrated. The end, he noticed, had a pointed quality, as if it was good at cutting; a tongue that could hurt, that enjoyed slitting into something alive, tormenting it, and making it beg for mercy. That was the part it liked most: to hear the pleas. The teeth, too, white and sharp . . . made for rending.

He shivered.

"Do I bother you, Arnie?" the girl murmured. She had, by degrees, slid her body along the desk so that now—he could not understand how it had been accomplished—she rested alomst entirely against him. My God, he thought, she's —it was impossible.

"Listen," he said, swallowing and finding his throat dry; he could hardly croak out the words. "Get going and let me read my newspaper." Grabbing up the paper he held it between himself and her. "Go on," he said gratingly.

The shape ebbed a little. "What's the matter, Arnie?" her voice purred, like metal wheels rubbing, an automatic sound coming forth from her, like on a recording, he thought.

He said nothing; he gripped his paper and read.

When he next looked up the girl had gone. He was alone. *I don't remember that,* he said to himself, quaking inside, down deep within his stomach. What kind of a creature was that? I don't get it—what was happening, just then?

He began automatically to read an item in the paper about a ship which had been lost in deep space, a freighter from

Japan carrying a cargo of bicycles. He felt amused, even though three hundred people aboard had perished; it was just too goddamn funny, the idea of all those thousands of little light Jap bikes floating as debris, circling the sun forever. . . . Not that they weren't needed on Mars, with its virtual lack of power sources . . . a man could pedal free of cost for hundreds of miles in the planet's slight gravity.

Reading further, he came across an item about a reception at the White House for—he squinted. The words seemed to run together; he could hardly read them. Printing error of some kind? What did it say? He held the newspaper closer. . . .

Gubble gubble, it said. The article became meaningless, nothing but the gubble-gubble words one after another. Good grief! He stared at it in disgust, his stomach reacting; his duodenal ulcer hurt worse than ever now. He had become tense and angry, the worst possible combination for an ulcer patient, especially at meal time. Darn those gubble-gubble words, he said to himself. That's what that kid says! They sure spoil the article in the paper.

Glancing through the paper he saw that almost all the articles devolved into nonsense, became blurred after a line or so. His irritation grew, and he tossed the paper away. What the hell good is it like that he asked himself.

That's that schizophrenia talk, he realized, Private language. I don't like that here at all! it's O.K. if he wants to talk like that himself, but it doesn't belong here! He's got no right to push that stuff into my world. And then Arnie thought, Of course, he did bring me back here, so maybe he thinks that does give him the right. Maybe the boy thinks of this as his world.

That thought did not please Arnie; he wished it had never come to him.

Getting up from his desk he went over to the window and looked down at the street of Lewistown far below. People hurrying along; how fast they went. And the cars, too; why so fast? There was an unpleasant kinetic quality to their movements, a jerkiness, they seemed either to bang into one another or to be about to. Colliding objects like billiard balls, hard and dangerous . . . the buildings, he noticed, seemed to bristle with sharp corners. And yet, when he tried to pinpoint the change—and it was a change, no doubt of that—he could not. This was the familiar scene he saw every day. And yet—

Were they moving too fast? Was that it? No, it was deeper than that. There was an omnipresent *hostility* in everything;

things did not merely collide—they struck one another, as if doing it deliberately.

And then he saw something else, something which made him gasp. The people on the street below, hurrying back and forth, had almost no faces, just fragments or remnants of faces . . . as if they had never formed.

Aw, this will never do, Arnie said to himself. He felt fear now, deeply and intensely. What's going on? What are they handing me?

He returned, shaken, to his desk and sat down again. Picking up his cup of coffee, he drank, trying to forget the scene below, trying to resume his routine of the morning.

The coffee had a bitter, acrid, foreign taste to it, and he had to set the cup back down at once. I suppose the kid imagines all the time he's being poisoned, Arnie thought in desperation. Is that it? I got to find myself eating awful-tasting food because of his delusions? God, he thought; that's terrible.

Best thing for me, he decided, is to get my task here done as fast as possible and then get back to the present.

Unlocking the bottom drawer of his desk, Arnie got out the little battery-powered encoding dictation machine and set it up for use. Into it he said, "Scott, I got a terribly important item here to transmit to you. I insist you act on this at once. What I want to do is buy into the F.D.R. Mountains because the UN is going to establish a gigantic housing tract area there, specifically around the Henry Wallace Canyon. Now you transfer enough Union funds, in my name of course, to insure that I get title to all that, because in about two weeks speculators from—"

He broke off, for the encoding machine had groaned to a stop. He poked at it, and the reels turned slowly and then once more settled back into silence.

Thought it was fixed, Arnie thought angrily. Didn't that Jack Bohlen work on it? And then he remembered that this was back in the past before Jack Bohlen had been called in; of course it didn't work.

I've got to dictate it to the secretary-creature, he realized. He started to press the button on his desk that would summon her, but drew back. How can I let that back in here? he asked himself. But there was no alternative. He pressed the button.

The door opened and she came in. "I knew you would want me, Arnie," she said, hurrying toward him, strutting and urgent.

"Listen," he said, with authority in his voice. "Don't get

too close to me, I can't stand it when people get too close."
But even as he spoke he recognized his fears for what they
were; it was a basic fear of the schizophrenic that people
might get too close to him, might encroach into his space.
Nearness fear, it was called; it was due to the schizophrenic's
sensing hostility in everyone around him. That's what I'm
doing, Arnie thought. And yet, even knowing this, he could
not endure having the girl come close to him; he got abruptly
to his feet and walked away, back once more to the window.

"Anything you say, Arnie," the girl said, in a tone that was
insatiable, and despite what she said she crept toward him
until, as before, she was almost touching him. He found
himself hearing the noises of her breathing, smelling her, the
sour body scent, her breath, which was thick and unpleasant. . . . He felt choked, unable to get enough air into his
lungs.

"I'm going to dictate to you now," he said, walking away
from her, keeping distance between the two of them. "This
is to Scott Temple, and should go in code so they can't read
it." They, he thought. Well, that had always been his fear;
he couldn't blame that on the boy. "I got a terribly important
item here," he dictated. "Act on it at once; it means plenty,
it's a real inside tip. The UN's going to buy a huge hunk of
land in the F.D.R. Mountains—"

On and on he dictated, and even as he talked a fear as-
sailed him, an obsessive fear that grew each moment. Suppose
she was just writing down those gubble-gubble words? I just
got to look, he told himself; I got to walk over close to her
and see. But he shrank from it, the closeness.

"Listen, miss," he said, interrupting himself. "Give me that
pad of yours; I want to see what you're writing."

"Arnie," she said in her rough, dragging voice, "you can't
tell anything by looking at it."

"W-what?" he demanded in fright.

"It's in shorthand." She smiled at him, coldly, with what
seemed to him palpable malevolence.

"O.K.," he said, giving up. He went on and completed his
dictation, then told her to get it into code and off to Scott at
once.

"And what then?" she said.

"What do you mean?"

"You know, Arnie," she said, and the tone in which she
said it made him cringe with dismay and pure physical disgust.

"Nothing after that," he said. "Just get out; don't come

back." Following after her, he slammed the door shut behind her.

I guess, he decided, I'll have to contact Scott direct; I can't trust her. Seating himself at the desk he picked up the telephone and dialed.

Presently the line was ringing. But it rang in vain; there was no response. Why? he wondered. Has he run out on me? Is he against me? Working with them? I can't trust him; I can't trust anybody. And then, all at once, a voice said, "Hello. Scott Temple speaking." And he realized that only a few seconds and a few rings had actually gone by; all those thoughts of betrayal, of doom, had flitted through his mind in an instant.

"This is Arnie."

"Hi, Arnie. What's up? I can tell by your tone something's cooking. Spill it."

My sense of time is fouled up, Arnie realized. It seemed to me the phone rang for half an hour, but it wasn't at all.

"Arnie," Scott was saying. "Speak up. Arnie you there?"

It's the schizophrenic confusion, Arnie realized. It's basically a breakdown in time-sense. Now I'm getting it because that kid has it.

"Chrissake!" Scott said, outraged.

With difficulty, Arnie broke his chain of thought and said, "Uh, Scott. Listen. I got an inside scoop; we have to act on this right now, you understand?" In detail, he told Scott about the UN and the F.D.R. Mountain. "So you can see," he wound up, "it's worth it to us to buy in with all we got, and pronto. You agree?"

"You're sure of this scoop?" Scott said.

"Year, I am! I am!"

"How come? Frankly, Arnie, I like you, but I know you get crazy schemes, you're always flying off at a tangent. I'd hate to get stuck with that dog's breakfast F.D.R. land."

Arnie said, "Take my word for it."

"I can't."

He could not belive his ears. "We been working together for years, and it's always been on a word-of-mouth confidence basis," he choked. "What's going on, Scott?"

"That's what I'm asking you," Scott said calmly. "How come a man of your business experience could bite on this phony nothing so-called scoop? The scoop is that the F.D.R. range is worthless, and you know it; I know you know it. rybody knows it. So what are you up to?"

"You don't *trust* me?"

"Why should I *trust* you? *Prove* you got real inside scoop stuff here, and not just your usual hot air."

With difficulty, Arnie said, "Hell, man, if I could prove it, you wouldn't have to trust me; it wouldn't involve trust. O.K. I'll go into this alone, and when you find out what you missed, blame yourself, not me." He slammed down the phone, shaking with rage and despair. What a thing to happen! He couldn't believe it; Scott Temple, the one person in the world he could do business with over the phone. The rest of them you could throw in the ocean, they were such crooks. . . .

It's a misunderstanding, he told himself. But based on a deep, fundamental, insidious distrust. A schizophrenic distrust.

A collapse, he realized, of the ability to communicate.

Standing up, he said aloud, "I guess I got to go to Pax Grove myself and see the abstract people. Put in my claim." And then he remembered. He would have to first stake his claim, actually go to the site, in the F.D.R. Mountains. And everything in him shrieked out in rebellion at that. At that hideous place, where the building would one day appear,

Well, there was no way out. First have a stake made for him in one of the Union shops, then take a 'copter and head for the Henry Wallace.

It seemed, thinking about it, an agonizingly difficult series of actions to accomplish. How could he do all that? First he would have to find some Union metal worker who could engrave his name for him on the stake; that might take days. Who did he know in the shops here in Lewistown who could do it for him? And if he didn't know the guy, how could he trust him?

At last, as if swimming against an intolerable current, he managed to lift the receiver from the hook and place the call to the shop.

I'm so tired I can hardly move, he realized. Why? What have I done so far today? His body felt crushed flat with fatigue. *If only I could get some rest,* he thought to himself. *If only I could sleep.*

It was late in the afternoon before Arnie Kott was able to procure the metal stake with his name engraved on it from the Union shop and make arrangements for a WWU 'copter to fly him to the F.D.R. Mountains.

"Hi, Arnie," the pilot greeted him, a pleasant-faced young man from the Union's pilot pool.

"Hi, my boy," Arnie murmured, as the pilot assisted him into the comfortable, special leather seat which had been built for him at the settlement's fabric and upholstery shop. As the pilot got into the seat ahead of him, Arnie said, "Now let's hurry because I'm late; I got to get all the way there and then to the abstract office at Pax Grove."

And I know we won't make it, he said to himself. There just *isn't enough time.*

sixteen

The Water Workers' Union 'copter with Goodmember Arnie Kott in it had hardly gotten into the air when the loudspeaker came on.

"Emergency announcement. There is a small party of Bleekmen out on the open desert at gyrocompass point 4.65003 dying from exposure and lack of water. Ships north of Lewistown are instructed to direct their flights to that point with all possible speed and give assistance. United Nations law requires all commercial and private ships to respond."

The announcement was repeated in the crisp voice of the UN announcer, speaking from the UN transmitter on the artificial satellite somewhere overhead.

Feeling the 'copter alter course, Arnie said, "Aw, come on, my boy." It was the last straw. They would never get to the F.D.R. range, let alone to Pax Grove and the abstract office.

"I have to respond, Sir," the pilot said. "It's the law."

Now they were above the desert, moving at good speed toward the intersect which the UN announcer had given. Niggers, Arnie thought. We have to drop everything we're doing to bail them out, the damn fools—and the worst part of it is that now I will meet Jack Bohlen. It can't be avoided. I forgot about it: now it is too late.

Patting his coat pocket he found the gun still there. That made him a little more cheerful; he kept his hand on it as the 'copter lowered for its landing. Hope we can beat him here, he thought. But to his dismay he saw that the Yee Company 'copter had landed ahead of him, and Jack Bohlen was already busy giving water to the five Bleekmen. Damn it, he thought.

"Do you need me?" Arnie's pilot called down from his seat. "If not I'll go on."

In answer Jack Bohlen called back, "I don't have much water for them." He mopped his face with his handkerchief, sweating in the hot sun.

"O.K.," the pilot said, and switched off his blades.

To his pilot, Arnie said, "Tell him to step over here."

Hopping out with a five-gallon water can, the pilot strode over to Jack, and after a moment Jack ceased attending to the Bleekmen and walked toward Arnie Kott.

"You wanted me?" Jack said, standing there looking up at Arnie.

"Yes," Arnie said. "I'm going to kill you." He brought out his pistol and aimed it at Jack Bohlen.

The Bleekmen had been filling their paka eggshells with water; now they stopped. A young male, dark and skinny, almost naked under the ruddy Martian sun, reached backward, behind him, to his quiver of poisoned arrows; he drew an arrow forward, fitting it onto his bow, and in a single motion he fired the arrow. Arnie Kott saw nothing; he felt a sharp pain, and looked down to see the arrow protruding from his chest, slightly below the breast bone.

They read minds, Arnie thought. Intentions. He tried to pull the arrow out, but it would not budge. And then he realized that he was already dying. It was poisoned, and he felt it entering his limbs, stopping his circulation, rising upward to invest his brain and mind.

Jack Bohlen, standing below him, said, "Why would you want to kill me? You don't even know who I am."

"Sure I do," Arnie managed to grunt. "You're going to fix my encoder, and take Doreen away from me, and your father will steal all I've got, all that matters to me, the F.D.R. range and what's coming." He shut his eyes and rested.

"You must be crazy," Jack Bohlen said.

"Naw," Arnie said. "I know the future."

"Let me get you to a doctor," Jack Bohlen said, leaping up into the 'copter, pushing aside the dazed young pilot to inspect the protruding arrow. "They can give you an antidote if they get you in time." He clicked on the motor; the blades of the 'copter began to turn slowly and then more quickly.

"Take me to the Henry Wallace," Arnie muttered. "So I can drive my claim stake."

Jack Bohlen eyed him. "You're Arnie Kott, aren't you?" Getting the pilot out of the way, he seated himself at the controls, and at once the 'copter began to rise into the air. "I'll take you to Lewistown; it's closest and they know you there."

Saying nothing, Arnie lay back, his eyes still shut. It had all gone wrong. He had not staked his claim and he had not anything to Jack Bohlen. And now it was over.

Those Bleekmen, Arnie thought as he felt Bohlen lifting him from the 'copter. This was Lewistown; he saw, through pain-darkened eyes, buildings and people. It's those Bleekmen's fault, from the start; if it wasn't for them I never would have met Jack Bohlen. I blame them for the whole thing.

Why wasn't he dead yet? he wondered as Bohlen carried him across the hospital's roof field to the emergency descent ramp. A lot of time had passed; the poison surely had gone all through him. And yet he still felt, thought, understood . . . perhaps I can't die back here in the past, he said to himself; maybe I got to linger on, unable to die and unable to return to my own time.

How did that young Bleekman catch on so fast? They don't ordinarily use their arrows on Earth people; it's a capital crime. It means the end of them.

Maybe, he thought, they were expecting me. They conspired to save Bohlen because he gave them food and water. Arnie thought, I bet they're the ones who gave him the water witch. Of course. *And when they gave it to him they knew. They knew about all this, even back then, at the very beginning.*

I'm helpless in this terrible damn schizophrenic past of Manfred Steiner's. Let me back to my own world, my own time; I just want to get out of here, I don't want to stake my claim or harm anybody. I just want to be back at Dirty Knobby, in the cavern with that goddamn boy. Like I was. Please, Arnie thought. Manfred!

They—someone—was wheeling him up a dark hall on a cart of some kind. Voices. Door opening, gleaming metal: surgical instruments. He saw masked faces, felt them lay him on a table . . . help me, Manfred, he shouted down deep inside himself. They're going to kill me! You have to take me back. Do it now or forget it, because—

A mask of emptiness and total darkness appeared above him and was lowered. No, Arnie cried out. It's not over; it can't be the end of me. Manfred, for God's sake, before this goes further and it's too late, too late.

I must see the bright normal reality once more, where there is not this schizophrenic killing and alienation and bestial lust and death.

Help me get away from death, back where I belong once more

Help, Manfred
Help me

A voice said, "Get up, Mister, your time has expired."
He opened his eyes.

"More cigarettes, Mister." The dirty, ancient Bleekman priest, in his gray, cobweb-like robes, bent over him, pawing at him, whining his litany again and again against his ear. "If you want to stay, Mister, you have to pay me." He scratched at Arnie's coat, searching.

Sitting up, Arnie looked for Manfred. The boy was gone.

"Get away from me," Arnie said, rising to his feet; he put his hands to his chest and felt nothing, no arrow there.

He went unsteadily to the mouth of the cavern and squeezed out through the crack, into the cold midmorning sunlight of Mars.

"Manfred!" he yelled. No sign of the boy. Well, he thought, anyhow, I am back in the real world. That's what matters.

And he had lost his desire to get Jack Bohlen. He had lost his desire, too, to buy into the land development of these mountains. And he can have Doreen Anderton, for all I care, Arnie said to himself as he started toward the trail up which they had previously come. But I'll keep my word to Manfred; I'll mail him to Earth first chance I get, and maybe the change'll cure him, or maybe they have better psychiatrists back Home by now. Anyhow, he won't wind up at that AM-WEB.

As he made his way down the trail, still searching for Manfred, he saw a 'copter flying low overhead and circling. Maybe they saw where the boy went, he said to himself. Both of them, Jack and Doreen, must have been watching all this time. Halting, he waved his arms at the 'copter, indicating that he wanted it to land.

The 'copter dropped cautiously until it rested up the trail from him; in the wide place before the entrance to Dirty Knobby. The door slid aside, and a man stepped out.

"I'm looking for that kid," Arnie began. And then he saw that it was not Jack Bohlen. It was a man he had never seen before. Good-looking, dark-haired, with wild, emotional eyes, a man who came toward him on a dead run, at the same time waving something that glinted in the sunlight.

"You're Arnie Kott," the man called to him in a shrill voice.

"Yeah, so what?" Arnie said.

210

"You destroyed my field," the man shrieked at him, and, raising the gun, fired.

The first bullet missed Arnie. Who are you and why are you shooting at me? Arnie Kott wondered, as he groped in his coat for his own gun. He found it, brought it out, fired back at the running man. Then it came to him who this was; this was the feeble little black-market operator who had been trying to horn in. The one we gave that lesson to, Arnie said to himself.

The running man dodged, fell, rolled over, and fired from where he lay. Arnie's shot had missed him, too. The shot whistled so close to Arnie this time that for a moment he thought he was hit; he put his hand instinctively to his chest. No, he realized, you didn't get me, you bastard. Raising his pistol, Arnie aimed and prepared to fire once more at the figure.

The world blew up around him. The sun fell from the sky; it dropped into darkness, and with it went Arnie Kott.

After a long time the prone figure stirred. The wild-eyed man crept to his feet cautiously, stood studying Arnie, and then started toward him. As he walked he held his pistol with both hands and aimed it.

A buzzing from above made him peer up. A shadow had swept over him and now a second 'copter bumped to a landing between him and Arnie. The 'copter cut the two men off from one another and Arnie Kott could no longer see the miserable little black-market operator. Out of the 'copter leaped Jack Bohlen. He ran over to Arnie and bent down.

"Get that guy," Arnie whispered.

"Can't," Jack said, and pointed. The black-market operator had taken off; his 'copter rose above Dirty Knobby, floundered, then lurched forward, cleared the peak, and was gone. "Forget about him. You're badly shot—think about yourself."

Arnie whispered, "Don't worry about it, Jack. Listen to me." He caught hold of Jack's shirt and dragged him down so that Jack's ear was close by. "I'll tell you a secret," Arnie said. "Something I've discovered. This is another of those schizophrenic worlds. All this goddamn schizophrenic hate and lust and death, it already happened to me once and it couldn't kill me. First time, it was one of those poisoned arrows in the chest; now this. I'm not worried." He shut his eyes, struggling to keep himself conscious. "Just dig up that kid, he's around somewhere. Ask him and he'll tell you."

"You're wrong, Arnie," Jack said, bending down beside him.

"Wrong how?" "He could barely see Bohlen, now; the scene had sunk into twilight, and Jack's shape was dim and wraith-like.

You can't fool me, Arnie thought. I know I'm still in Man-fred's mind; pretty soon I'll wake up and I won't be shot, I'll be O.K. again, and I'll find my way back to my own world where things like this don't happen. Isn't that right? He tried to speak but was unable to.

Appearing beside Jack, Doreen Anderton said, "He's going to die, isn't he?"

Jack said nothing. He was trying to get Arnie Kott over his shoulder so that he could lug him to the 'copter.

Just another of those gubble-gubble worlds, Arnie said to himself as he felt Jack lift him. It sure taught me a lesson, too. I won't do a nutty thing like this again. He tried to explain that, as Jack carried him to the 'copter. You just did this, he wanted to say. Took me to the hospital at Lewistown to get the arrow out. Don't you remember?

"There's no chance," Jack said to Doreen as he set Arnie inside the 'copter, "of saving him." He panted for breath as he seated himself at the controls.

Sure there is, Arnie thought with indignation. What's the matter with you, aren't you trying? Better try, goddamn you. He made an attempt to speak, to tell Jack that, but he could not; he could say nothing.

The 'copter began to rise from the ground, laboring under the weight of the three people.

During the flight back to Lewistown, Arnie Kott died.

Jack Bohlen had Doreen take the controls, and he sat beside the dead man, thinking to himself that Arnie had died still believing he was lost in the dark currents of the Steiner boy's mind. Maybe it's for the best, Jack thought. Maybe it made it easier for him, at the last.

The realization that Arnie Kott was dead filled him, to his incredulity, with grief. It doesn't seem right, he said to himself as he sat by the dead man. It's too harsh; Arnie didn't deserve it, for what he did—the things he did were bad but not that bad.

"What was it he was saying to you?" Doreen asked. She seemed to be quite calm, to have taken Arnie's death in her stride; she piloted the 'copter with matter-of-fact skill.

Jack said, "He imagined this wasn't real. That he was blundering about in a schizophrenic fantasy."

"Poor Arnie," she said.

"Do you know who that man was who shot him?"

"Some enemy he must have made along the way somewhere."

They were both silent for a while.

"We should look for Manfred," Doreen said.

"Yes," Jack said. But I know where the boy is right now, he said to himself. He's found some wild Bleekmen there in the mountains, and he's with them; it's obvious and certain, and it would have happened sooner or later in any case. He was not worried—he did not care—about Manfred. Perhaps, for the first time in his life, the boy was in a situation to which he might make an adjustment; he might, with the wild Bleekmen, discern a style of living which was genuinely his and not a pallid, tormented reflection of the lives of those around him, beings who were innately different from him and whom he could never resemble, no matter how hard he tried.

Doreen said, "Could Arnie have been right?"

For a moment he did not understand her. And then, when he had made out her meaning, he shook his head. "No."

"Why was he so sure of it, then?"

Jack said, "I don't know." But it had to do with Manfred; Arnie had said so, just before he died.

"In many ways," Doreen said, "Arnie was shrewd. If he thought that, there must have been some very good reason."

"He was shrewd," Jack pointed out, "but he always believed what he wanted to believe." And, he realized, did whatever he wanted to. And so, at last, had brought about his own death; engineered it somewhere along the pathway of his life.

"What's going to become of us now?" Doreen said. "Without him? It's hard for me to imagine it without Arnie . . . do you know what I mean? I think you do. I wish, when we first saw that 'copter land, we had understood what was going to happen; if only we had gotten down there a few minutes earlier—" She broke off. "No use saying that now."

"No use at all," Jack said briefly.

"You know what I think is going to happen to us now?" Doreen said. "We're going to drift away from each other, you and I. Maybe not right away, maybe not for months or possibly even years. But sooner or later we will, without him."

He said nothing; he did not try to argue. Perhaps it was so. He was tired of struggling to see ahead to what lay before them all.

"Do you love me still?" Doreen asked. "After what's happened to us?" She turned toward him to see his face as he answered.

"Yes, naturally I do," he said.

"So do I," she said in a low, wan voice. "But I don't think it's enough. You have your wife and your son—that's so much, in the long run. Anyhow, it was worth it; to me, at least. I'll never be sorry. We're not responsible for Arnie's death; we mustn't feel guilty. He brought it on himself, by what he was up to, there at the end. And we'll never know exactly what that was. But I know it was something to hurt us."

He nodded.

Silently, they continued on back to Lewistown, carrying with them the body of Arnie Kott; carrying Arnie home to his settlement, where he was—and probably always would be—Supreme Goodmember of his Water Workers' Union, Fourth Planet Branch.

Ascending an ill-marked path in the arid rocks of the F.D.R. Mountains, Manfred Steiner halted as he saw ahead of him a party of six dark, shadowy men. They carried with them paka eggs filled with water, quivers of poisoned arrows, and each woman had her pounding block. All smoked cigarettes as they toiled, single file, along the trail.

Seeing him, they halted.

One of them, a gaunt young male, said politely, "The rains falling from your wonderful presence envigor and restore us, Mister."

Manfred did not understand the words, but he got their thoughts: cautious and friendly, with no undertones of hate. He sensed inside them no desire to hurt him, and that was pleasant; he forgot his fear of them and turned his attention on the animal skins which each wore. What sort of animal is that? he wondered.

The Bleekmen were curious about him, too. They advanced until they stood around him on all sides.

"There are monster ships," one of them thought in his direction, "landing in these mountains, with no one aboard. They have excited wonder and speculation, for they appear to be a portent. Already they have begun to assemble themselves on the land to work changes. Are you from them, by any chance?"

"No," Manfred answered, inside his mind, in a way for them to hear and understand.

The Bleekmen pointed, and he saw, toward the center of

the mountain range, a fleet of UN slave rocket vehicles hovering in the air. They had arrived from Earth, he realized. They were here to break ground; the building of the tracts of houses had begun. AM-WEB and the other structures like it would soon be appearing on the face of the fourth planet.

"We are leaving the mountains because of that," one of the older Bleekman males thought to Manfred. "There is no manner by which we can live here, now that this has started. Through our rock, we saw this long ago, but now it is here in actuality."

Within himself, Manfred said, "Can I go with you?"

Surprised, the Bleekmen withdrew to discuss his request. They did not know what to make of him and what he wanted; they had never run across it in an immigrant before.

"We are going out into the desert," the young male told him at last. "It is doubtful if we can survive there; we can only try. Are you certain you want that for yourself?"

"Yes," Manfred said.

"Come along, then," the Bleekmen decided.

They resumed their trek. They were tired, but they swung almost at once into a good pace. Manfred thought at first that he would be left behind, but the Bleekmen hung back for him and he was able to keep up.

The desert lay ahead, for them and for him. But none of them had any regrets; it was impossible for them to turn back anyhow, because they could not live under the new conditions.

I will not have to live in AM-WEB, Manfred said to himself as he kept up with the Bleekmen. Through these dark shadows I will escape.

He felt very good, better than he could remember ever having felt before in his life.

One of the Bleekman females shyly offered him a cigarette from those she carried. Thanking her, he accepted it. They continued on.

And as they moved along, Manfred Steiner felt something strange happening inside him. He was changing.

At dusk, as she was fixing dinner for herself and David and her father-in-law, Silvia Bohlen saw a figure on foot, a figure that walked along the edge of the canal. A man, she said to herself; frightened, she went to the front door, opened it, and peered out to see who it was. God, is wasn't that so-called health food salesman, that Otto whatever his name was again—

"It's me, Silvia," Jack Bohlen said.

Running out of the house and up to his father excitedly, David shouted, "Hey, how come you didn't bring your 'copter? Did you come on the tractor-bus? I bet you did. What happened to your 'copter, Dad? Did it break down and strand you out in the desert?"

"No more 'copter," Jack said. He looked tired.

"I heard on the radio," Silvia said.

"About Arnie Kott?" He nodded. "Yeah, it's true." Entering the house he took off his coat; Silvia hung it in the closet for him.

"That affects you a lot, doesn't it?" she said.

Jack said, "No job. Arnie had bought my contract." He looked around. "Where's Leo?"

"Taking his nap. He's been gone most of the day, on business. I'm glad you got home before he goes; he's leaving for Earth tomorrow," he said. Did you know that the UN has started taking the land in the F.D.R. range already? I heard that on the radio, too."

"I didn't know," Jack said, going into the kitchen and seating himself at the table. "How about some iced tea?"

As she fixed the iced tea for him she said, "I guess I shouldn't ask you how serious this job business is."

Jack said, "I can get on with almost any repair outfit. Mr. Yee would take me back, as a matter of fact. I'm sure he didn't want to part with my contract in the first place."

"Then why are you so despondent?" she said, and then she remembered about Arnie.

"It's a mile and a half from where that tractor-bus let me off," he said. "I'm just tired."

"I didn't expect you home." She felt on edge, and it was difficult for her to return to preparing dinner. "We're only having liver and bacon and grated carrots with synthetic butter and a salad. And Leo said he'd like a cake of some sort for dessert; David and I were going to make that later on as a treat for him, because after all he is going, and we may not see him ever again; we have to face that."

"That's fine about the cake," Jack murmured.

Silvia burst out, "I wish you would tell me what's the matter—I've never seen you like this. You're not just tired; it must be that man's death."

Presently, he said, "I was thinking of something Arnie said before he died. I was there with him. Arnie said he wasn't in a real world; he was in the fantasy of a schizophrenic, and that's been preying on my mind. It never occurred to me before how much our world is like Manfred's—I thought they were absolutely distinct. Now I see that it's more a question of degree."

"You don't want to tell me about Mr. Kott's death, do you? The radio just said he was killed in a 'copter accident in the rugged terrain of the F.D.R. Mountains."

"It was no accident. Arnie was murdered by an individual who had it in for him, no doubt because he was mistreated and had a legitimate grudge. The police are looking for him now, naturally. Arnie died thinking it was senseless, psychotic hate that was directed at him, but actually it was probably very rational hate with no psychotic elements in it at all."

With overwhelming guilt, Silvia thought, The kind of hate you'd feel for me if you knew what awful thing I plunged into today. "Jack—" she said clumsily, not sure how to put it, but feeling she had to ask. "Do you think our marriage is finished?"

He stared at her a long, long time. "Why do you say that?"

"I just want to hear you say it isn't."

"It isn't," he said, still staring at her; she felt exposed, as if he could read her mind, as if he knew somehow exactly what she had done. "Is there any reason to think it is? Why do you imagine I came home? If we had no marriage, would I have shown up here today after—" He was silent, then. "I'd like my iced tea," he murmured.

"After what?" she asked.

He said, "After Arnie's death."

"Where else would you go?"

"A person can always find two places to choose from. Home, and the rest of the world with all the other people in it."

Silvia said, "What's she like?"

"Who?"

"The girl. You almost said it, just now."

He did not answer for such a long time that she did not think he was going to. And then he said, "She has red hair. I almost stayed with her. But I didn't. Isn't that enough for you to know?"

"There's a choice for me, too," Silvia said.

"I didn't know that," he said woodenly. "I didn't realize." He shrugged. "Well, it's good to realize; it's sobering. You're not speaking about theory, now, are you? You're speaking about concrete reality."

"That's correct," Silvia said.

David came running into the kitchen. "Grandfather Leo's awake," he shouted. "I told him you were home, Dad, and he's real glad and he wants to find out how things are going with you."

"They're going swell," Jack said.

Silvia said to him, "Jack, I'd like for us to go on. If you want to."

"Sure," he said. "You know that, I'm back here again." He smiled at her so forlornly that it almost broke her heart. "I came a long way, first on that no-good damn tractor-bus, which I hate, and then on foot."

"There won't be any more," Silvia said, "of—other choices, will there, Jack? It really has to be that way."

"No more," he said, nodding emphatically.

She went over to the table, then, and bending, kissed him on the forehead.

"Thanks," he said, taking hold of her by the wrist. "That feels good." She could feel his fatigue; it traveled from him into her.

"You need a good meal," she said. "I've never seen you so—crushed." It occurred to her, then, that he might have had a new bout with his mental illness from the past, his schizophrenia; that would go far in explaining things. But she did not want to press him on the subject; instead, she said, "We'll go to bed early tonight, O.K.?"

He nodded in a vague fashion, sipping his iced tea.

"Are you glad now?" she asked. "That you came back here?" Or have you changed your mind? she wondered.

"I'm glad," he said, and his tone was strong and firm. Obviously he meant it.

"You get to see Grandfather Leo before he goes—" she began.

A scream made her jump, turn to face Jack.

He was on his feet. "Next door. The Steiner house." He pushed past her; they both ran outside.

At the front door of the Steiner house one of the Steiner girls met them. "My brother—"

She and Jack pushed past the child, and into the house. Silvia did not understand what she saw, but Jack seemed to; he took hold of her hand, stopped her from going any farther.

The living room was filled with Bleekmen. And in their midst she saw part of a living creature, an old man only from the chest on up; the rest of him became a tangle of pumps and hoses and dials, machinery that clicked away, unceasingly active. It kept the old man alive; she realized that in an instant. The missing portion of him had been replaced by it. Oh, God, she thought. Who or what was it, sitting there with a smile on its withered face? Now it spoke to them.

"Jack Bohlen," it rasped, and its voice issued from a mechanical speaker, out of the machinery: not from its mouth. "I am here to say goodbye to my mother." It paused, and she heard the machinery speed up, as if it were laboring. "Now I can thank you," the old man said.

Jack, standing by her, holding her hand, said. "For what? I didn't do anything for you."

"Yes, I think so." The thing seated there nodded to the Bleekmen, and they pushed it and its machinery closer to Jack and straightened it so that it faced him directly. "In my opinion . . ." It lapsed into silence and then it resumed, more loudly, now. "You tried to communicate with me, many years ago. I appreciate that."

"It wasn't long ago," Jack said. "Have you forgotten? You came back to us; it was just today. This is your distant past, when you were a boy."

She said to her husband, "Who is it?"

"Manfred."

Putting her hands to her face she coveerd her eyes; she could not bear to look any longer.

"Did you escape AM-WEB?" Jack asked it.

"Yesss," it hissed, with a gleeful tremor. "I am with my friends." It pointed to the Bleekmen who surrounded it.

"Jack," Silvia said, "take me out of here—please, I can't stand it." She clung to him, and he then led her from the Steiner house, out once more into the evening darkness.

Both Leo and David met them, agitated and frightened. "Say, son," Leo said, "what happened? What was that woman screaming about?"

Jack said, "It's all over. Everything's O.K." To Silvia he said, "She must have run outside. She didn't understand, at first."

Shivering, Silvia said, "I don't understand either and I don't want to; don't try to explain it to me." She returned to the stove, turning down the burners, looking into pots to see what had burned.

"Don't worry," Jack said, patting her.

She tried to smile.

"It probably won't happen again," Jack said. "But even if it does—"

"Thanks," she said. "I thought when I first saw him that it was his father, Norbert Steiner; that's what frightened me so."

"We'll have to get a flashlight and hunt around for Erna Steiner," Jack said. "We want to be sure she's all right."

"Yes," she said. "You and Leo go and do that while I finish here; I have to stay with the dinner or it'll be spoiled."

The two men, with a flashlight, left the house. David stayed with her, helping her set the table. Where will you be? she wondered as she watched her son. When you're old like that, all hacked away and replaced by machinery. . . . Will you be like that, too?

We are better off not being able to look ahead, she said to herself. Thank God we can't see.

"I wish I could have gone out," David was complaining. "Why can't you tell me what it was that made Mrs. Steiner yell like that?"

Silvia said, "Maybe someday."

But not now, she said to herself. It is too soon, for any of us.

Dinner was ready now, and she went out automatically onto the porch to call Jack and Leo, knowing even as she did so that they would not come; they were far too busy, they had too much to do. But she called them anyhow, because it was her job.

In the darkness of the Martian night her husband and father-in-law searched for Erna Steiner; their light flashed here and there, and their voices could be heard, business-like and competent and patient.